Disclaimer

Grandma is a fictional character. Some of her stories are based from actual events and some are completely made up. All characters have fictional names.

The photos were collected to illustrate the story and are used with permission and credit given.

THE GRANDMA CHRONICLES

Annie Keys

DEDICATION

This book is dedicated to everybody's Grandma.

And to everybody who loves their Grandma.

Credits and Permissions

Proof reader: A special thank you to my proof reader, Shirley Peters, you make me look good! *Thanks*!

Photography all photos are used with the permission of the photographer and/or the subject.

I appreciate all the photographers who contributed to this work of heart. Thank you.

Photos were taken by both amateur and professional photographers (listed alphabetically by **first name**)

Avi Ben Zaken, **Cynthia** Robinson, **Ed** Reichtag, **Jim** Swaringen, **John** Hadden, **John** Keys, **Julia** Bogle, **Katrin** Bell, **Natalie** Beidler Mayhew, **Pam** Bell, **Rose** Ann Keys, **Stanley** Kozma, **Suzanne** Willis, and **Tom** Robinson

Honoring the beautiful women, a few gentlemen, and a couple of pets whose portraits illustrate The Grandma Chronicles. (Alphabetical order by last name)

Loosi Anna and Hambone **Anderson**, Cindy **Ashby**, Pam **Bell**, Clara **Caldwell**, Millie and Bob **Carter**, Theresa **Daily**, Dr. SueEllen **Garner**, Courtney **Greathouse**, Brenda **Hadden**, Margie **Hutcherson**, Celia **Johnson**, Annie and Dan **Keys**, Claude **Keys** (Greg and Cara's cat), Madeline **Kozma**, Gail and Hubert **Lee**, Mary Nell **Overton**, Laura **Peacock**, Beth and Ed **Reichtag**, Frances **Robinson**, Micki **Smith**, Vicki and Charlie **Stone**, Charles Michael **Stone III**, Deb and Jim **Swaringen** and Mary **Thayer** with her beloved doggie, Maggie.

Cover Photography by John Keys

Front Cover Model: Merry Keys **Back Cover Model**: Annie Keys and Ladybug

Cover Designed and arranged by Dan Keys and Annie Keys

A timeless quote by Mr. George Bernard Shaw

"You don't stop laughing when you grow old.

You grow old when you stop laughing."

Table of Contents

Chapter Title   **Page number**

Chapter Title	Page number
Disclaimer	002
Dedication	004
Credits and Permissions	005
Quote on aging by George Bernard Shaw	006

Part 1: Getting to Know Grandma

Chapter Title	Page number
Prologue	012
Who Is That Old Lady?	014
Grandma Wants to be Dangerous	017
The Comedy of My Life	019
Grandma's Thoughts on House Cleaning	022
Warm Fuzzy Technology	024
Things That Annoy Grandma	026
Rearview Mirror Faith	034
Another Use for Duct Tape	038
Grandma's Miracle Tan	039
Grandma's Cookie Blog	041
Grandma's Skinny Doctor	045
Grandma's Moustache	047

A Dead Man-- Where?   049

Food Police Alert   052

Grandma Gets Drug Busted   054

Chapter Title   **Page number**

Grandma's Paean   057

One Size Fits All?   060

Mrs. Eberheart's Amazing Song   062

Old Age is an Adventure   065

The Saga of the Red Dress   069

Grandma's Wild Ride   072

The Anointing Crisco   074

NO Peach Cobbler   078

Grandma's Teeth Get Away   081

Grandma Needs Adult Supervision   083

A Random Journal Entry   085

The Drive Through Mumble Special   086

The Once a Year Time Travel Adventure   088

Do You Brush Your Teeth   090

Chasing Contentment   092

Grandma, the Plant Killer   094

Today, I Wait   097

Wrong Place Right Time   101

Got Mouth   103

The Great Broccoli Soup Adventure   104

Grandma Can't Multitask	107
Crazy for Evangelism	109
The Adventure Begins	110
Antique Hutterly for Sale	113

Chapter Title	**Page number**
A Home for Old Bibles	115
A Time to Break Things	118
The Tiki Bar Sign and Grandma's Coffee Cup	121

Part 2: The Move

Truth Is--	124
Hello, My Name Is Rebecca	126
Grandma's Spin Cycle Class	129
Living In the Highlighter	132
Shopping for Necessaries	134
Growing Up is Not Mandatory	137
Whose Box is This?	139
The Importance of Scheduling	140
Grandma's Never Fail Filing System	142
Hell is for Everybody	144
Grandma Wants to Learn to Yodel	147
Wedding Adventures	150
You Don't Need a Lucky Shirt	155

Part 3: Life Changes Fast

The Widow's Might	160
Look at Me	163
Midnight Cupcake Madness	168
Grandma's Gift of Great Worth	175

Chapter Title   **Page number**

Grandma's New Friend Has Four Feet	177
The Mourning Class	180
Life Goes On So Will Grandma	184
Grandma's Friends	187
The Floppy Red Frog	195
Commitment to Fitness	197
For the Love of Carolyn	200
The White Water Rafting Adventure	207
Life Can be Dangerous	212
Grandma Has Anger Issues	214
Where are the Memories?	216
Saga of the Dead Mousie	218
Worshipping Till You---Laugh?	220
Grandma Learns to Juggle and Wrap	223
Common Sense Maintenance	227
Hot Car or Antique Roadster?	230
The Final Chapter in Grandma's Journal	233

Part 4: Pages Grandma Promised You

Grandma's Extreme Chocolate Chip Cookie Recipe   236

Skit: GOT MOUTH?   237

Other Books by Annie Keys   242

Prologue:

Grandma doesn't know where to start. My friends have told me that I should write a book because my life is so funny. Oddly, Grandma has not noticed all this humor going on, but, never the less, my friends tell me it exists. Mercy, I *do* know how often Grandma can make a mess of things and those messes **can** be ridiculously crazy.

Maybe these messes are what my friends refer to as---funny? I call these things an unavoidable part of everyday life. But then, I'm living through these things instead of seeing them as a casual observer. Of course, there are some wild adventures in my journal along with the funny mishaps. Grandma also has a serious thought now and then and that will be included too.

Grandma loves pictures, so I will also have pictures of my friends, things that I love and, well, just—whatever my story needs to illustrate the moment. Never the less, as I start this journal about Grandma's life adventures and ponderings, I hope that you, the reader, enjoy the funny stories, the life lessons Grandma has learned and the good photos that are sure to be included in, *The Grandma Chronicles*.

With all the Love in Grandma's heart,

Rebecca Grace (also known as Bitsy)

PART 1: GETTING TO KNOW GRANDMA

Who Is That Old Lady?

Today, in the decorating section of the local department store, the items were being rearranged for an upcoming big sale. Distracted with trying to find a red tablecloth, I glanced to my left and saw the feet and legs of an old lady reflected in a mirror that had been sat on the floor.

Realizing that I was probably in her way, I turned to face her and excuse myself for blocking her path. Once turned around, I noticed that there was no old lady behind me; the legs in the mirror were---mine. Stunned, I looked down and observed that my feet and legs looked the same to me from the top looking down as they always had. Obviously, age can only be seen from the side--.

The shock of looking old isn't the worst of it. Here lately, I've started to realize that many of the things on my bucket list that I'd planned on doing at some point in my life, just flat out, are never going to happen. Like learning to sword fight and learning to yodel; probably not happening.

It seems like just a short time ago that I had a lot of time ahead of me to accomplish all that I had to get done. Stunningly, I find the "life goals" that I had set as markers slipped by more or less unnoticed; my kids grew up, got married, had kids of their own and ---now THEIR kids are at the age where they are getting married. Interestingly, it seems that my grandchildren have grown up much faster than my own offspring did.

My parents have both been in heaven for nearly two decades and every time one of my brothers visits me, I think, "who is this old man and why is he calling ME sissy?" This is strange since both of my brothers are younger than me—things that make me say, "hmmmmm."

It is a real head knocker when your grandchildren grow to be adults. Grandma _expected_ her children to grow up, but I thought grandchildren were forever to be, little kids. Wasn't it just a few years ago that I took my grandson, Gerald, to the amusement park and he ate his cotton candy face first? He had wisps of blue fluffy candy threads floating out from his ears on the summer breeze.

I loved his ears, they were too big for his head and with such fine hair, when you looked at him from the back, he looked like a Volkswagen with the doors hanging open. Having watched many children grow up, I knew he'd grow into those ears one day. He was so cute as I held him on my lap while I got wet wipes out of the bag to clean the blue sticky off his ears and out of his eyebrows.

This morning, I looked over at Gerald as he stood in the shed pouring gas in my lawn mower so he could mow the yard for me; he's such a precious young man. His linebacker shoulders tanned and his biceps like baseballs, he hefted the five gallon gas can like it was an empty container. He stood up to his full six feet and I shook my head, nope, it was certainly more than a few years ago since we shared that blue cotton candy. And, I had been right; he had for sure grown into those ears. Mercy, where does time go?

Old age is one of those things that you fight and work hard to do everything the commercials on television and the magazine in the beauty parlor say to do so it doesn't happen. My friend since childhood, Fiona, (actually her name is Fanny, but once she got her college degree, she changed it to "Fiona") invested in creams and lotions and gym memberships and dried her skin only on white cotton bath towels to avoid damaging her skin with artificial dyes that might possibly cause her to age prematurely .

She drank only bottled water that, according to the label, is actually the tediously collected tears of young alpaca that graze on the level heights of the Andes of southern Peru. Of course, she always *always* used excessive amounts of sunscreen with the maximum UV protection. And guess what; after all that effort and expense; she looks as old as I do. Grandma thinks that is a HOOT!

Age---happens. No matter how much money you spend in damage control, how healthy you eat, or what vitamins you take, age---happens. Grandma loves Fanny, er, I mean Fiona, even though I know for a fact her copper red hair comes out of a bottle, no matter WHAT she says.

She keeps asking me how I keep the skin under my eyeballs so firm, I tell her it is because grandma has shmeared a swipe of preparation H under each eye before going to bed at night for the last 40 years. Then, I tell her to---read the label, it says, "shrinks delicate tissues."

The look of horror on her face, oh mercy sakes. And no, I do *not* do that---but I love telling her I do. In truth, I think the skin under my eyes stays tight because I'm overweight most of the time. Now and then, I do manage to get down to "thin," but it never lasts long. If I was as tiny as she is all the time, my eyeballs would have saggy skin too.

One afternoon my young granddaughter was looking through the photo albums in the box under my bed. Her mom, my daughter, was trying to find a certain picture her memory said I had in an album somewhere. I overheard my daughter say, "Look there's momma, when I was a little girl sitting on the beach!" My granddaughter leaned over and wrinkled her brows. "Ok, who is that babe in the black silky swim suit sitting with you, momma?"

My daughter said, "Oh, that's grandma." My granddaughter got a shocked look, grabbed up the photo album, and studied it carefully. Then looking over at me folding the laundry, she whispered, "That's GRANDMA? WHAT HAPPENED TO HER?" My daughter and I laughed till we both had wet eyeballs. Mercy; what, indeed, happened?

Life is constantly changing, rearranging, maturing and moving on. The one thing that has remained constant in my life is the foundation that I stand on---Jesus.

Grandma Wants to be Dangerous

Grandma's grandson, Billy, is only 7 years old and says that he is an inventor. One of his recent projects is a "new and improved envelope, easily opened yet totally sealed and completely waterproof." I encourage him as he researches for this invention. Grandma has gotten more than a few cards in the mail box that look like they were dragged across the bottom of the river on the way to their destination. Mercy, this is an invention whose time has come.

While at my house this last weekend, little Billy spent a lot of time with pencil and paper. Then, carrying a collection of 'supplies,' he disappeared into the guest bathroom wearing his "invention glasses." These marvelous glasses had been bought by Grandma at the dollar store.

The glasses have black frames and a big plastic nose attached. Over the glasses frame tops are two huge bushy black "eyebrows" that are reminiscent of Groucho Marx. As soon as Billy saw them, he announced that those were just what he'd been looking for *all of his life*; "crazy scientist invention glasses." Grandma had no idea he'd been looking for these—if I'd only known.

Later, when Grandma went into the bathroom to check on the progress of the new and improved waterproof but totally sealed envelope, I observed his "work site." He had empty spools of tape, a roll of plastic wrap, a bottle of glue and numerous sheets of paper folded in many different shapes all neatly arranged on the sink counter top. Oh, and mercy sakes, there was water <u>everywhere</u>.

Each carefully folded homemade envelope had been given a number and had an accompanying slip of paper listing the pros and cons of that particular envelope design. Quite an accomplishment for a seven year old, even though Grandma does tend to be a bit prejudiced when judging such things. The design problems were described in little boy terms, "wet instide," "still wet instide," "wet instide agan."

I asked Billy if he'd had any success with his invention. He said, "Not yet, but I'm making progress." After a moment of deep thought, he confided to me that he wasn't sure, but I probably should keep my eye on him because he *might* be <u>very</u> dangerous. His serious little face, wearing those big black glasses with the fuzzy eyebrows; it was all Grandma could do to escape the "crazy scientist laboratory experiment room," with a straight face. I held my laughter till I got to the kitchen.

As I fixed a cup of coffee, a sudden realization came to my mind, I want to be dangerous too! Grandma wants to be so dangerous for Christ that when I wake up in the morning, the gates of Hell tremble and the devil's imps moan, "ohhhhh noooo, she's awake again—-".

Grandma is fully aware that Satan will do everything he can to side track me from my plan. But Grandma knows an intimate relationship with Jesus will defeat the wiles of the enemy.

But right now, I want to bake my little inventor his favorite chocolate chip cookies. Actually, I think I'll take a plate full of prayed over cookies to work with me tomorrow. Grandma has been and will continue to be---very—dangerous.

The Comedy of My Life

If I were to chronicle all the times in my life that I've done something ridiculous and embarrassed myself; Grandma could publish that topic alone as a book. That book of only foolish and embarrassing events would have hundreds, maybe thousands of pages.

When I was very young, I was easily embarrassed; if there was a mess, I was usually involved in the making of it. My dear Daddy told me that the best way to handle embarrassment was to hold my head up and view the situation as a casual on-looker instead of adding the personal pain of involvement to the whole event. That simple transference removed the personal humiliation and enabled me to laugh at myself.

That ability to laugh at myself takes me from being a victim to being a victor. My Daddy was very wise and the result has been that, for the rest of my life, I've laughed at my own foibles. Consequently, I've had much to laugh about through my life. These are just a few of the more --- ridiculous--- silly things-- Grandma has done unawares; embarrassing things.

One Sunday after church, my husband and I were enjoying dinner with a missionary at my pastor brother in-law's house. My beloved husband, Walter, was sitting across from me at the table. I slipped my shoe off and began playing with his foot. It amused me that he didn't even look up, such a stoic. So, I played with his foot all the more, watching him for that twinkle in his eye that says, "You silly thing, I love you too." After a few more unfruitful attempts to play footsie wootsie, I put my foot on top of his and just let it rest there.

Awhile later, my husband excused himself and left the table to get more coffee. To my horror, my foot was still resting on top of "his" shoe! Three decades later, my brother in-law still razzes me about the Sunday I played footsie with the missionary---. I was embarrassed.

Then, there was the time I mistakenly grabbed my green eyeliner pencil and outlined my lips with it, thinking it was my lip liner. My daughter was a makeup consultant and had talked me into using an array of pencils to outline everything. My eyes, my lips; who knew a bit of color could do so much for beauty enhancement.

Grandma soon learned that busy people need organizational skills so the proper liner pencil is used on the proper facial surface. The looks I got at the mall that day; my grandson described the effect perfectly, "you have fish lips, mamawl." Indeed, when I finally found a mirror to look in, my pink lips outlined in green did look like a fish. I was embarrassed.

Then, there was the day I went bowling---and yes, I'd read all the "how to do it" books I could find before I actually went to the bowling alley. There is a fine line, a side step, if you will, from head knowledge to practical knowledge. I threw that bowling ball with so much force it liked to have taken my arm with it. In fact, it did take my arm with it. The ball failed to leave my hand and I threw myself down the alley---sliding to a stop a few feet down the smoothly polished lane. I was embarrassed.

A few years ago, Grandma was asked to be a speaker at a small Bible College's Sunday morning service. The college was old school Pentecostal and required that all female speakers wear skirts/dresses and heels to speak on the platform. My feet are a size ten and a half, a heeled shoe in that size is like balancing a barge on stilts. Converse tennis shoes or flip flops are Grandma's personal footwear choice.

The night before I was to speak, my sister in-law helped me to practice walking on my new "stilt shoes" without tripping or falling. We both laughed till our ribs ached. But, I was finally able to take a few steady steps. Finally, she prayed with me about my speaking engagement the next morning, asking God to help me to stand up strong, spiritually, emotionally AND physically.

The next morning, I was introduced as the guest speaker and as I rose to my feet and walked toward the podium, my ankle turned. I grabbed for the pew beside me and thankfully did not catapult onto the floor. Experience had taught me that even though I might MAYBE able to make it to the podium with no further mishap, I'd not be able to stand or walk in those heels for the hour I was to speak.

I pulled myself together, smoothed my out of kilter skirt, smiled my loveliest most confident smile, reached down, slipped off my shoes and carried them to the podium and sat them on the floor beside me as I spoke.

Afterwards, the wife of the District Superintendent hugged me so tight I thought I would break in half. As she hugged me she murmured, "Well done, perfect cover, I love you!" Obviously, she and I shared in the sisterhood of clumsy mishaps. I was embarrassed but I did not fall down—that time.

If there is a bump in the floor, a protrusion in any surface, my feet will find that and I will throw myself unceremoniously onto my face. I've torn the sleeves off of blouses catching the cloth on the latch going through the door. I've stumbled into rooms and knocked over lamps, tables and potted plants.

There have been times in my life where I actually thought about introducing myself as "clumsy." Maybe, "Hi, my name is Rebecca, my friends call me Bitsy but everybody who knows me calls me Clumsy." My Dad always said I'd outgrow the clumsy stage. Sadly, that is one of the very few times my dear Daddy was mistaken. Early on in my life, I learned to laugh at myself. Why not? I have to admit that to a bystander, it's often like I'm a one person comedy act.

However, there is one time when I know that I won't be embarrassed, though. On that day when I stand before my Lord to be judged, I will have no fear of shame. The book of life will be opened to the page where all of the naughty and selfish things that I've ever done are recorded.

At that moment, my Lord, Jesus, will step in front of me and the page of my iniquity, and all of the embarrassing moments when I failed will "poof" and be gone. I will stand before the God of the universe with no shortcomings, no inadequacies; clothed in the righteousness of Christ and ---I will, for once, **not** be embarrassed.

Grandma's Thoughts on House Cleaning

Grandma hates to clean the house. However, like so many other of life's mundane chores, house cleaning is a necessary nasty. Usually, I think of something I can bake then set the ingredients out on the counter top; as soon as cleaning is done, baking will be my reward.

Let me state up front that Grandma does _understand_ the need for a clean and organized home. We live in a cultured society and such things are important. And I do make every effort to keep my house at the very least----in order. Interestingly, have you ever noticed that a great housekeeper and a great cook very rarely inhabit the same body?

When I walk into a friend's house that is spotlessly clean with not even a trace of dust or a magazine out of place on the coffee table---I know that we should go out to share a meal and not expect to eat at her house ---or I should plan to have the friend over to my house to eat. There are a few exceptions to this rule. I have several friends who love to cook and have spotlessly clean and tidy homes. They hire a housekeeper to come in once a week. Grandma takes her housekeeper money and spends it on kitchen gadgets.

All that said, I do have a few housekeeping hints for those who don't have time to clean EVERY day, but do want the house to at least look like it is inhabited by responsible humans. Just remember, it is important that the house actually be cleaned thoroughly ---now and then. Just like faking living a Christ centered life, you can't fake good housekeeping for long periods of time. After a while folks just---know.

Leave the vacuum in the middle of the floor—cord in a tangle. Visitors think that they must have just interrupted you as you were getting ready to clean. This works great for the casual drop in visitor. However, if you invite guests over, this won't work because you should have cleaned hours ago... This also works with a mop bucket and a mop. But I've found a bucket full of water sitting in the middle of the floor is a disaster waiting to happen. Don't ask me how I know this.

If dusting is not one of your favorite pastimes, be very careful to not move any of your little keepsakes out of their original spots. As long as you leave them all exactly where they've been, your shelves and end tables don't look dusty. The dust simply gives the illusion of a soft patina, but, I must emphasize, do not move any of your knick knacks because you'll never get them back in the exact spot.

Grandma always tries to keep the foyer of her home spotlessly clean. Most unexpected guests never get past the entry way of the house; when that small area is shiny, spotlessly clean, guests assume that the rest of the house is equally spotless. Only close very intimate friends should ever be allowed passed the front doorway into the main living area.

The girlfriends who know me well enough to get beyond that special clean entry way know what kind of housekeeper Grandma is anyway and besides, if I know them that well, I know what their little failures are too. Nobody is perfect. Lilly Sue is not going to ever mention the dust on my coffee table when she knows I'm aware of how she always slices the bottoms off her cupcakes before she ices them ---to remove the burned bottoms. No way is Ms. Lilly going to say *any*thing bad about my housekeeping---absolutely--nope.

One of Grandma's favorite Bible readings is the one about sisters Mary and Martha. One was busy about the house making everything all clean---and the other was sitting at Jesus' feet, feasting on the love and wise counsel of her Lord. Jesus Himself pointed out that the sister sitting at His feet had made the better choice. I do note that Jesus never said it was wrong to clean the house, He just pointed out that the most important thing is spending time with Him.

So, there you go. Grandma absolutely does not miss her daily time for Bible study and prayer, even if it means that now and then the vacuum only gets run in the middle of the rug. We have to have priorities and priorities must be set to maintain not only a reasonably clean and welcoming home but a Christ centered home as well. It's ALL good.

Warm Fuzzy Technology

My daughter in-law, who lives in England, wanted a cookbook. Happy to help, I made my selection from a web site and proceeded to "check out." The site would not accept the APO address. I clicked the box that stated, "Problems? Try our on line chat with a live representative." Relieved to have personal contact, I clicked the button.

"Hello, my name is Jill, can I help you?" popped up. I typed in my problem. Jill responded that she needed my credit card information. I quipped "You promise you won't use it to get a condo on the beach?" Jill responded, "I don't understand your request." This response seemed strange, but, ok, after all, she's at work. I typed the information and waited. Time passed, I typed, "Hello? Is anybody there?"

Jill typed, "I don't understand your request." Frustrated, I told Grandpa, who was on his back under the kitchen sink fixing a leaking pipe, that it would have been faster if I'd have wrapped the book, traveled to England and hand delivered it to my daughter in-law's front door myself.

Weary of waiting, I added, "It doesn't help that the rep I'm working with has the personality of a stump." Grandpa laughed, saying, "There's no rep there, honey! It's all computer generated; certain words are recognized and the appropriate response is given. You are talking to a computer generated program."

In disbelief, I turned back to my computer, where I was still waiting for "Jill" to finish the paperwork to make my purchase. Timidly, I typed, "Are you real?" She typed back, "I don't understand your request." Horrified, I realized that Walter could possibly, ---MAYBE---be right.

Still not entirely convinced, I typed, "There's no company representative eager to serve me, is there?" Jill immediately responded, "Thank you for choosing to shop with us." Feeling totally betrayed, I typed, "Your mamma is a circuit board." Jill responded quickly with "I don't understand your request."

Sighing in resignation, Grandma typed, "Never mind, I'll buy one at the bookstore downtown and mail it myself." Jill quickly typed, "Thank you for allowing me to be of service, I hope our communication made your shopping experience more enjoyable."

One of the many things that Grandma's heart cherishes is that when I speak to the Lord, He hears me. He doesn't tell me he's busy or give me a number and tell me to get in line. He <u>ALWAYS</u> hears me and understands me.

My Lord never hands me off to an automated program. He is there, first time, every time, all the time. My Lord loves me, hears me and answers me. That's not customer service; that's a close friend, a confidant. That's a RELATIONSHIP.

Things That Annoy Grandma

Grandma has an issue with cords. In a world that is full of technology—why do we still have electrical cords? My grandson tells me lots of electronics don't have cords now, but cordless equipment is expensive. Seriously, I can use my cell phone to call my friend on the other side of the country and my TV remote can turn on the television from across the room.

So, with all of this techno, why can't Grandma push a button and the vacuum, the toaster, the lamp and the mixer, all turn on without all these—cords? Don't say I said so, but Grandma thinks it may be because it isn't the men who use these household appliances, so the "need" is not even noticed. As I said---the TV remote changes the channel without cords and the mouse on the computer doesn't have a cord. Boom.

An interesting thing that Grandma has noticed---Grandpa thinks imaginary people live with us. I know he believes this because whenever anything comes up missing, he doesn't say, "I wonder where that could be?" or "Where was I the last time I used that?" No, instead he says, "SOMEBODY has lost (item)." Since nobody lives here but Grandpa and me, he obviously thinks there are invisible people here; people who get up at night and move his things.

The day he looked high and low for his eyeglasses, mumbling about how SOMEBODY moved them from their usual place beside his recliner in the den; Grandma found them lying on the bathroom counter, beside his pill bottle. Then, there was the day SOMEBODY moved his coat, it was not where he left it---. When he got to the office, *whoever* had taken it had left it on his desk chair.

Last week, after many years of living with that mysterious "somebody," Grandma said, "Do you mean me? Do you think that I moved your cell phone?" Grandpa looked at me confused, "No, darling, I didn't mean that at all." I smiled and said, "Then do you believe there are invisible people who live here with us that took your phone?" Grandpa looked sheepish and said, "No, no of course not. And I don't believe you took it either. But if you did, you did it by accident."

Slightly amused at myself to have finally called my beloved's annoying blame habit out, I teased, "Oh, so you think I may have *accidentally* picked up your cell phone and took it away---what do you imagine that I thought it was?" Grandpa sighed and said, "I'm sorry. I know I misplaced it. It's just easier to say 'somebody' than admit I don't know what I did with it."

Of course, I hugged him and kissed him and told him I loved him and he said he'd try to not say, "SOMEBODY" took it when he loses something. Through the years, Grandma has found a lot of things that annoy married couples are simply because of idly spoken words. Words that are said out of frustration and an unwillingness to accept responsibility can, over time, hurt a relationship.

Grandma needs to be careful of that too because I know Grandpa is not the ONLY one in the house who says careless things. I'm pretty sure I do too. And I'm sure Grandpa can tell me what they are if I really want to know—

There is one thing that so many women complain about that puzzles me; the toilet seat up "thing." Grandma was raised as the only girl in a family of boys. I had two brothers and a Dad—and then there was mom and me. So, statistically, the boys had majority rule. It was common sense that before one of us girls plopped our bare bottom down on the toilet, we took a quick back look to make sure the "girl guard" was in place.

Even in a home where there is one man and one woman that is equal preference for toilet seat positioning. So, why do so many women get angry that their husband leaves the toilet seat up? Doesn't it make just as much sense for the seat to be up as down?

When was the last time you ever heard a man complaining about the toilet seat being left down so he had to raise it to use the bathroom? Exactly. Doesn't it make sense that if the men are to put the seat down for the women—then the women should put the seat up for the men? Of course it does. Or, we could each simply adjust as needed.

Grandpa is severely OCD. Since he is a mechanical engineer and attention to even the tiniest detail is his life's blood, this personality type works well for him. However, what is a blessing and a Godsend for an engineer can be a curse in everyday life. I was amazed to learn that it MATTERS to my beloved how the toilet tissue unrolls off the roll.

Now some of you reading this are gritting your teeth and going "Ngngngngn, I KNOOOOW!" The rest of you are like me, you are squinting your eyeballs and muttering, "Whaaaat? Are you kidding me?" This "what way does the tissue hang off the roll" controversy has an easy remedy.

Grandma sits the roll of toilet paper on top of the holder and lets *Grandpa* put it on. That way the paper ALWAYS comes off the roll *any way that he wants*. Because I simply do not care---all I care about is that there IS toilet tissue within reach of the work station.

Out of curiosity, I asked Grandpa if there were other things that I give no thought to that have particular ways to be done. His dear old face lit up all smiles and he began to tell me how to fold the towels so they face the same way in the linen closet and how to vacuum the floor all in one direction so the nap on the carpet all goes the same way.

When Grandpa started telling me how all the silverware in the kitchen drawer should face the same direction, Grandma realized how difficult it must be for such a particular man to live with a "never mind" spouse. Mercy, how much this dear man must love me to have put up with my total disregard for order and organization all these years.

I put my arms around him and hugged him tight and told him I loved him and asked if he wanted some ice cream. Of course he did, bless his heart. Grandma did NOT ask him if it mattered how I put the ice-cream in the bowl. Somethings you just don't want to know.

Through the years, Grandma has figured out how to make Grandpa's OCD work FOR me. The severe OCD makes my beloved absolutely obsessed with things like---how the sheets on the bed are made up. They have to be perfectly straight, no wrinkles, the exact amount of sheet on each side of the bed. Now, I could get all worked up and have a hissy because every time I make the bed, grandpa re-makes it.

But, knowing that OCD is real, and Grandpa's mental anguish is genuine, I decided to make it work FOR me. Years ago, I lovingly told him that I couldn't make the bed perfect, and like him, I did so love a *perfectly* made bed. Ok, so that was a tiny little exaggeration—the only thing Grandma cares about is that the bed has sheets and blankets ON It---period. Never the less, I asked him, kindly, not sarcastically, if he would please make the bed—perfectly--just for me.

Well, he did. In fact, he was delighted to make the bed for me. It takes him twice as long as it takes me—and he even measures the length of the sheet hangover with his hand to make sure both sides are exactly the same. I go make him a bowl of cereal to enjoy before he goes to bed while he gets the bed all made—absolutely--perfectly.

Then, when we go to bed, I always tell him how beautiful the bed is---"look at those blankets, no wrinkles, not even one." The pillows are stacked as only an engineer can stack them. The sheets with a perfect over hang that is consistent all the way around the bed. I truly appreciate this bit of housekeeping help and I always kiss him and tell him how much I enjoy sleeping in our—perfectly made---bed.

I love this old man, for a few years when we were first married, he drove me crazy, but, in time, I learned to make many of his idiosyncrasies work for ME, not annoy me. Grandma can't change anybody but herself---and I'm a handful. Mercy. Oddly, I've discovered that when I change, most often, so does Grandpa, because we influence each other. It just takes some time.

Like all of our friends married and single, we are becoming the representatives of Christ; each considering the needs of the other, honoring Jesus, one day at a time.

These are some photos of our friends. If you ever see them out and about, hug their neck and tell them you know Grandma.

Rearview Mirror Faith

This afternoon, Grandma was in the car with my lovely young teen granddaughter, Betty Jean. She was being very animated in telling me that she didn't like her hair, or her eyes or---ANYthing about herself. Obviously, she was having one of those awkward "too big to be little but too little to be big" moments that make adolescence such a painful time of life.

When she was done with her list of 'stuff' that she hated about herself, I assured her that she was not only very beautiful now but one day; she'd be a beautiful woman as well. With a frustrated sigh, she proclaimed, "But Grandma, by then, <u>you'll</u> be DEAD!" While that is a stunning thought, it could prove to be true. I made a mental note to spend more time with Betty Jean; she will be out on her own in just a few years. Grandma must make memories while time is at hand.

It is hard to imagine that in just a few years, my precious granddaughter will be out in the world, on her own. Grandma feels a fear in the pit of my stomach when I think about it. She is so naïve' yet so grown up. Naïve about how to handle life's issues in the wisdom and love of Christ but she is very much aware of the things the world offers. She is at a cross roads, the decisions she makes now will have direct influence on the rest of her life.

It strikes Grandma as---strange---that the biggest decisions that determine our life outcome are made when we are young and naïve. Who we marry, who our close friends are, our career path, our faith, our lifestyle; many of these decisions are made while we are, as the saying goes, "young and clueless." Wouldn't it make better sense if these decisions were made later on when we have gained some experience and wisdom?

Thanks to television, movies, and just the world life style in general, young women today are far older than their years. I know for a fact from the very open conversations my granddaughter and I have had together that this woman child knows more about sex now than Grandma did on her wedding night. Not because she is promiscuous, heaven's <u>no</u>.

This too soon maturity has come because she lives in a Godless world that has worldly pursuits at every turn. The world has robbed her of her childhood; her hedge of innocence has been removed. She is daily facing things that Grandma never faced till in her mid-20s, if ever at all. Indeed, some of the things she tells me of leave my old eyeballs going, "blink blink."

Forget the influence of movies, media and television programming. A full education in all things adult can be had simply by watching commercials and seeing advertisements in magazines. How can purity be kept when the world is determined to invade and influence even the youngest most innocent of minds?

Is there ANY reason why a young person, not even old enough to drive, whether male OR female, should be well informed about erectile dysfunction, the wide selection of catheters available, vaginal dryness or the possibility of having to cope with the loss of bladder control? Grandma does not think so. Yet, those are the products that are advertised in commercial breaks during prime time family viewing on television.

The media, both television and movies, is jam packed with examples of rebellion and loss of family values. Most of the sitcoms spotlight families that are not Godly in any way shape or form. The adolescents and teens are in charge of the households, making their own life decisions without parental direction. Often times, adult supervision is not even depicted, just the teens doing whatever is "good for today." The husbands are belittled by the mother and mocked by the children. Often, both parents are portrayed as idiots and the teens are in charge.

Careless irresponsible living, lying, stealing and every kind of fornication, pornography and sexual dysfunction that can be thought of are presented as a normal part of life on almost every sit-com. What's worse, now, even some people who are in church think these things are---acceptable—in *Christian* homes.

Leave It to Beaver, Lassie, and the Mary Tyler Moore show are no longer the markers for life in America. In today's world, the idea of watching television for examples of how life is well lived is a joke; there are no standards set by society and God's standards are mocked.

The stuff that is going on in the world today has not taken God by surprise. In fact, the Bible even describes what is going on today—in definite words, not vague illusions. II Timothy 3 says, "But mark this: There will be terrible times in the last days. People will be lovers of themselves, lovers of money, boastful, proud, abusive, disobedient to their parents, ungrateful, unholy, without love, unforgiving, slanderous, without self-control, brutal, not lovers of the good, treacherous, rash, conceited, lovers of pleasure rather than lovers of God—having a form of godliness but denying its power. Have nothing to do with such people."

No matter what circumstances look like in the world around us, His Word assures us that He will do everything there is to be done to give our children, grandchildren and others we love---*direction and opportunity* to come to serve Him. God is able to not only keep their hearts focused on Him, but also will use the bad things they experience to strengthen them.

Sometimes, the only way we will see the full extent of God's faithfulness is through the "rearview mirror" of eternity. We, as grandmother's who love God with all of our heart---must continue to stand strong in prayer. Come quickly, Lord Jesus.

Another Use for Duct Tape

Today, I spent the afternoon with three of our grandchildren. All day long, I kept looking at my eleven year old grandson, Henry, trying to figure out what was different about his appearance. Today, as he was reading his library book, it struck me what the difference was.

Casually, I said, "Hey, Henry, what happened to your eye brows?" At the same time he said, "Nothing," his little sister said, "I didn't MEAN to, mamaw!" For the last two days, I had noticed that she would obediently do whatever he asked. This, in itself, was <u>totally</u> unheard of. Something was very _very_ strange and it had to do with my grandson's eyebrows, **or the lack of them**.

Once more, I said, "Hey, what happened to your <u>eye brows</u>, bud?" He got an _extremely_ annoyed look on his face. He glared at his sister, who was again mumbling about how it was an **ACC*ID*ENT**. He took a deep breath and with obvious controlled annoyance said, "I was sleeping on the couch and SHE put duct tape on them." He scowled at his sister, who was muttering, "Well, I didn't know it would do THAT."

In disbelief, I started shaking my head and saying "oh no, no; she **<u>didn't</u>**!" He responded, "Oh yes, she **DID**, she put duct tape on my eyebrows while I was asleep then she _<u>pulled the tape off.</u>_" His forehead was a telltale shade of pink, obviously still suffering from the consequences of such a crude depilatory act.

Glaring at his sister, with no eyebrows for expression, he had this wide-eyed look of permanent amazement. He shrugged and said, "I want a cold drink." His sister turned and ran to the kitchen and got the cold drink, opened it and humbly handed it to her brother. I could tell it was going to be a long 'payback' for my granddaughter–.

Grandma knows that when we ask God to forgive us for something we did; <u>God </u>has no payback. However, we are often left to deal with the life consequences caused by our sin. And like Henry, sometimes innocent people are left to suffer the consequences of our sin as well. But, thankfully, God provides us ALL with the Holy Spirit to direct us toward reconciliation. Taking another sip of my hot tea, Grandma can't help but to laugh. She duct taped his eyebrows? _SERIOUSLY_? OH, mercy **sakes**---.

Grandma's Miracle Tan

According to the television commercials, one of the most important goals every woman has for this summer is to get a gorgeous tan. The perfect answer to the busy woman's desire for a golden tan is, tan in a tube. A tanning cream that can be applied like lotion and within a few hours, a perfect golden tan develops. Personally, Grandma thinks it would be a far better choice to lay on the beach and get a tan, but, I don't have time for that and science says it isn't healthy.

Grandma knows how to cook and I know what is really happening with a natural "tan." You are lying out on a big towel slathered in coconut oil and letting the sun fry your skin to a golden brown. Seriously, that is what is happening---all that is missing is a pinch of salt and pepper; but you don't hear very many people refer to tanning as frying.

So, a tan in a tube delivered as a smooth as silk, easy to apply cream, seems to be a much healthier, safer way to accomplish that delicious golden brown color. What's not to love? And, it certainly takes less time. Grandma is all about getting things done without wasting precious time. I went to the pharmacy and bought two large tubes of self-tan it; Grandma is a big woman.

After Grandpa went to bed Tuesday night, I quietly slipped into the bathroom, shut the door and fetched the two tubes of self-tan it out from under the sink. Stripping down to the bare essentials, Grandma picked up the tube and found the print was too small to read. Not wanting to get dressed and go hunt for my reading glasses, I figured, what could be so difficult, I'd watched the TV model apply it on the commercial, let the tanning proceed.

I squirted a handful of the white cream into my hand and began to liberally smear it all over my body. How could white cream turn my skin into a golden brown? We'll see, I doubt it, but, we'll see. The cream vanished into my skin making it difficult in knowing what skin had been smeared and what skin had not.

Squirting more cream into my hand, I continued lathering myself, being careful to go back over questionable application areas. I did not want to end up spotted. The first tube of self-tan used up just as I finished the process. I was pleased that I'd have the second tube for a second tan for another day.

As I stood in the middle of the bathroom, impatiently waiting for the cream to totally dry, I realized I'd not applied any tan cream to my face. None. I got the second tube of cream, squeezed out a handful and slathered it all over my face. Still having an ample amount in my hand, I went ahead and smeared it down my arms and across the front of my legs, if a little is good, more would only be better, right? Finally, my skin felt dry and I turned out the light and tippy toed to bed.

The next morning I woke to the sound of laughter. Grandpa was standing beside me as I lay in bed, laughing till the tears fell out of his eyeballs. Before I could ask what was so funny, he left to make coffee hollering, "You need to go look in the mirror."

Leaping out of bed the first thing I noticed was a light brown body print on the bed sheet. There was a perfect Grandma silhouette, in the palest of brown imprinted on the linen. It looked like one of those crime scene people marks. Oh, great, I thought the cream had been dry when I got in bed. I hoped ALL the tan had not rubbed off on the sheets.

Unfortunately, I got what I had hoped for; there was still tan on my body—lots of tan and places that had no tan and other places that had a little tan. Tan in swirls, tan in squiggles, tan in different shades of brown. It seems the two tubes of lotion were not the same color. Who knew tan came in colors? The tv commercial had not mentioned that.

Digging out the thrown away empty tube and the just opened tube, I found one was "deppest dark tan" and the other one was, "soft golden tan." I looked like I'd been dipped in vanilla, then caramel then chocolate. HORRIFIED, I jumped in the shower. The water and soap never faded the tan a bit. Then, another attack of horror---my bed sheets; it the tan doesn't wash off in the shower---will it wash off the bed sheet in the laundry?

A good washing with bleach took the tan crime scene Grandma shadow off the sheet. It took a week before the tan started to fade on my body. During that time, every time Grandpa looked at me, he snickered. My friends giggled at church and my co-workers giggled at the store. Even strangers snickered at my---tan. Grandma wondered why I'd even cared what the world thought about whether or not I had a tan in the first place.

The world has turned "self" into a life style. Self-worth, self-esteem, self-respect; it's all about "me." Surprisingly, God also thinks "self" is important. But, with a slightly different slant---.

Jesus said that the second most important commandment is to <u>love our neighbor *as our self*</u>. What we feel about our self motivates how we treat others. And when you get right down to it---whether Grandma or you have a good tan has nothing to do with anything. Nope. Beauty comes from the inside, not the outside.

Grandma's Cookie Blog

If you know Grandma and you are familiar with my ineptitude with ALL things techno, this will make you laugh. As I was going to the kitchen to make cookies, a crazy thought surfaced in my mind; I want to write a cookie blog. Yes, I know, I know; I'll give you time to stop laughing before I continue with my writing. Women today have so much responsibility that they have no time to bake cookies. The lack of gooey homemade cookies in today's busy society could be the problem causing many of our stress disorders.

Last week, Grandma heard one of the teens at church talking about stuff they learned on a blog site AND I'd heard her say that she had stuff she had put on her own blog. Obviously this blog thing is recognized as a source for information and must not be too complicated to create. After all, Grandma is a writer, so, that has to be helpful at least on some level. I hope.

Because I love God so much, my heart wants to include Him in everything that I do. Grandma has to create a blog that says something about Jesus, ***without*** being "preachy," and include cookie recipes and baking tips. To start with, what exactly is a blog, can I use it for recipes? I've heard the word, blog, and I've heard about how useful it is, but I don't really understood what it means or is. Grandpa has a computer at his office, maybe he'd know?

Hoping for help, I went into the den and asked Grandpa what he thought of when I said, "blog." He looked at me over the tops of his bifocals and quipped, "I think of a long haired unemployed hippy with a scrappy beard living in his mama's basement writing about how useless his life is and how it's somebody else's' fault." Allllrighty then, I'm guessing that Grandpa has NOT had a good blogging experience. So, I guess I'd better get on line and see what I can learn on my own about a blog and how to make one.

All I know about a blog is that it's done on a computer. Not wanting to bother my teen aged granddaughter who is busy behind piles of homework books at the dining room table, I googled, even Grandma knows how to Google, and found rules for creating a blog. Experts say the first thing that I must do is, choose a subject and a title. I know what the blog is about, so on to choosing a title. Grandma is grateful there are rules for every step.

Rule #1: A blog title should not be underwhelming (?). The title should be unique, yet clearly state the content and draw the reader "in." "Grandma Bakes With Jesus?" No. Well, I mean I DO, but that's not a good title; no mention of cookies and it makes Jesus sound like an ingredient like sugar or chocolate chips. Ok, how about, "Grandma Blogs About Baking Cookies With Jesus." No, too long and it still has Jesus sounding like a cup of sugar.

Wait, statistics say the most commonly used title word for a blog is; "blog." The blog site tutorial says that because of the common use, I should, therefore, _not_ use it. Whaaaaat? This means that, "Grandma's Cookie Blog" with, or without, mention of Jesus, is not a good title choice. Oh my, maybe blog making isn't going to be as easy as I'd hoped. Grandma wishes she'd baked a pan of cookies for herself before she started learning about blogs; just saying— research is hard work. Mercy.

My Thesaurus is found and an alternate word for "blog" is--? Blog is NOT IN my desk Thesaurus. Back to Google search, I learned that "blog" didn't exist until April (maybe even May), 1999. I made a paste it note to buy a more current version of Roget's even though the pages on this one don't look worn in spite of frequent use. Technology happens so fast.

Hoping for help, I asked my granddaughter what SHE thought a good blog title would be. She looked up at me over the top of a stack of school books and quipped, "Blog title? I thought you were going to bake us some cookies." (Sigh) Obviously, she isn't going to be any help at all—at least not until I get cookies baked.

Rule #2: Identify the kind of people that will be reading my blog. Obviously, that would be young women who want to bake but don't have time. They need time saving hints. AND, with such busy lives, they need encouragement in Christ. Grandma must combine Jesus with baking cookies and helpful time saving hints; this is a challenge. Help me, Lord, to put all this together.

Rule #3: Use vivid words to lure the casual reader in. How do I make a blog about baking cookies ---vivid? With all this new technology, Grandma wishes that somebody had invented smellavision. Now THAT would lead the reader in. I'm no wiser than I was to start with, but all this research and thought has made me feel 'snacky' and Betty Jean is expecting cookies.

I pull out my mixing bowl; Grandma thinks better while she is baking. Instinctively, I dump the ingredients into the bowl and turn my mixer on. Fiddle faddle, I'm out of chocolate chips. Not to mind, I'll make snicker doodles, another favorite.

Back to my blog; a vivid title that doesn't use common words yet lures the reader in. Oh, and without using the word, "blog" and doesn't make my Lord sound like a cup of flour. Grandma has baked for more years than computers have existed; the cookie dough comes together with little thought and much prayer.

No matter how busy life gets, the joy of both baking and eating homemade cookies never goes away. I remember when I was a young mom; the list of chores was daunting and I didn't even work outside the home. Mercy sakes. I can't even imagine working full time AND keeping up the house and kids. What can I do with this blog to encourage these girls who are carrying such a heavy load?

Then, it came to me. Today's young women don't need a blog on how to make baking easier. What they need is an old granny to bring them a plate of warm, prayed over cookies. As I pull the last pan of cookies out of the oven, I see young Janice, next door, pulling into her driveway.

Two cranky preschoolers in tow, her weariness is clearly seen on her young face. Grandma isn't waiting for those weary young women to have time to read a blog. Giving the weary even more to do on top of what they already MUST do---that just---is not—ministry.

I'm taking cookies baked with the love of Jesus, TO them. Pulling out an inexpensive yet decorative plastic party platter from the cabinet, I pile cookies on the plate, praying over them as I build a giant cookie mountain. I'm careful to leave a dozen cookies for Grandpa and Betty Jean.

With one more prayer of blessing and direction breathed over the plate piled high with cookies I head out the door. From the end of my driveway, I wave at Janice, hold out the cookie mountain plate and shout, "I baked cookies for you today, honey!" Janice looks up, surprised, then, oh mercy sakes, she begins to---cry.

"Thank you! Thank you SO much! You just don't know what this means to me tonight!"

Baking is a ministry---yes. I Peter 4:10 comes to Grandma's mind, "Each of you should use _whatever_ gift you have received to serve others, as faithful stewards of God's grace in its various forms." Baking is Grandma's "_whatever_."

(Grandma's special Extra Chocolatey Chip Cookies recipe, the ones I usually make for taking to folks, is at the end of this book--- this is not a recipe that I share often---please, enjoy. Everybody has a recipe for snicker doodles, so I'll just include my special chocolate chip recipe.)

Grandma's snicker doodles turned out pretty enough for a picture---so before I took them to the sweet girl next door, I took a picture. Mercy, I wish there was scratch and sniff for books!

Grandma's Skinny Doctor

Grandma hates to go to the doctor. I do not have time for all that. However, my doctor seems to think I should stop by and check in with him at least every 4-6 months. I humor him. Since I have to be there, I figure I may as well enjoy the journey.

Why does the doctor need to weigh Grandma? My weight goes back and forth; when I starve and exercise, I lose weight. However, eventually all the weight I lost comes right back on and brings friends. It would make more sense if the nurse just wrote, "still fat," or "fat again," in my chart and let it go. Those crazy doctor scales are never accurate. It is humanly impossible for Grandma to gain weight while in transit from my house to his office—yet—every time this is what happens.

Since the doctor's scales are so sensitive, I remove any possible source of excess weight before I mount the scales. I set down my purse—which weighs as much as a bowling ball all by itself—take off my shoes---my jewelry—and this last time, I took out my teeth. Still didn't help, the extra few pounds were still manifested on the digital read.

Frustrated, I jumped off the scale, pointed at it and hollered, "LYING SCALE! LYING SCALE!" You see, this last four months, Grandma has exercised faithfully, three times a week at the YMCA. Also, I walk a mile every evening---measured on my car mileage and confirmed on a local map. Today should be one of the times that I weigh less. So, after walking a mile a day, working out at the gym three days a week AND still---Grandma weighs exactly the same as she did last time? The scales are rigged, I know they are.

Not only has Grandma been exercising, I've also been taking major effort to cut down on carbs, calories and fat in our daily diet. Grandpa loves ice cream. He thinks the day is not over with until he gets a bowl of ice cream each evening. Now, Walter gets a huge bowl with three or four healthy dips in it and Grandma gets ONE small dip in a custard cup. Guess who doesn't gain weight and who does? Life is not fair.

Grandma read that the best way to deal with avoiding desserts is to make it inconvenient to *have* dessert. So, I started not buying any dessert items. I told Grandpa from now on, if he wanted dessert, we'd have to get our shoes on, get in the car, drive across town and go to the ice cream store. No longer is it convenient to grab a dish of ice-cream—it will now take quite a bit of effort.

I suspected that this plan was not working as well as I thought it would when the little clerk at the ice cream store down town started calling Walter, "Grandpa" and knew what flavors he liked and started dipping them when we walked in the door. Obviously Grandpa was making more than the now and then trip to the ice cream store.

Yes, I agree that our daily eating habits should be healthy. I've always cooked healthy meals. It is only in the last decade that we've started losing the battle with weight. Always before, eating sensibly kept us at a reasonable weight. Now, with the onset of age, it's like our metabolism has totally shut down. If I'd been serving up cakes, pies and biscuits every day, it would make sense to cut back. But when you've maintained a fairly healthy diet all your life, there is no wall to back up against.

Healthy magazines and knowledgeable people tell me that eating well and exercise will lengthen my life. My issue is that now, those extra years of life added on are not going to be good quality years. If those added years would have been added on when I was say, 30-50, that would make sense. But, instead those extra years will be added on at the end, so I'll live to be 95 instead of 90. What's the point? Obviously these nutrition gurus have not thought this "health" thing through.

So, Grandma has come up with a conclusion. My doctor is a tiny, thin man. Obviously, he has no idea what Grandma goes through just to stay at the current level of fat. He has no concept of the struggle of dieting to be thin then before you know it, you're being fat again. Those rare times when I do show up thin at my appointment, he doesn't dance or sing, blow a horn, doesn't even clap his hands for me. He just says, "You lost some weight, good."

Maybe I should take a picture the next time I'm thin and show it to him when he's going on about being overweight since he doesn't seem to remember those times I HAVE lost weight. I've told the dear man that as I've aged I've had to give up so many pleasures it is insane. The list of things Grandma either can't do or can't have grows longer and longer.

The last thing on my list of "fun to do/have" is dessert. I've allowed the other fun things to fall to the wayside without too much whining. But, Grandma has standards. You will NOT take my tiny little slice of pie, eaten at the buffet after Sunday dinner when church lets out, away from me. Nope.

Grandma's Moustache

Tonight Grandma enjoyed a very special dinner at the BBQ shack in celebration of her birthday. My oldest son and his family and one of my daughters and her family were with us. After dinner, my little grandson was sitting on my lap. He looked at me with those big brown 4 year old eyes and very seriously said, "Mamawl, kiss me on the lips." Amused by his childish demand, I told him, no, but I'd kiss him on the cheek, and I did.

After a few minutes, he looked up at me and insisted, "Mamawl, I want you to kiss me <u>right on my lips</u>." And he puckered up his little mouth. I hugged him and said, "Honey, someday you will kiss your girlfriend on the lips and later, your wife on the lips, but Mamawl is not going to kiss you on the lips."

He squinted his eyes and said, "Oh." Then, a few moments later, he said, "Well Mamawl, then can I lick your lips with my tongue?" Momentarily I was stunned speechless — recovering, I said, "WHAT? WHY on earth would you want to lick Mamawl's LIPS?" He shrugged his shoulders and said, "Because I want to see if the hair on your lip tickles me like Daddy's does".

My son laughed so hard he had to stand up to keep from falling out of his chair. My daughter in-law covered her face with her hands and laughed till her shoulders shook. The waitress who was serving our drinks at the time of the proclamation, laughed so hard she splashed tea all over Grandpa. My little grandson, with no idea why everybody was laughing gave a deep sigh and said, "I guess this means no."

Later that night, I sat with my cup of coffee and just shaking my head, still laughing at my little grandson's before dinner revelation. On the way home, I had stopped at the pharmacy and bought a box of those "hair removal wax strips." It's so easy to miss things in our lives that are very obvious to others!

As I sat quietly contemplating how I could have missed something so obvious—and yes, when I got home, I looked in the mirror and it WAS that—obvious. Yet, I'd not even realized, had honestly never noticed. As I picked up my Bible to read before turning in for the night, the Holy Spirit began to speak to my heart.

Perhaps since it is so easy to overlook such an obvious physical problem, perhaps I should take a good look inside my heart regularly as well. An attitude of self-righteousness, a selfish heart, an arrogant spirit; all these things are easily seen by those around us but most often not noticed within ourselves.

I certainly do not want to have anything hiding in my heart that can harm the reflection of Christ through me. And mercy sakes, I hope that removing those unnoticed, pesky sins from my heart is less painful than removing the hair from Grandma's upper lip. Ouch!

A Dead Man-- Where?

Today, while Grandma was at work, I got a strange phone call from a neighbor. My friend who lives next door to me called and said, "You need to come home right now, there's a dead man on your roof. The coroner said to tell you he can't pronounce the man dead till YOU give permission for him to climb onto your roof and pronounce the death."

My first reaction was to hold the phone out from my head and look at it---making confirmation that I was actually having this conversation on a real telephone, not a stunt prop. Putting the receiver back to my ear I said, "Is this a joke? Because if this is a joke, I don't think it is very funny and I'm busy, I don't have time for this right now." The familiar voice of my friend whispered, "I know it sounds crazy, but, I swear to heaven, the coroner is standing here and says you can't even give him permission on the phone, you have to say "it's ok" looking right in his face."

Well, I was pretty much sure this WAS a joke; my neighbor is always laughing and plotting some kind of crazy venture---but I really was curious how she could arrange such a crazy drama. I had to go home and look anyway, because according to her, if I didn't come home of my own free will, they would send a police car to my work place to pick me up and bring me. Crazy as it all sounds, if true, Grandma does not need that kind of drama at work. So, I locked the office and headed for my house.

As soon as I turned down my street, I saw a fire truck, a police car and the coroner's wagon sitting in front of my house. First, I gasped, then I fought the urge to laugh; it wasn't a prank, it was --- real. The confirmation of reality was even crazier than fantasy could ever be. There—was--- actually--a---dead---man---on—my---roof. Grandma pulled into the driveway and slowly got out of the car, still looking cautiously around for any sign of an elaborate Candid Camera type set up.

A large man in a City Government shirt came toward me, clip board in hand, and introduced himself as the County Coroner. I had no idea what my response to the situation should be so I smiled and asked him if I could please see his ID. He looked at me for a moment, expressionless, not even blinking. Then, he said, "Why certainly, ma'am." and reached into his pant pocket and pulling out a well-worn leather wallet, fumbled through the contents then handed me a photo identification that declared the holder to be---in fact—the County Coroner. I thanked him and handed the ID back, signed the necessary paper work and stood with the small crowd of curious people now gathered in my yard.

The dead man on my roof was one of the roofing crew that was replacing my roof. At noontime, the workers, except for the one now lying on my roof motionless and very pale, had gone to get lunch. The worker left behind had said to bring him a sandwich, he'd finish the block of shingles he was working on then come down and eat when they returned.

When the roofers returned, they found their co-worker lying motionless on the roof. When he could not be roused, they had called 911, who had sent the customary array of first responders and the coroner. The coroner, after a quick examination to confirm death, stated that it looked like the dear man had a massive heart attack and was DRT (Dead Right There). He did not fall down and die, he died and fell down.

Later as Grandma sat on the sun porch sipping a cup of hot tea, the uncertainty of life was very clear. The scripture says that we are never promised another day, but to have such a personal illustration was a bit unnerving. This dear man had been at home this morning; he kissed his wife and children good bye, petted his dog and left for work.

Neither he nor his family had any idea that would be the last time he would be at home alive. It was a day like any day and he was a healthy middle aged man, active and involved with life. He had plans and goals. That he could be dead now, with no warning, was just---unbelievable. I'd heard one of his co-workers saying that he loved Jesus and was active in his church—that comforted me.

Precious in the eyes of the Lord is the death of His saints---and youth is not a guarantee that there is still much time ahead of us. Another reason to live each day to the fullest, never walk away angry and always hold those you love close to your heart---none of us knows what day will be our last. Grandma started sipping the tea and listened to the crickets in the woods chirping. Thank you, Lord, for giving me another day.

Food Police Alert

Grandma has heard a lot of jokes made about the food police. A few folks have allegedly levied law suits against prominent fast food eateries for making them fat. This cracks Grandma up because I've never had anybody any place order my food for me or make me eat something I didn't order. A side of fries or an ice cream now and then is not going to make me fat; such treats are---treats—not an everyday diet. And if I get fat, I do it to myself; I certainly don't need anybody to help me.

Never the less, I've heard that a few people have even won those 'you made me fat' lawsuits. As a result of those law suits, some reports say that more and more eateries are downsizing their menus and some are even advising their wait staff to point out more healthy food choices in the hopes that their establishment will not be the next to be sued for making a patron---fat.

Grandma has often wondered if these stories about people's dietary choices being interfered with were actually true. The media these days loves to major in the minors and minor in the majors, if you know what I mean. Different cities have different businesses and different types of people; maybe it is a location thing, not a nationwide trend?

Maybe it's different where those folks go for their hamburgers, but every place I've ever been there was a menu, usually with very large detailed posters hanging on the walls clearly illustrating the hot and juicy wares they were peddling. Anybody with half a brain knows 'hot and juicy' is fast food speak for 'hot and greasy.' Place your order or go home and make yourself a salad. This is America, land of the free; eat what you want for lunch people. Even more importantly, let everybody else eat what they want.

My son in-law and our daughter along with our young adolescent grandson, Henry, had a real life run in with a member of the Food Police the other day. And, the enforcer was not wearing a uniform. In fact, she seemed to be more busy body than concerned about healthy meal choices. First, let me tell you a bit about my grandson so you know what led up to the encounter.

Young Henry wears braces on his teeth. Even though he's had them for a while, every now and then, his mouth gets really mad about the whole 'braces thing.' His orthodontist told his mom to give him ibuprofen for the inflammation. After a painful brace realignment, Henry's mom would gently remind him, "Braces are not a fashion statement, they are a medical treatment and sometimes medicine isn't easy. Sometimes good results are painful to accomplish."

In the beginning, the orthodontist told our daughter that, not often, rarely, but every now and then when the braces really make a statement in suffering, there would be times when a milk shake would be permissible as a meal--. Such things *are* allowed and even authorized by a doctor—now and then. Now, back to the moment; young Henry and his parents stopped to get the aforementioned milk shake.

Henry's mouth was swollen, he was pale and flushed and even his lips were poking out from the painful adjustment his braces had just under gone earlier that morning. The doctor recommended that a milkshake was definitely a good choice for lunch.

Henry and his mom and dad sat down at a table and a waitress came over and asked what they wanted. Henry mumbled that he wanted a large side by side milkshake vanilla/chocolate with extra whipped cream and a side car of fudge. (Grandma just now gained two pounds typing the words--)

The waitress jutted her hip out to the side, shook her finger in admonition, pursed her lips, and said, "NO. That is not healthy; you can't have a milkshake for lunch."

Our son in-law, with an inquiring look, leaned over to our daughter and said, "What did she just say to *my* boy?" Our daughter looked at the waitress and saw a serious look, not a joking look. Henry said he knew that look his mom was getting on her face, that first surprised then furious brown eyeballs flashing fire look and he sat there thinking, "Ohhhhhhhh man, this can't be good."

Henry's mom said she took a deep breath --smiled sweetly and said, "Yes, he **can**." His Dad turned to his mom again and repeated his question, "Did she just tell **MY** boy he couldn't *HAVE* a milkshake?"

Both mom and dad looked the waitress in the eye; Henry said he squinted his eyes shut----. Our son in-law said he was getting ready to tell the self-appointed food police that the stud in the tip of her tongue couldn't be healthy either, but it wasn't any of HIS business, was it? When the waitress shrugged and wrote down their order and that was the end of that. Talk about a timely miracle of intervention; mercy.

I asked Henry if he got his milkshake. He grinned, "Yeah, and you better believe I drank that baby fast!"

Grandma Gets Drug Busted

You KNOW how Grandma loves to help with Children's Church. A new class series is starting soon! In preparation, I had been singing the kids' song for the puppet play again and again. I'd put the audio tape in my car and I sang along with it wherever I went. After several weeks, I finally had the words committed to my brain.

After all the weeks of practice, one day, I was not singing it when I picked the grandkids up. Noticing the silence, my grandson, said HE **WANTED** to sing it some MORE! I took this as encouragement because a child---like the ones in my class, was so excited about the song; he WANTED to hear it again. A bit of encouragement is always good to hear.

Before I could get all heady about this moment, his older brother quickly responded, "Ok, but do you want to sing it the way mamawl sings it ---or the way it's ***supposed*** to sound?" After the initial stun of what was said, I couldn't' stop laughing.

After I dropped the kids off and I was driving home, the thought came; the world is watching to see how we handle everyday life as Christians. Is my life "sounding" the way Jesus REALLY sounds? Or have I made up my own version of the way Jesus "sounds?" Wow! What an eyeball opening revelation!

With this heavy thought on my mind, I see a police check point up ahead of me on the highway. As I put my brakes on, I look in the windshield mirror to make sure I'm not going to be rear-ended. My eyeballs see my little granddaughter's car seat, still strapped in my back seat.

I mentally acknowledge that my daughter only has one car seat and it is strapped in my car. Obviously, I need to turn around and take that seat back to her house or she'll have no way to take the kids to Day Care before work in the morning. As I'm slowing down for the traffic check ahead, I see a dirt road to the left; put my signal on, turn into the road and then right back onto the highway, back towards my daughter's house.

As I'm driving up the street, I notice flashing blue lights coming up fast behind me! THREE police cars are on my tail; I realize I need to get out of their way because they are coming up behind me fast, sirens shrieking. I pull off to the side of the road to allow them to pass. To my astonishment, the cops' cars pull in behind me, in front of me and beside me. Grandma's mind is going, "Whaaaaaat?"

I'm sitting there wondering what on EARTH when two of the officers appear beside my window, guns drawn. By this time, I'm wondering what on earth I'd done; was it illegal to turn onto that dirt road then go back the other way? And how could a simple illegal turn instigate such a crazy response?

The officer demands that I keep my hands in sight and get out of the car. I do so, my heart pounding like a jackhammer in my chest. I'm so skeert all my mind can do is pray and I'm so bumfuzzled that the only prayer I can pray is in tongues. Now, people, you KNOW that is some kind of serious scared, right there. Mercy.

A female officer pats me down, while a male officer asks me what I have in my car. My tongue is so scared I could barely mumble, "What? Nothing---what? Why did you stop me?" The officer asks me why I was in such a hurry to get away from the traffic stop.

Finally, Grandma realizes why all this is happening and I stutter, "Ohhhh, no, I slowed down and when I looked in the rearview, saw my granddaughter's car seat in the back. I knew her mom had to have it in the morning, so I turned around and was going back to drop the baby's seat off."

The officer tells me to stand "right there" while they search through Grandma's car, opening the trunk and the hood and feeling up underneath the seats. Now, a K-9 unit shows up and a dog is led over to my car and starts sniffing. After a thorough sniff, the doggie sits down and just sits there. The dog's handler gives him a doggie treat. The officers are on their cell phones, calling people, asking me questions and relaying my answers.

Grandma is really scared now, but not because of any kind of law breaking. Those two cups of coffee I drank an hour ago are showing up and my bladder is at maximum capacity---and for an old lady, this is never good. This police encounter needs to end and it needs to end fast or somebody is going to have to get a mop.

One of the officers asks for my daughter's name, address and phone number. I'm doing my best to tell all that---but Grandma's mind is concentrating on one thing and that is bladder control, not addresses. The lady officer calls my daughter's house and asks a few questions. Satisfied with the answers, she says a few words to her fellow officers and they start packing up to leave, shaking my hand and giving apologies and explaining about how "suspicious" my actions had looked.

As the police cars pull out, Grandma's son in law pulls up in his truck. He comes over, hugs me tight. I notice that he is shaking---I'm deeply moved that he is so concerned that he is crying over me—when I realize he is not crying. He is LAUGHING. He laughed and laughed and LAUGHED. Grandma was NOT amused, but laughter is contagious—and I started laughing with him.

After assuring himself that I was ok, in spite of the trauma, he helps me get into my car and gets the car seat out. As he walks away I hear him saying into his cell phone, "You aren't gonna believe this, my mother in law just got stopped in a drug search---yeah, I know, crazy! Scared her so bad she almost wet her pants."

Grandma's Paean

Yesterday, as I was doing my every day Bible reading, David's Psalm 136 caught Grandma's eye. What makes this Psalm different than all the others is that every other line is the repeated phrase, "His mercy endures forever." Why did David repeat the same line--to the point of making the phrase, itself, a paean?   As ever, I ask God to show me the truth in His Word. Even this repetitive line must have some root in reason? God sends no revelation and I finish my prayer time and go about my day.

Today, as I engage in my daily routine, I find myself consumed with care for my loved ones, the church and the world. As I work, play, rest and sleep, I find my heart's prayer a reminder of whose I am. My friends and loved ones need Jesus; I've wearied them with my constant witness. They turn and hide when they see me coming. My voice is like fingers grating on a black board to their ears, or so I've been told. Never the less, my heart whispers, "I love you, my Lord; I trust you and I will see your salvation in the hearts of those I love."

The economy is shaking. My dollars pay for less and less. The cost of living escalates day by day. A loaf of bread and a gallon of milk costs more than a week's groceries did when I was a child. My job is uncertain; I don't know if there will be a pay check next week. My heart confidently speaks, "I love you, my Lord; I trust you and am eager to see your provision."

The government is corrupt; officials mock the name of my King and belittle his son, Jesus Christ. Those who praise you openly and give thanks are ridiculed and mocked. It is against the rules to carry your precious Holy Word into our work place, our schools. My heart boldly states, "I love you, my Lord; I trust you and am eager to see your Kingdom come."

The fools who do not know you predict the end of time will be soon. The calendar of the ancient ones ends leaving those of weak faith to declare there is no future. Earthquakes and great storms ravage the countryside; who knows what will happen next? My heart speaks with reassurance, "I love you, my Lord; I trust you and am eager to be surrounded by your protection."

How can I doubt your strength when I look into your face and see the fire in your eyes? The world crumbles, the economy shakes, the people rebel, yet I will not be afraid because you are my Lord and I will keep my eyes on you and you alone. My heart stands strong and shouts, "I love you, my Lord; I trust you and am eager to be consumed by your peace."

Tears streaming down my face, Grandma must stop to worship. The concerns of life, the fears of the day, the worrisome sounds of rebellion against your name weary my ears. But, my heart rejoices because I know YOU. My hands must lift in praise because you have shown yourself victorious through the ages and continue to be the victor even in the present age. I love you, my Lord; I trust you and am eager to be consumed by your praise.

King David was just as we are today—sure, he wore different clothes, walked on different streets, but his strength, resources and protection were provided by his God. Shouldn't my heart also be consumed with the acknowledgement of my Lord's presence? Indeed, from this moment on; it will be. Now, *now* I fully understand the Psalmist David's repetitious phrase.

Psalms 136: 26 Give thanks to the God of heaven. *His love endures forever.*

One Size Fits All?

Since entering that stage of life where kids call me mamawl, a lot of things have changed. The two most annoying changes are having to wear false teeth and I've put on some weight. The false teeth, I could do nothing about. My dear momma had always told me if I did not eat sweets, brushed and flossed my teeth every day, I'd never have to get dentures. She was mistaken; chalk it up to one of those things in life that aren't fair. Whatever. It's been a month and Grandma is STILL trying to get used to wearing dentures---but I'll leave that for another day's chronicle.

My weight, however, is an ongoing battle, I fought my weight for my entire life and now that I'm old, the weight is winning. As a hefty non-dressy grandma, it's really difficult to find clothes that look good....or should I say, look good ON me. I had not realized that the tastes of young women are so different from the style choices of the older women, like me. In fact, I'd not even noticed that my tastes had changed.

Then, today at the mall, I overheard my daughter and my teen aged granddaughter giggling as they looked at dresses. They did not see me coming up behind them and I heard my daughter ask, "How does this look?" She was holding a lovely multi flowered dress up to her svelte figure. My granddaughter rolled her eyeballs and giggled, "Seriously, mama, no, that looks like something grandma would wear."

About that time, they saw me and held out the dress for my opinion. I looked the garment up and down then said, "Why, it's lovely." They laughed and told me they'd just said that they bet I'd like it. Particular styles are for particular ages and body builds and obviously as the body matures, so does our fashion choices.

Fashion pros say that there are certain styles and prints that I can wear that will make me look thinner. Unfortunately, these garments don't change my physical dimensions; they only draw attention away from the obvious. Well-endowed women should never wear horizontal stripes; they make us look like we bought our clothing from Omar the tent and awning maker.

However, when I wear a dress with vertical stripes I look like a field with a fence around it. In the dotage of my old age, I just have to remember that it doesn't matter what pattern is on my garment---underneath it, I'm still not thin. A garment I put on is not going to change me and make me smaller, it will just make the dress look "busy" as my artist friend would say.

As I stand in line with my daughter while she pays for her purchase, the Holy Spirit whispers to me that there is a garment that I can wear that <u>does</u> change me; the garment of a servant. Like any other garment, I must choose to put it on. Lots of people make much ado about <u>wanting</u> to be a servant. But they don't understand that God does not make us into a servant; it is something *I must choose* to do.

I love how the Holy Spirit uses every day events and circumstances to show God's way for my life. We live in a very goal oriented society; giving to get is the standard. God has set a higher standard; it is a conscious choice that I must make—to serve—not to always be served. However, today, Grandma wishes that somebody somewhere wanted to serve me by making lovely slimming dresses for fat old ladies.

Mrs. Eberheart's Amazing Song

This weekend, Handel's Messiah will be presented at the big church down town. Grandma's memory goes back to when my Aunt Violet would take me to hear this masterpiece. I loved my Aunt Violet, she did all she could to give me a sense of wonderment for the arts, particularly music.

She never understood that I can't find the beat in a song even if you handed it to me in a bucket. She stared at me blankly when I told her I had to watch people standing beside me so I'd know where to clap. I did love the accoutrements of the Christmas music, though. I love shiny and bright and Handel's work gave way to much splendor.

Handel's amazing work is an oratorio, which is like an opera only without the theater part. Opera is considered to be musical theatre and an oratorio is just orchestra and voice. It is believed by some that when the Hallelujah chorus part of the music was written, Handle actually saw the heaven's open up and heard the angels sing. If you ever heard the chorus---you'd know why that is said. Grandma is not even a music loving person and that part of the performance always makes goosebumps come on my arms.

The presentation of *The Messiah* was always the first Saturday and Sunday in December. Living in West Virginia, it was pretty much a sure bet that the weather would be cold and crisp. The sky was an expanse of black velvet with the stars shimmering in the darkness like rhinestones. It was the kind of cold where my nose could smell it.

Aunt Violet took me to hear Handel's great master piece every year, it was a very special night for us; we dressed in our Sunday clothes. One year, I was just beginning to approach young womanhood and Aunt Violet had bought me a small tube of light pink lipstick and showed me how to apply it so my lips looked like a bow. I felt very lovely.

Of all the years we went together to see Handles greatest work, I vividly remember the year of the tube of pink lipstick. It was an Epiphany in my young life. I have no idea why, I just know in my heart that year, something happened that gave me direction for my life. Don't ask me what, I don't know. I just know---it did. Something happened inside of me that night at the annual performance of Handel's Messiah when Mrs. Eberheart sang her amazing song.

The orchestra tuned up and the lighting dimmed so that only the stage was brightly lit. The gowns were fabulous, the music unlike any other music anywhere. My skin tingled as the performance progressed. Then, Mrs. Eberheart, the soprano soloist, floated onto the stage. She wore an ethereal dark blue gown that sparkled with jewels when she moved. It wafted about her legs like dark clouds making it look like she floated across the stage.

Her solo piece was always, at least in my young adolescent mind, the high point of the entire performance. Mrs. Eberheart was the main reason I loved to attend this annual Christmas celebration. My aunt insisted that the soprano was *not* a fat lady, but I knew she was a long way from thin.

My Aunt Violet confided in me that the reason Mrs. Eberheart could sing with such intensity and range was because of her very ample bosoms. I never questioned this reasoning because oh mercy---yes, *very* ample. And somehow, in my adolescent mind, it **did** make sense.

That year, I couldn't help myself, as she flowed across the stage, I looked down the front of my own, still quite flat, chest and wondered for just a moment what it would be like to walk and not be able to see the floor. How did she not trip and fall? Did she have to do special practices to be able to walk without seeing the floor? I *could* see the floor perfectly fine and I tripped; her ability to flow across that stage with not so much as a stumble amazed me.

The vast auditorium became silent, not a sound could be heard as she stood, head bowed, silently praying for God's annointing, or so my Aunt Violet always told me---. Every year she sang the same song, "Rejoice Greatly." The big choir and the orchestra backed her up but she was the only voice that could actually be heard personally. I remembered her voice was so big I could always feel it vibrate the metal chair I was sitting on when she hit the high notes. It made my butt cheeks tickle and I would try not to giggle.

As Mrs. Eberheart began to sing there was a sparkle of light that would dance across her chest. It was a butterfly with diamond wings on a thin gold chain. It wasn't flat; the wings were at an angle so it looked like it was actually sitting on her skin, ready to take to flight. When her ample bosom would rise and fall with the music the butterfly would dance, catching the light and sparkling as it flittered from one abundant side of her chest to the other. It was—mesmerizing.

When the part of the song was reached where the one word, "rejoice," would stretch out into a whole song unto itself, I would lean forward in my seat, holding my breath marveling at how she could stretch one word out into so many levels. A few times, I even tried to hold my breath till the one word was completed and found I could not.

Every year, Mrs. Eberheart, in one breath, belted "rejoice" out making it go high then low then high then run it along then high and low—and that sparkling butterfly flying from one side of her expansive chest to the other. Mercy! No matter how many times I heard that song, by the time it was finished, I'd have sweat on my forehead and my heart would be pounding.

That year, even with all of that anticipated emotional response, it was-- different. As she sang her highly acclaimed, "rejoice" solo, an unspeakable joy and an intimate awareness of something so vast I couldn't comprehend washed over me and I shivered from head to toe. At that moment I knew that I loved Jesus more than anything or anyone in the entire world.

Mercy, Grandma's heart is beating fast just remembering about it! When the song was finished, nobody said a word. No clapping, no whistling, no stomping or anything. Just---breathless silence. The song about rejoicing left every person standing to their feet in deafening silence. Some would wipe tears from their eyes, others just stood with heads bowed.

There was more music, more singing and of course the most magnificent of all music, the Hallelujah Chorus at the ending. But, for me, the evening was over when Mrs. Eberheart finished her song. The rest of the music, in my mind, was a completely separate event. The evening was over when Mrs. Eberheart sang.

Many years later, as Grandma sat in church, my heart hurting so bad I could not breath, I didn't know how I could continue to live. Life hurt too badly. In my mind, the show was over. I'd prayed, I'd sought God for answers and my eyeballs saw nothing. I had come to the conclusion I had to choose; would I believe what God's Word said, would I believe the promises that the Holy Spirit whispered to my heart OR --not? I squinted my eyeballs shut and whispered, "I choose to believe. I choose to go on. I—choose—to stand strong."

The burden I'd been carrying for so long suddenly lightened and my throat stopped aching. Circumstances had not changed, my view point had. I chose to look through the eyes of faith, not the eyes of every day sight. Then, out of nowhere, God whispered to my heart, "Hang on my child, Mrs. Eberheart has not sung yet." Now, I'd not thought of her in---over forty years, maybe more. Yet, God's voice was clearly heard. I know I did not make it up because I'd never ever have even thought of such a thing.

Only God knew that was the earmark I'd made for the end of the performance so long ago. Confirmation of God's sovereignty can sometimes be very personal, very precious. Oh, and by the way, what I had waited for has still not come to pass. But, it will. I know it just like I knew that when Mrs. Eberheart floated out onto the stage wearing the sparkly butterfly it meant that—the waiting had ended . Yes.

Old Age is an Adventure

One of the adjustments that getting older often requires is the acquisition of dentures. It doesn't sound like such a big deal, "Hey, I have dentures now." But you soon discover that having dentures changes your entire life, not just your mouth.

Strangely, every action your mouth does includes your teeth and when your teeth are strangers you feel like the comedian on a reality show. You have no idea how much stuff you do with your teeth until your teeth aren't yours anymore.

Words that used to be so easily said now get tangled up and I find myself searching for words that are more simply spoken. Food tastes different, smiling and laughing feel weird and I feel like my teeth are as big as a picket fence. Whenever I smile I feel like somebody left the front door wide open and the porch light is on.

So many new things all at once! I've lived my entire life the way I was and suddenly, everything I do is different. If you don't have dentures (yet) you have no idea what I'm talking about and I'm happy for you; bless your heart. Mark this chapter in Grandma's journal so you can come back to it. When your time comes, you'll need to come back and laugh with the rest of us. As you age, you simply MUST keep your sense of humor. You stop laughing and you stop living.

Another thing I've noticed about aging is that my joints don't cooperate anymore. It used to be when I went to stand up I just---stood---up. Now, I find I have to sit up straight then rock a bit to get some momentum going. Finally, I have enough leverage that I can stand up. Embarrassingly, the noises my body makes with the effort is another point of anguish.

At church the song leader up front doesn't like to keep folks standing for very long, so they sing two songs then we sit down for 5 minutes. Then stand up again. Then sit down again. When you are old, it is easier to be up than to get up. By the time I get up, it's time to sit down. When you see the old people sitting through the song service, it isn't because they are not involved; it's just that it takes too much effort to get up and down.

My glasses hide on top of my head and my shoes are never where I left them. When I finally find my shoes, the floor is a lot farther away than it was when I took my shoes off. Alongside losing my glasses and not finding my shoes; I find the older I get the more I think about the hereafter. I walk into a room and wonder what I was here after.

Nobody wants to listen to old people. Sometimes, I can't say that I blame them. There is an old saying about how wisdom comes with age. But, Grandma has noticed that sometimes age comes alone. Young folks wonder why old folks repeat the same stories over and over. It's because young folks don't stay around to listen long enough to finish the story---.

The next time it is easier to just start over than remember where the last time left off. Consequently, the young people only hear the first part of the story—again---and—again. If they sat down and spent some time they'd find this isn't mental deficiency on the elder's part; it's patience with the short attention span of youth.

There are a lot of things that Grandma had on her bucket list that I kept putting off thinking, "I'll do that someday." Now, I find that a lot of the stuff in the bucket isn't worth the energy it would take in the doing. Too much energy spent for the pleasure gotten, however there are a few things in the bucket Grandma still insists I will do—even if I die trying.

Things like learning to sword fight, to yodel and to call an auction. I'd also like to learn to juggle. Maybe Grandma will address doing those things on another day for another journal entry. When I sat down to write in my journal this morning, I was feeling all melancholy and frustrated about getting old.

Maybe a bit of my angst is caused by the "back of my mind" knowledge that as I age, roles will change. Instead of being the care giver, Grandma will become the cared for. The thought of my loss of independence, the loss of my ability to care for my own self hurts my pride. No, more than that, it hurts my heart. Grandma has always had the mind set that if there are things to do, I should do them, not let them be done. To have that taken from me and become mentally and physically confined to another person's will and care will be hard.

Later in the day, as Grandpa and I are walking on the beach, the mist is rolling in. The air is so quiet that the sound of the birds calling to each other echoes eerily. As I watch the birds pecking for food in the wet sand, the Holy Spirit brings to my mind a scripture. The one about how if God cares for the birds, how much more will He care for His own children who He loves? Grandma is going to praise God for the many blessings my life has received. Today, Grandma is going to remind myself of the birds and how God provides for them.

Now, I feel rejuvenated, maybe because I've sorted things out in my mind. Some things won't get done, some things will get done or I'll know the reason why. It's good to put thoughts on paper and read them back to yourself. Life is not done yet; there are still things to do, people to meet, places to go. When the time finally comes, I will remember how my Lord provides for the birds and know that He will certainly take care of—me. Grandma's pity party is officially D-O-N-E.

The Saga of the Red Dress

Today, I had taken my ten year old granddaughter to the Dr. for painful surgery on her fingers. It was a grueling procedure that she endured stoically; eyes squeezed tight shut allowing only a minimum of tears to slip by. My heart broke at her pain and my mind ached with the knowledge that there was not a single thing I could do to lessen her suffering.

We'd finally gotten back to the car and she looked at me with those big brown eyes, still glistening with unshed tears. Her fingers were individually bandaged and lay quietly in her lap. I expected her to say something about the pain she had just been subjected to. Instead, she said, "Mamaw, would you make me a special dress to wear to my school party Thursday?"

I have a sewing machine and I do mending---but--sew a dress? I told her I was not a seamstress; I just couldn't do something like that. She said, "Oh, please mamaw? Made by you just for me?" She never asks me for anything; the one time she does ask me for something, I'm going to turn her down? Not a chance. So, we went straight to the mall and searched pattern books to find the easiest "any idiot can do this" pattern. Thursday's party is only two days away and half of today is already gone by.

After we had agreed on a simple yet attractive A-line pattern--she chose a shiny red satin cloth with silver sparkles on it for her dress. She said she loved it because it looked like a Christmas tablecloth on the fourth of July. Looking at it, I realized that her description of the cloth was perfect. It did, indeed, look exactly like that.

As soon as we got to the house, she helped me spread out the cloth, and watched me pin on the pattern and cut the dress pieces out. She went happily home; clueless that tomorrow would be a very difficult day for her Grandma.

I can cook just about anything, but, sewing takes me to the very edges of my fortitude. My heart was willing but my ability was sadly lacking. The next morning, it wasn't long before I was sobbing in frustration. I prayed in the Spirit while I struggled to make sense of words that had nothing to do with cooking.

Bias? Binding? Gusset? Dart? Overlay? These words mean nothing to me. I sat down with a cup of coffee and as I sipped, I wondered if a seamstress would struggle with the terms from my world; words like, garnish, gratin, par boil and julienne. Probably, I mean, why would these words mean anything to somebody who never cooked? They would be as alien as sewing words are to me.

Interesting, I'd never considered such things before. The Holy Spirit nudged my thoughts; I love it when he does that. I'm just sitting minding my own business and I'm interrupted by a question whispered to my conscious mind. A question that I would never have even thought of, a question that requires me to search before I give an answer.

"When you talk about Me with your neighbors, strangers and co-workers, what do you sound like to them?" Caught off guard, I focused on my "witnessing words." Words. What words do I use? Born again. Eternally secure. Streets of gold. Blood bought. Redemption. Rapture. Sin sacrifice. Salvation.

All of these words and phrases make perfect sense to me. I know exactly what and why each phrase is used—and where to find the scripture to back the concept up. The Spirit continued His gentle query to my heart, "Do those church words mean anything to somebody who has not been in church, doesn't read their Bible and has no idea about the Christ life?"

Stunned, I think about my co-worker. She has never been receptive to anything I've tried to tell her about Jesus. She won't EVEN let me finish my sentence when I try to talk about Christ or church or anything. Instead, she talks to, and sometimes even cries on the shoulder of, another unchurched co-worker.

If given the unlikely opportunity to share Christ with this friend, would those "church words" mean anything to her? With shocking new clarity, I realize, *probably*—**not**. The epiphany was like a light bulb coming on in my mind, I fall back onto my chair in stunned awareness of my own ineptitude.

The Holy Spirit whispered, "I will open the door for you to talk with her, when I do, use words that she understands. Words like, "I care about you, how can I help?" Before you can show her MY love for her at Calvary, you must show her YOUR love for her, as my representative."

Given much to think about as I sewed, I futilely tried to follow instructions that made absolutely no sense at all, unstitching more than I'd stitched. Each sewing term and direction emphasized what the Spirit had whispered into my heart earlier. Nearing exhaustion, hours later; the dress was, finally, completed.

Tonight, my beautiful granddaughter, her fingers still bandaged, came over to pick up her dress to wear tomorrow at the party. She will wear her sparkly red dress and nobody will even notice the bandages on her fingers. The love sewn into each seam, the tears of sacrifice that dried invisibly into the cloth would never fully be understood by my granddaughter. Decades from now, she will remember how her mamawl loved her enough to step out of her comfort zone and risk looking foolish simply because---Grandma cared.

And even more important, Grandma will watch for that opportunity that God said He would provide me to show the LOVE of Jesus to my co-worker.
I will step out of my comfort zone again and risk looking foolish simply because---Jesus cares enough about her to send me to her as His representative.

Grandma's Wild Ride

It was supposedly a "kiddy" ride at the amusement park. One of those amazing, startling, 3D effect happening in your face, carnival rides. Whatever all that means, Grandma isn't sure. As we entered the auditorium sized building, an attendant handed each of us a pair of glasses and instructed us to put them on before the ride started.

As I put the glasses over my eyeballs, I notice that they really didn't do anything and I wondered what they were for. When the ride operator's voice said, "Please strap yourself into the seat and secure all loose objects," I began to have doubts as to our ride choice and thought perhaps I knew why they had given us protective eye wear.

I heard my 8 year old grandson in the seat beside me, holler, "Hang on to the handles mamaw, so you don't go flying out of your seat and hurt yourself!" Wait, go flying out of my seat? What? Nobody mentioned flying out of seats to Grandma when we got in the long line outside the building. Grabbing for the aforementioned handles, I knew, I _knew_ I was in _trouble_. I was in serious, big going to regret this with ice packs and analgesic creams and lotions, trouble.

As my seat was jerked from side to side, I held on with all my might. Stationary objects became weapons of visual assault because of the break neck speed we were spinning. The walls hurled at me like slabs of dark concrete, cartoon characters came flying through the air throwing virtual reality foods. Imaginary but clearly seen hamburgers were flying through the air and somersaulting around me. Even though I KNEW none of it was real, it all seemed not only real but bigger than life.

I instinctively threw up my hands to swat at a shower of pickle slices that was flying through the air. A ridiculous song about sponges and somebody named, Bob, and living underneath the sea screamed at me as I was hurled around and down gasping for air! The noise was deafening.

Then, I remembered a friend of my granddaughter, who had taken ballet, had told me that if you could just focus your eyes on something stationary, the wild spinning around would stabilize. The whole world was gyrating, my seat was jerking violently from side to side, try as I might, I could not find anything stationary to latch my eyeballs onto. Then, I caught a fleeting glimpse of a green glowing line that seemed stationary.

I lowered my head and riveted my eyeballs on my grandson's shoe, firmly planted in the foot trough beside mine. In the dim lighting, his glow in the dark lime green shoestrings captured my focus and held tight. The world around me was still spinning, but my mind quieted with the comfort of the stationary glowing double knotted bow. My focus riveted, I memorized every fiber, every piece of lint, every curve on that little green bow tie.

After the ride, my grandson took my hand and said, "Mamaw, we need to go get a cold drink now because you used a LOT of energy screaming and praying in there." *Mercy!* Was I screaming? And praying? I honestly could not remember. Sitting in the cool quiet of a snack bar booth, sipping on an icy cold beverage, Grandma fought to regain her equilibrium.

My young grandson was still holding my hand in his, murmuring soothing words meant to console me. My heart was touched at his genuine concern. I was rather amazed that his 8 year old little self had actually enjoyed the ride. Quite frankly, I had not thought I was going to live to tell about it.

As I sat thinking about the unexpected trauma I'd just endured, I was reminded of how our life as a Christian can often be like a wild ride at the amusement park. We are living uneventfully when suddenly; life as we know it goes crazy! We feel like we have lost all control and one horrible thing after another assaults us.

We struggle to get right side up again but we feel we are trapped where we are and there is no escape! Emotionally and mentally exhausted, we search for some focal point that will steady us amidst the chaos. Life can be rough, bad things DO happen to good people. Jesus said there would be times like this. Only when we make our mind stop looking at the tumult and focus on Christ, can we find a place of peace.

The world is still crashing and screaming but our focus is no longer on the "noise and motion." When we force ourselves to focus on Jesus instead of what's going on, satan's effort to rob us of our peace is made pointless. Grandma loves how the Holy Spirit makes every moment a teaching moment. There is a lesson to be learned in every life experience.

Happy that even though I've been traumatized, a life lesson has been reinforced, I finish my beverage. I sloo00oowly rise from the table. My old knees still feel a bit wobbly.
As my grandson and I clean off our table and throw our trash in the can, he looks at me and says, "See, now, that wasn't so bad after all, was it, Mamawl? Do you want to go do it again now?" I throw back my head and laugh. No. No, I do **NOT**. Mercy sakes.

The Anointing Crisco

It's weird how things happen and bring to mind something that happened many many years ago. Events that had gone by so long ago that memory didn't even have it in storage anymore. Something happened and boom, the long forgotten event was in full view again. Grandma wonders how that happens, is it a memory system reboot or what?

Like this afternoon, I was looking for my old gray sweater; it had, without use, migrated to the very back of my closet. Finally, after much searching, I found it and wrapped it around my shoulders. Even though it was too warm for a sweater, the hospital was chilly and I had decided to find something warm to take with me when I returned tonight.

Grandpa had taken a tumble last week and had broken his hip. Actually, the Doctor said most likely Walter did not fall down and break his hip. No, far more likely, his hip broke and he fell down. Old age is like that; suddenly, things just start breaking and not working right. The machine wears out.

Anyway, now, as I sit at the foot of Grandpa's hospital bed, and pulled the sweater around my shoulders, I noticed that a button was dangling, ready to fall off. It was that button that took my mind back, far back, decades back to when Grandpa and I were first married.

As a new bride I had thought marriage was all about forever love, laughter, happiness and endless joy. It was such a shock to find out that marriage was a lot of work. Physically, emotionally, and spiritually, marriage was a commitment that I was not as ready for as I had thought. I remember thinking, "This must be why the marriage vows say, "for better or worse." However, it seemed that there had already been a lot more worse than there had been better.

In my youthful innocence, I thought marriage was supposed to be 50-50; then a wise elder friend had told me that was not right. Divorce was 50-50 marriage was 100-100. And, it did not matter if my spouse didn't keep his 100% going, I still had to. It never crossed my mind that maybe he felt the same way, until he told me later. As I sat at the foot of my beloved's hospital bed, I remembered another loose button. A loose button that God had used to change my entire mind set and save my marriage.

\--------------------

The button on my old red coat was driving me crazy, hanging by a thread; head down like it's watching for a good place to jump off. Honestly, I've sewn it back on my coat so many times that I've lost track of counting! And, now, here I sit, on the grumbling old greyhound bus, hoping the stupid button didn't fall off --again.

I'd had this problem since childhood, my coat buttons are always falling off. Most the days of my youth, I'd greeted my Mom with, "The button fell off my coat AGAIN." Mom had always shook her head and admonished me that if I'd just listen to her directions to use three strands of thread to sew it back on this time instead of the customary two, there would be no more issue with missing buttons.

What she said made no sense at all. If the metal shank on the button could cut its way through one or two threads, why would a third matter? Wouldn't the shank simply cut through that thread as well? But, she'd always insisted the "three strand thing" would work.

Now, years passed childhood, my button and my heart dangled by a thread. I sat toying with the button crying as the mile markers rushed by my window. Enough, I'd simply had enough of fussing, empty promises and brokenness. I'd tried, for months, no let's be honest, years, to live with Walter. Life had been good for the first few years; what had changed?

My head ached almost as much as my heart; when DID things start to fall apart? Angrily I wiped my tears with the back of my hand. The time for crying was over; it was time for action! Strangely, I thought the act of leaving would bring release. Instead, I felt even more trapped in my escape than I had in my assumed captivity.

Earlier today when I closed the door and left the house key under the mat, I intended not to return. Walter was out of town on business, by the time he got back to the empty house, I would be far away. I'd not left a note; he could figure it out himself.

My mom wasn't expecting me, I probably should have called her and at least let her know that I'd left Walter and was heading to her house. I couldn't stay at Walter's house anymore, yet, I knew I wouldn't be able to return to my child hood and "fit" again either. Odd, I just noticed that I'd called "our home," "Walter's house." When had I started thinking of it that way? Certainly it was long before I locked the door behind me this morning.

How had Dad and Mom stayed married for so many years? Living with Daddy couldn't have been easy; he was so strong willed. Musing, I smiled; mom had always said I was just like my Dad. When HAD things started to unravel with Walter? When we first married, we were so in love; we did everything as a couple; we even taught a Sunday school class together. Church, now, I can't even remember the last time Walter and I went to church together.

First, Walter had stopped going, he had so much work to do; Sunday was the only time he had to catch up. Then, in time, I too stopped going to church. I'd never considered myself to be a religious person anyway. My mom had always talked about how Christianity wasn't a religion, it was a relationship. Mom always made a "Jesus connection" to everything. There are times when I think mom was a little overboard with her "living for Jesus" stuff.

As I'd watched her sew, she'd even told me that anchoring a button with three threads instead of two was like making Jesus part of your home. The sharp edges of life can make the fragile threads of relationship fray and fall apart. But, when you add that "Jesus thread;" the buttons hold tight. As I wiped a tear, the dangling coat button dropped off onto my lap in silent reference.

Maybe mom was right after all? Perhaps I should, finally, sew the button on my coat as per her instructions. And, maybe that's what was wrong with Walter and me; we'd never used that Jesus thread to anchor our marriage. Maybe we were losing our buttons? I sputtered through my tears and stifled a giggle.

As soon as I got to Mom's house, I called Walter, and told him I was "spending the weekend with Mom; she's going to tell me how to keep my buttons tight."

Grandma smiled at the memory. I had been so young, so eager, so hopeful, so naive. I'd thought it was my husband's responsibility to lead in Christ. And, scripturally, it is the man's appointed position to be the head of the home. But, God has shown me that sometimes it is necessary that the wife be the neck that turns the head. It is the wife who creates the atmosphere in the home; either by making it a normal part of everyday life to honor Christ, or a normal part of life to shove the Lord to the bottom of the basket and get Him out only when it suits us.

As the setting sun cast shadows on the hospital room floor, I laugh as I remember how, sitting in church one Sunday, before my beloved, Walter, had started going with me again, I had heard the preacher talk about anointing the doorposts with oil. Once home, I was determined to anoint every doorway, every, room with oil and prayer, *every day*.

Times were tough, good quality olive oil was expensive. All I could afford was a big bottle of Crisco. Crisco oil, olive oil, anointing oil, what difference does it make? I consecrated a new bottle of vegetable shortening to be "anointing oil," and kept it on a shelf separate from the everyday cooking stuff. I remembered from Sunday School that sanctified means to "set aside for a particular purpose." So, in my hope for a Christ centered home, I sanctified that bottle of oil to be used only for anointing. Grease, oil, it's all shortening and once sanctified, holy.

Each morning after Walter left for work, I'd go through the house, praying, putting a smear of Crisco oil over each door. Sometimes the prayer would be so intense I'd be hoarse by the time I'd gone through the whole house. And let me tell you, there were a lot of tears shed over that bottle of oil. Mercy sakes. Grandpa could be a handful when he was misbehaving! But, I held my peace; my tongue beat my eyeballs black and blue many a time. Only the Holy Spirit knew the intensity of the prayers Grandma prayed over that man! And the cat. Yes, the cat knew---I scared that cat a few times. Just saying, poor kitty.

It took some serious prayer for direction, some tongue biting and some pride swallowing, (Grandma often gets choked when I swallow my pride, but, it was necessary and I did it!) but in time, Walter was sitting beside me in church again. I did not badger him into going, no. I simply made my Lord a part of my everyday life. I spoke openly of how much God meant to me. God's faithfulness prevailed. From that point on, through hard times and fun times, we served God *together*.

Grandpa moaned and I quickly went to his bedside. He smiled at me and squeezed my hand. "What you doing, praying for me over there in the corner?" I nodded and leaned over to kiss his forehead. He winked at me and whispered, "Did you sneak your bottle of Crisco in with your sweater?" Mercy, I love this old man.

NO Peach Cobbler

You KNOW how much Grandma loves peaches. A couple of years ago, Grandpa planted a peach tree in the corner of the back yard. All spring and most of the summer, I've watched as the first buds have gone from tight bud to flower to green fruit to ripen. As I watched the fruit's progression, I thought about the wonderful sweet, juicy fresh peach dessert that would be my reward at summer's end.

Finally, the day when the fruit is perfectly ripened has come! What a blessing that Grandpa comes home from the hospital tomorrow just in time to enjoy the first cobbler off of our tree. As I had my morning coffee I scanned through my recipes for yummies made with fresh peaches.

Cobbler? A wonderful cobbler? No, peach pie, oh my goodness, a delicious peach pie. Wait— fresh peach ice-cream; oh, be still my heart. And there is my beloved Aunt's recipe for hand held peach pies; she won a ribbon for that "Peach Hand Pie." My eyeballs keep going back to that fresh peach cobbler; I think my decision has been made.

Overjoyed, I gathered my harvest and went to my kitchen to prepare the cobbler. To my dismay, when I opened the fruit, it was full of worms! Peach after peach had to be thrown into the garbage. All the fruit had looked great on the outside. But, inside, the worms had gnawed away the flesh until all that was left was rot.

As I stood in dismay over the pile of bad fruit, a childhood memory surfaced. Many *many* years ago, my Aunt's neighbor, a gardener, had showed me a wonderful peach that was ruined inside by worms. He had told me that there is more to growing fruit than letting it get ripe. The tree must be cultivated; protected from destructive vermin and blight.

I had not thought of the old farmer in decades, but his advice was clearly remembered as I stood before the bucket of wasted fruit. This next year, I will carefully cultivate the tree and have an abundant crop of sweet fruit. Why, oh WHyyyyyyy didn't I remember that old farmer and his wise words early in the spring?

After supper, with NO peach cobbler, I sat down with a cup of peach tea to do my devotions and talk to Jesus. The tea is yummy, not fresh peach cobbler yummy, but, better than nothing— yummy. As I open my Bible, my eyeballs notice that tonight's devotion scripture is talking about fruit. Spiritual –fruit.

Grandma loves it when God uses everyday things to show me Biblical principles. He could have used a lot of things to illustrate a Christ like attitude and demeanor. But, He chose to use something that all people, from all times, of all sexes, races and beliefs, would understand. He— chose-- fruit.

The *fruits* of the Spirit are love, joy, peace and self-control and I personally struggle with that last one more than I care to admit. Grandma finds it interesting that church people rarely even mention the fruits and focus on only a few of the <u>gifts</u> of the Spirit. Of the eight gifts listed, people view prophesies tongues and miracles as the most desirable —all things that make "us" *look* special.

The list of gifts *also* includes knowledge, discernment, faith and wisdom. But we don't hear about those too often. Grandma has never thought about that before; I wonder why we neglect the growing of fruit and focus on the getting of gifts. The obvious answer is because gifts are freely given and growing fruit requires discipline and work.

The fruits are what make us humble and Christ like. Grandma knows the work required to produce good fruit and I also know if I don't do that work, the fruit, if it even grows, is not good. That's why I had no peach cobbler tonight; I did not do the work necessary to have the fruit.

Just like fertilizing and caring for the peaches, it is up to Grandma, with the help of the Holy Spirit, to prune out the sinful nature that would prevent the growth of good spiritual fruit in my life. Our fruit shows Jesus to the world. The world is looking for that fruit, not the drama of a few select-- gifts. The gifts *are important* but the fruit is vital. Mercy, now that is a *lot* of contemplation for somebody who was denied fresh peach cobbler tonight.

And the peach tea, while it was very tasty did NOT satisfy Grandma's longing for peach cobbler. I think there may be a good lesson illustration hiding in there—but---Grandma will save that thought path for another day. Time for bed, tomorrow I will, of course, continue to work on cultivating the fruit of the Spirit in my life AND I will get what garden supplies I need to cultivate good fruit on my peach tree so this peach of a lesson never has to be learned—again.

Mercy, Grandma wishes she had a good dish of hot fresh peach cobbler tonight. Tomorrow, as soon as Walter gets home from the hospital, I'll buy a basket of fresh peaches and make us one. Bless his heart, after all these days in the hospital eating food that tastes like gruel mixed with styrofoam, a big dish of hot peach cobbler with a melting dollop of vanilla ice cream nestled on top will help make him feel better.

Grandma's Teeth Get Away

Grandma is STILL trying to get adjusted to having false teeth. In concept, it seems so simple but in reality, it is very complicated. After weeks and weeks of wear, I've finally gotten so I can speak without muffling and chew without biting myself. I thought I had the art of wearing "falsies" mastered. In fact, I was feeling so confident that I'd even started singing in church again.

You may think that is funny, but trust me, it is quite a learning experience to figure out how to keep your teeth from jumping out of your mouth. It's like the denture feels trapped and fights to get out. With time your tongue and muscles learn to work together to keep the denture in proper position. But, mercy, that learning curve is tough.

Last Sunday at church, Grandma's throat was tickling so I was leaning over searching for a mint in my purse. As my fingers traced over every item in the bottom of my pocketbook I suddenly sneezed. Before I could put my hand over my mouth, both my top and bottom denture went flying out. They skittered across the floor at my feet and came to rest just out of my reach underneath the chair in front of me. Aghast, I crouched there, staring at my teeth. They lay there, a broken smile, mocking me, just beyond the reach of my fingertips.

Sitting back up in my chair, I peered around the big hat on the lady sitting in front of me whose chair now sheltered my teeth. If she was old, I could have handed her a Kleenex and asked her to please pick up my teeth and hand them to me. She probably would have dentures and know full well what had happened.

She would have discreetly plucked them from between her feet, cloistered my denture in the tissue and handed them to me. After church we could meet formally, laugh together about the pains of aging and gone for coffee and some lunch. Boom, disaster turned into friendship opportunity. Unfortunately, she was—not-- old.

In fact, she was young, say, 30 or there abouts. I tried to imagine what her reaction would be at my asking her to hand me my teeth. She would have no clue about such things and question my mental acuity. Depending on her personal fortitude and whether or not she had a grandmother, she might even gag or gasp. And certainly her worship experience would be ruined before it even started. No, I dare not risk such a request.

I simply stood; tucking my tongue behind my lips so my mouth would stay poked out and not sink in to reveal my toothless state. I did not care to sing toothless so instead, I tried to worship silently. But, what I found myself doing was quietly praying that the young woman in the big hat would not step on my teeth. Or worse yet, stumble over them and scream. It was going to be a long hour, sitting there praying for God to protect my teeth, but what else could I do?

The sermon was about being yourself, God loving us as we are; I guess, even—toothless. I love to laugh and I don't smile, I grin. So I had to keep reminding myself that no matter how humorous the Pastor's adlibs were, or who winked, waved or smiled at me, I HAD to respond with a straight lipped smile.

Grandma is relieved that Walter is still watching the live feed version of the church service from the house. Because if his hip was all well now, he'd be sitting beside me and oh mercy, I'd never live this down. Never. The young man taking up the offering handed me the plate and whispered, "bless you sister." Before I could stop myself, I grinned—a big---toothless –grin. I didn't realize what I'd done till the young man jumped and dropped the offering plate.

I was so thankful for generous people who drop paper money into the offering plate instead of coins that roll and clink on the floor. The money was quickly retrieved and the usher moved on. I couldn't tell if his shoulders were shaking from laughter or shock—but I knew I might possibly be the subject of conversation at his dinner table later today.

The remainder of the church service passed without event. The young woman sitting over my teeth gathered her things from the seat beside her and left without noticing my smile underneath her chair. I leaned over, picked up my purse and snatched my teeth in one smooth move.

Once in the car, I bowed my head and thanked God for mercy. Sometimes, mercy comes in big doses to cover our biggest baddest sin. And sometimes mercy comes in small doses to cover our humanity and silliness; but every day of our lives we all need—mercy.

Grandma Needs Adult Supervision

Grandma is not allowed to go back to the college computer lab without an adult to supervise me. First, let's start with an explanation for those of you who do not know Grandma personally. If you have known me through the years, you know that according to all the tests I'd taken in school, Grandma was -- average. My Dad, God love him and rest his soul in heaven, explained to me how important "average" is.

Average means there are people smarter than me AND people not so smart as me. The "average" person sets the standard. Everybody is either on one side of me or the other. The intellectual prowess of all people everywhere is determined by---me, the one who is, average.

My Daddy went on to tell me how very important it is that I always do my very best, study hard, and hand in every assignment, every test, so the standard for intelligence will always be high. Now you know one of the many reasons why my beloved Daddy was always my hero. That explained, on to how Grandma got banned from the computer lab---.

Somehow, I'd always thought by the time you had grandchildren, you were old, done, finished, and waiting on the next bus to heaven. Now, that I'm a grandmother, I'm surprised to discover that I'm NOT old. Indeed, I have many years ahead of me to live, love be happy and ---learn. So, Grandma enrolled in the Community College. I decided to take a computer class, Word Processing.

Don't laugh, I know I'm totally a mess when it comes to anything techno related, but, I'm sure that is because I simply have never availed myself of education to learn about technology. Since I'm a slow learner, I'd only signed up for a few classes to start with. If all goes well, I thought maybe I could continue my studies and eventually get a degree and even start a second career. My family all raised, life is filled with possibilities.

All had gone well for the first few months of class. My professor was a woman my age and spent a lot of time with me after class helping me struggle through the techno. At the end of the semester, we were assigned a project that would be a major part of our course grade. Grandma was confident, with all the extra tutoring and hours and hours of study, I felt I could do this project without any issues. Silly silly—silly---me.

The project was to create a business letter then make a mailing list and use the computer mass mail program to insert each person's name and information in the appropriate space in the letter, print a matching envelope and then print a list of the recipients of the mass mailing. There were 1,000 letters to be printed in my assigned mass mailing, each with their own personal name, information and envelope.

After much prayer, Grandma went to the computer lab while it was quiet and worked on the project. It took me MANY days to get the two page letter created, the list made and the appropriate information in the cue to print in the letters.

Finally, all of the "needs be" done, I made sure one of the "heavy job" printers down the line from me had the right letter head stationary loaded. Each line of work stations had their own printer and there were three "heavy job" printers that could be selected from every work station for those big projects. With a deep sigh of relief that my project was about to be d-o-n-e, I pressed "print." Nothing happened.

I waited a few moments---went and checked the printer—everything was fine, printer was on, paper ready, ink cartridge read full. Sitting back down at my computer, I clicked "print" again. Nothing. I clicked it again and again and again and again. About the time I was in tears and so frustrated I thought I was going to collapse from anxiety, the entire computer lab shut down. The entire lab---fifty work stations---fell silent and their blinking lights went out.

As I stood wondering what on earth had just happened, a wild eyed man with hair like bozo the clown came running into the lab. Looking frantically around and seeing I was alone in the computer lab, he pointed his finger at me and yelled, "IT WAS YOU WASN'T IT?"

To make a long—painfully long—story short, I had managed to select the wrong heavy job printer. The printer in the lab on the next line of work stations had started printing. The problem was, I had kept pushing print and the tally of copies kept adding up until finally, the system over loaded and the whole lab went dark.

At my disciplinary counseling session, I learned the final count on my print demand was over ten thousand copies. It was decided that I could no longer be in the computer lab without having a professor or a student mentor alongside me to oversee my every move. And THAT, boys and girls, is *why* Grandma is not allowed in the computer lab without adult supervision.

A Random Journal Entry

This morning, Grandma was on my way to the hairdresser for a haircut. My hairdresser and I have known each other for 25 years; we've shared, celebrated and mourned life events together. As I turned onto the highway, my cell phone rang.

It was Malia, my hair girl; she asked me if, while I was on my way, could I please stop and get her a biscuit. "Certainly." I said, and happily did, because I had a relationship with her.

Because of that intimate familiarity, I would not only stop and get the breakfast sandwich she asked for; I also knew *exactly* what kind of biscuit she wanted. She wouldn't call a stranger or even an acquaintance to get her a biscuit—but, she could call me. When we have a relationship with a person, we are not inconvenienced by unscheduled requests.

God often makes unscheduled requests of those who love Him. He knows that, even though busy, His friends will make time to do whatever He asks. Things like calling a person who hasn't been in church for a while, or visiting somebody that we'd not usually think needed a 'home call.'

God knows that He can depend on those who love him, just as we depend on those who know and love us. There are some people who scoff at the idea that God "asks" us to do things like that for Him. There are also some people who scoff at the idea of their beautician asking them to bring them breakfast too---.

That's Grandma's journal entry for today. Bet you didn't even know that I could write a short story, did you? Probably not even necessary to tell of such an ordinary life event, but, somehow, I just feel in my heart that needed to be mentioned. Grandma doesn't really even know how to conclude this short entry—other than maybe just a side note that I got Malia a steak biscuit-- with tomato. And---a large sweet tea.

The Drive Through Mumble Special

Grandma is not awake yet, but, I can feel eyes staring at me. Struggling to rise above a dream state, I open one eyeball. My beautiful eleven year old granddaughter, Maddy, stands beside my bed, already dressed, her soft brown curls pulled up in a perky ponytail. She whispers, "Are you awake, mamawl?"

"NoOoooOOo." Trying to ignore her effort to bring me to consciousness, I sigh and turn over pulling the sheet over my head as I flop to my left side. Giggling, Maddy grapples with the top sheet, "C'mon mamawl, get up or I'll tickle you!" Rising up suddenly, I grab her and pull her onto the bed with me, making big show of my toothless state as she squeals in protest, "Ewwwwww, toothless old lady breath, ewwwww." As I reach for my chenille robe, I tell her to go start the coffee while I get dressed.

Coffee enjoyed, we debate on what to do about breakfast. Looking at each other, we simultaneously proclaim, "Drive through mumble special!" Jumping up, Maddy shouts, "Last one in the car has to pay for breakfast!" Shaking my head, I grab my beat up old pocketbook and follow her out the door.

Pulling into the fast food drive up, we giggle as if we were BOTH schoolgirls. This is one of our favorite breakfast treats when we spend a "girls only" night together; the always astonishing drive through mumble special.

We all know how those drive through speakers work---nobody can understand anything from either end of the conversation. Looking away from each other in a futile attempt to silence our giggle fest, I pull up to the "order it" station at the fast food restaurant. Maddy, holding her hand over her mouth to contain gales of silent laughter squeezes her eyes tight shut and buries her face in the soft sides of my old purse.

The fuzzy, indecipherable voice of the speaker cues me to place our order. Leaning out the window, I shout, "mufrrmphl shlerlong farrplltdt mroshprpght." The "order it" responds with static and then emits a responding indiscernible comment. Using my free hand to wave Maddy into continued silence, I shout an additional instruction, "Ahh, bmr fumblegrb Ahhh, fsrhtft."

After a few moments of electronic fuzzing, the voice says something that can only be guessed to be, "Pull around." I maneuver the car into the "pick it up" side of the drive through and the smiling clerk tells me, "That will be $9.46." After making the payment, I hand the overstuffed bag of breakfast goodies to my bright eyed, still giggling granddaughter and drive across the street to the park.

Maddy and I had invented the amazing "drive through mumble special" one rainy morning after a futile attempt at ordering through the drive up. Our order had been entirely wrong but we discovered we liked the wrong order better than what we had ordered to start with. We had enjoyed our surprise food so much, we made a silly name for the process and had ordered wrong on purpose ever since.

Once we are uncomfortably settled at a dilapidated picnic table, bulging bag of who KNOWS what sitting before us, we bless our food. We both begin to giggle as we dump our treasure out onto the splintered slats of the battered wooden table. Maddy rubs her hands together, obviously enjoying the anticipation of the moment. "Hurry, mamawl, I can't stand it—WHAT DID WE GET THIS TIME?"

As I ceremoniously unveil our treasure, I identify a sausage egg and cheese biscuit, a ham croissant, a platter of pancakes and FOUR fried apple tarts. We giggle at our abundance, rolling our eyes and remembering the last time when we'd ended up with three black coffees and one hash brown.

Suddenly, as if spurred by the memory of the "coffee a plenty" mumble special, Maddy smacks her forehead and says, "Awl, mamawl, we forgot to order drinks!" We both make a pouty face and Maddy skips across the walk to drop change in the park's canned drink vending machine.

The birds laugh at us from the trees as we sit giggling, talking and enjoying our bounty. Having eaten until we are stuffed tight enough to pop, we gather our trash as we continue to reminisce about previous "astonishing drive through mumble specials." With another mumble success added to our list, we drive back to the house as the first drops of a late fall rain shower pelt the windshield. Tonight, when Grandpa calls from out of town, he will ask what we did today. Grandma's heart smiles.

The Once a Year Time Travel Adventure

Once a year, every year, Grandma visits the future. It has become an event that is planned for, anticipated and welcomed with enthusiasm. On this pre-determined day, Grandma will press the numbers that will connect her with a dear friend living in another day, another month and a different year than what I'm living in.

Last year, I'd told Walter to make sure I was awake when the time came but both of us fell asleep watching the evening news. Grandma missed this grand event, slept right through it and woke up the next day. I was totally devastated that my next opportunity for time travel would not be until next year. This year I have set alarms all over the house so that THAT will not happen again!

It's almost time, I'd better make a cup of coffee, no, I'll make tea. My friend who lives in the future drinks tea, so I will have my cup ready to sip as we chat. It will be a short conversation, but it is one of the silly adventures that Grandma looks forward to each year.

It's time. I punch the numbers into the key pad-----here we goooooo. "Hello? This is Grandma---how are you? Fine? Great! How is it in the future?" Grandma laughs and affirms, "Well, Jesus is still Lord---that's all that matters." As I sit down with my cup of tea in my comfortable chair, my friend and I share a few giggles and acknowledge our love for each other.

After a few moments, the time has come for the time travel adventure to come to an end. In a few hours, it will be time for Grandma to enter the future. Grandma smiles as she presses the off button—and goes to take a pan of cookies out of the oven, replacing them with a new pan to bake.

New Year's Eve, where has time gone? It was good to talk to my dear friend, Helen, in Australia. She celebrated New Year 's Eve hours ago---now, it is almost my time to enter the future. I pick up my Bible, turn to my favorite scripture, Jesus, the same yesterday, today, and tomorrow.

I look at the sheet of paper, at the top I've penned the words, "What I will do for God this year." A tradition with my Lord, I make a contract with Him every New Year's Eve. I tell him what I will do for Him this upcoming year. That way, I have it written on paper. A contract I must live by.

This is not a typical contract where big words crowd the page. The only thing I have on the page is the header, the page is blank, I'll let God fill in the 'will do' part. Taking a deep breath, Grandma picks up the pen and signs her signature on the bottom of the blank page as the clock strikes midnight. I'm ready for what EVER God has planned for me. Grandma knows beyond any shadow of doubt that this year will be the most exciting time I've lived for my Lord yet! BRING IT!

Do You Brush Your Teeth

Grandma loves to help in Children's Church. This week, the theme was, "What Time is It? It's Time to Get Serious About Serving God!" As my lesson illustration, I brushed my teeth. (You know and I know that Grandma has false teeth, but the children did not) I started brushing, then told the class, it didn't feel right, wait---and I put on my fuzzy pink bathrobe.

I started to put toothpaste on my brush and stopped, saying, "Nope, sorry, it still just isn't right." I pulled out a dainty pink overnight case, tied with a pink ribbon, and put curlers in my hair. (The kids were starting to laugh) Once again I started to brush my teeth.

Again, I stopped and told them "Nope, something still isn't quite right--." Fumbling around, I took a bottle of hand cream and pumped a TON of it into my hands. Then, I squinted my eyes shut and plastered it allllll over my face. The kids were falling out of their chairs they were laughing so hard!

Finally, I told them _**now**_, finally, I could brush my teeth. Of course, I brushed really good and hung my tongue out and brushed my tongue and then, of course, I gargled long and loud and spit it in the trash can. The kids were howling with laughter. While I'd brushed my teeth, I had one of my helpers time me. It took nearly 5 minutes to mess around and dramatically brush my teeth.

When the kids were settled down, I took prayer requests. After writing down the requests in a notebook, I asked them why they felt that sometimes we don't hear God when he speaks to us. The children all sat there, shrugging their shoulders and waiting for an answer to drop from the sky.

After reviewing the requests that had just been given, I told the kids to quietly sit and pray, telling them that we wouldn't pray long; we'd only pray for one fifth as long as it took to brush my teeth. I asked the kids if they thought one minute was a long time. They all, one hundred percent, agreed that ONE minute is not a long time.

Needless to say, for them, a minute in quiet prayer, even with a list of prayer needs, was an _eternity_. When a minute was FINALLY up, I told them that even without all the drama I'd had brushing my teeth, sometimes people spend more time brushing their teeth than they spend talking to God.

God wants us to take time to be with Him, to get to know HIM. He wants to hear everything we think and feel. He never gets tired of listening. AND, God talks back to us through His Word and sometimes in a quiet voice straight into our heart. The children liked the idea that God was—always—available to listen to them.

I asked the class why THEY thought it was so hard to hear God's voice sometimes; figuring my teeth brushing illustration would speak volumes about the need to make a PLAN to spend time just enjoying God's presence and listening. Little Billy held up his hand and said, "We don't hear God's voice cause we don't give him time to finish brushing His teeth so He can say something back." Not exactly what I was trying to illustrate; I'll have to work on that illustration before I use it again. But, obviously, the children were listening—sort of.

Chasing Contentment

Mercy, it's cold outside! Freezing temperatures with a harsh north wind, brrrrr. It seems the house temp won't rise above 70* no matter how high Grandma sets the thermostat. I'm standing here with my sweater on drinking hot beverages to get warmer. ONE of these DAYS, we are going to move to Florida; of course I've said this every winter since Walter and I were first married. But still, one day----.

The thought occurs to me that a few months ago, I was standing in this same spot, the thermostat on 70*. But, I was turning the air conditioner to colder because 70* was just too hot to bear inside the house. I was fanning myself and drinking <u>cold</u> beverages to get cooled down. Hmmmm. What is the difference between 70* in the winter and 70* in the summer? Grandma pauses to think about this. Maybe the only difference is---attitude?

It seems to be human nature to <u>not</u> be satisfied. In looking at my own lifestyle; I have more of everything than most other people on the planet. Grandma is pretty sure the majority of people fall in the same "slot" that I do. We have—stuff. LOTS of stuff.

Yet, we are all obsessed with "more." We work longer and harder to get more; then, we <u>still</u> *aren't satisfied*. Contentment. Having enough. What is the mark of arrival at that elusive place when we want no more? It has to be an emotional place since physically, we have plenty.

So, how do I get to this place in my life, emotionally, where I really do have-- enough? Since it seems to be human nature to want more, how do I get to this place of contentment? Grandma needs to get some coffee and have a sit down to think about it.

As I pour the coffee, my mind thinks of how often I hear folks say, "if I just had (??) I'd be happy." A better job. A spouse. Children. A bigger house. A lot of money. All of those things ARE good to have---but---none of those things make anybody—happy.

Happiness is not something Grandma can go shop for or find in a lifestyle. Not even Grandpa can make me happy, though heaven knows; he devotes himself to the effort. Happiness is not an unattainable goal; it is a ***<u>side effect</u>*** of a Christ centered life. That's a realization that should make us ALL smile.

Grandma, the Plant Killer

If you know Grandma, you KNOW I'm not a garden person. As a child, my parents always had a garden so I have the knowledge in my head on *how* to garden. But, plants have no friendship with me; none. My youngest brother has a gift for gardening and one of our daughters is officially the plant whisperer; but, obviously, this gift skipped Grandma.

My gardening skills are so lacking that our daughter teases me that when she is in process of planting her spring flowers, I'm not to even look at the plants as I walk by. At least, I *think* she is teasing when she says that.

Grandpa, on the other hand, has a gift for gardening that is so amazing it's just—silly. I've seen him take a small twig, graft another twig onto it then talk to it, care for it, plant it and in time, grow a thriving bush. He loves violets, even propagating his own plants to create the colors and petal shapes he wants. He has a violet stand he built out of nice wood—sanded and stained so it looks like furniture. On it are 45 violet plants, each in a different stage of bloom and development.

On Monday, as my beloved, Walter, left for a business trip, he kissed me and looking at the violet stand, said, "With a little sunshine over the next few days, that second row of violets will be in full bloom when I get home at the end of the week." Well, Grandma was so excited to know what would make Grandpa's beloved violets bloom; I could hardly wait till he pulled out of the driveway.

Carefully, I selected the violets with the tight buds and set them lovingly on the front walk where they'd get full sun during the afternoon. If you know anything about violets, you know this did not end well. Nope. (sigh)

The only word that Grandma can think of to describe the outcome is---well, I guess, crispy. Bless Grandpa's heart---when he got home and saw what I'd done; he swallowed hard, put his hands over his face for a moment then took me in his arms and whispered, "It's ok, baby, you were trying to make me happy." Is it any wonder I love this man?

Then, there was the time Grandma killed her friend's silk plant. Yes, you read that right. I killed a silk plant. My friend left me to tend her potted plant in her sun room while she was on vacation. I told her I was a plant killer but she said this vine was indestructible; it was a Heart-Leaf Philodendron. She promised me there was no way I could kill it in only a couple of weeks. She was right.

However, when I went to her house to water the ivy, I noticed that there was a lovely plant sitting beside it on the window. She'd not mentioned the second plant, which I thought was odd. Maybe she figured I'd just know to water it because it was there. I looked at the straw like stuff over the dirt in the pot and saw that it was dry as bones. It was a VERY good thing that I had come to water the philodendron that day because this other plant was so dry, it would not have lasted till next morning. I watered it generously. My friend had been right; the philodendron thrived and needed very little care. However, the "other" plant was much more labor intensive to care for.

After a few days, of constantly watering, the new plant looked a little sad. Oddly, the surface of the straw and peat moss in the pot was again horribly dry. I watered it generously this time, noticing that the pot itself was a little heavy. Concerned over the plant, I returned the next day to check on it. To my horror, the plant was laying limp across the pot and the straw in the top of the pot was once again, bone dry.

Oddly, the plant itself was still bright green, even though it had fainted, I guessed from lack of water. I watered it generously again, making note that the pot was even heavier this time than the last time and the straw on top of the soil was once again, bone dry. Grandma is NOT a gardener, but, it doesn't take a plant master to realize something just wasn't right.

The next day when I went over to check on the plant, it was still in a dead faint, still bright green and this time the straw on top was not dry. In fact, the straw was floating on a pool of water. I dared not water it again with all the water pooled on top of the peat moss like that. Instead, thinking maybe for some reason the plant was not able to drink deeply (root problem?), I heavily misted the plant in hopes that it would rally around before my friend returned the next day.

Mortified to have made such a mess of my friend's plant, I left her a note saying I would buy her a new one. My friend called me the following afternoon. To my surprise, she was laughing, not angry. She told me I was the first person she'd ever seen that killed a silk plant. Silk? A silk plant? Really? Grandma will never live that one down. Never.

Early this spring Grandma discovered a bright green vine growing up from the root of an old dead tree. Thinking it was wisteria, very abundant around the yard and grows into a beautiful purple flowering vine; I fertilized it and watered it every day. Wisteria is very sturdy, almost impossible to kill and grows fast. Since it was winding on a dead tree, there was no danger it would consume and choke out the "host" as Wisteria is so prone to do.

I knew if I watered it and tended it the lovely vine would grow even more quickly and be more beautiful. Every day I talked to the vine because I'd read that talking to plants can encourage them to grow. It was my hope that I'd lovingly care for this little vine and bring to an end the shame of having killed a silk plant just a few weeks ago.

The vine exceeded my highest expectations. It was crazy, all the other plants that I'd devoted myself to over the years had died, but this one thrived. I was just---thrilled---to finally have a plant that actually responded to my tender loving care. Each day that I talked to it and cared for it, I thanked God that the little plant was growing so big and beautiful.

Spring passed and the lawn man came to begin his weekly mowing and yard care duties. Today, as he was packing up to leave, I saw him studying my vigorous vine. Before he left, he knocked on my side door. I was certain, since he'd been looking at my vine so intently; he was going to praise me for how healthy it was. My daughter would be so surprised, and Grandpa would be even more surprised. Finally, a plant that I could grow.

I opened the door and the lawn man said, "That's about the healthiest poison sumac vine I've ever seen, missy. Stay away from it and next week I'll bring some spray to kill it. Have a nice day." Poison sumac? Really? (sigh)

Today, I Wait

Today, Grandma is waiting. I hate to wait. There are places I need to go, things I need to do, and people I need to see. This weekend, I'm going to a Women's Conference, I have much to do before I leave. Waiting is a waste of time; I hate to wait. Settling down in a chair provided for my---waiting---I pull my sweater around me closer. In retrospect, I realize that a great deal of my life is spent in waiting.

Waiting in line to make a purchase, for the light to change, waiting for an appointment, waiting for the oven timer to go off, a phone call to come, a package to arrive—it seems I'm always--waiting. Waiting is a common bond in our humanity; everybody rich and poor, young and old, waits.

Grandma has discovered that whether I have entered a physical waiting room for an appointment or I'm waiting on God for direction; waiting can be tedious. The best relief for tedium is being busy. Of course, silent prayer is always an option but in a quiet room where the ceiling lights hum if I close my eyeballs, I will fall on the floor and take a nap. So, perhaps I should occupy myself with magazines and books that might encourage me, maybe even teach me something, as I wait.

Many cooking techniques, gardening tips and ideas for vacation spots have been expounded upon while in a physical waiting room. I should get up, pick up a magazine from the overflowing rack across the room, and use this waiting time as a learning time. But, I don't WANT to learn something; I want to sulk about waiting.

A young man a few chairs over from Grandma sneezes directly into the magazine he's reading. After sneezing into the pages, he closes it and places it back into the magazine rack. Now, I'm SURE I don't want to read a magazine and—learn—something or more probably, catch a virus.

Grandma has friends who have the gift of evangelism; they can start up a conversation anytime anywhere with anybody---and talk about Jesus. This has never been one of my gifts. Oh, mind you, I've tried---but---nope. I can't even start up a conversation with a stranger about baking cupcakes, so it is no surprise that an evangelistic conversation is not likely to happen.

Sometimes, when I'm with a person I've already met, common ground is found and comfortable conversation might lead to an opportunity to speak about faith. However, Grandma has not ever been able to just jump in and start a conversation with strangers about ANYthing---not gardening, not baking--not even---Jesus.

So, what else can I do in order not to waste this---waiting—time? Pulling my sweater closer around my shoulders, I scowl; If I had coffee or a hot cup of tea, it would certainly be easier to wait. I pull my creaky old bones up and go to the magazine rack across the room, carefully avoiding the section where the sneezed in periodical rests. As long as I use hand sanitizer and don't touch my face, I should be safe from contamination from germs sneezed earlier.

Interestingly, I find a little devotional that somebody has left. It has pretty flowers on the cover and attracts my eyeballs. Oh, mercy sakes, it even has a devotional about—waiting. The first devo is about how waiting can be a time of personal reflection.

Taking a deep breath, I begin to personally reflect on losing weight, cleaning my house, weeding my flower garden---. Now, I'm annoyed at all the time that is being wasted—waiting. Grandma wants to be out and about---busy. Not—waiting.

Well, one thing for sure, Grandma does NOT want to wait any longer. It doesn't matter whether I use this waiting time as productive time or a time to sulk and pout, I'm still going to wait and it is starting to make me cranky. I guess this is one of those times when I choose my attitude and my choice determines my anxiety level, my opportunity and my productivity.

Choices, my attitude in *any* situation is all about ---choices. Grandma does NOT choose to wait--- but I can choose how I spend my "necessary time" waiting. So, at least I do have some little bit of control over my situation. Hmmphf. Nice pep talk, but Grandma is still waiting and annoyed.

Then, I see an elderly lady, much older than Grandma, come into the waiting room and quietly sit down. As she sits, I notice she wipes tears from her eyes. Maybe I can do something productive while I wait after all. Gathering my things, I move over to where the elder is sitting, quietly crying into what looks to be a hand embroidered handkerchief. Not a Kleenex, not a napkin—a handkerchief. Grandma gently touches the woman's hand. "What a lovely hanky, did you embroider it yourself?"

As the elder gentle lady looks at me I can see in her eyes that today, life hurts. She reaches for my hand and ---holds it. I say nothing. There is nothing that can be said. Sometimes it is the little things we have opportunity to do that mean the most to others and to God.

It does not require wise words, nor great knowledge not even boldness is needed to simply hold the hand of somebody who is hurting. Grandma is thankful for opportunity to minister while I'm in the ---waiting room.

Wrong Place Right Time

Grandma has had the most wonderful time this weekend! I went to a Women's Conference with two of my friends. The speaker was very well known and the event was well thought out, a good time was had by all. One thing is difficult to understand, the event was promoted as a "time to get away and renew."

Maybe Grandma is old, but, it seems that any retreat that speaks of renewal would not require a 7 a.m. wake up call, a quickly consumed inadequate breakfast, followed by a crowded bus ride, waiting in line and then sitting on hard metal bleacher seats for the entire day. But—since I paid a high dollar price tag for this event, I'm going to say I enjoyed it even though I thought I was going to die from weariness **_while_** I enjoyed it. Now, that is just between you and Grandma, ok, don't say I said that.

After two days of this exhausting "renewal," Grandma was so tired I could barely sit upright for the trip home. Yes, the conference was good, the speakers were substantive and even humorous, and the fellowship was great. But, it was also grueling; those bleachers were hard as, well, metal benches.

You'd think as big as Grandma's backside is, no matter where I sit, I'd have adequate padding, but, oddly, not true. The older I get the more my derriere and lower back needs substantial comfort and support. Thankfully, every two hours, they had everybody stand up and stretch for five minutes. But at this age, it takes more than five minutes to GET up, and way longer standing up to get my equilibrium back. Grandma's soul was fed and my heart uplifted but my body felt like it had been tumbled in a tub of rocks then stuffed in a sock drawer. Mercy.

The young women with us seemed to have a grand time and were telling each other how their "cups were running over." But Grandma was slap wore out and MY cup felt like it had been knocked over and then run over by a truck. Mercy, I'm too old for this "renewal." It was good to be heading home. I kept nodding off to sleep in the back seat during the drive back to the house. My friend's husband had agreed to drive us home and we were grateful.

Arriving at the house about nine at night, Grandma was groggy from exhaustion and was trying to find the bottle of saline to squirt in my eyeballs. As the car went slowly up the street, my friend and I both looking for my house, I see the familiar driveway and holler, "this is it!" My friend's husband pulls into the driveway, opens the back of his sedan and hauls my suitcase out onto the sidewalk.

As I'm digging in my purse for my house key, my eyeballs notice that while I was gone, Grandpa had bought new porch furniture. I can't find my key, so I banged on the front door to get Walter to come let me in—and I noticed he had replaced the front door with a newer—and I must say, much more attractive, door.

Then, at the very moment my mind yelled, "THIS IS THE WRONG HOUSE!" the front door opened and a little old lady in her night clothes stepped out onto the porch demanding to know what we wanted. My friend and her husband are laughing so hard they had to lean on their car as I'm trying to explain to the little woman in her flowered nighty ---that I'd gotten the wrong house.

The next day, I baked a pan of cinnamon rolls and took them, still warm, to the lady whose evening I'd interrupted by banging on her door. She laughed when I told her what had happened. Sometimes life's biggest embarrassments can end up being a blessing in disguise. I can't change circumstances, but I do have much control over what my responding actions are; I choose blessings.

Got MOUTH?

Grandma helps with children's church; sometimes I write skits and lessons for my class. Here lately, the kids have been fussing and saying things that are certainly not pleasing to God. There seems to be a spirit of "mean" and it's getting out of hand. I decided to take the issue to a higher authority.

After church last Sunday, Grandma prepared and served dinner. The necessities taken care of, I made a cup of hot tea, went to my bedroom, sat down in my recliner and told God the trouble I was having with the kids in my class. After a few moments of prayer, I figured God would just handle it, but instead, He asked me what I wanted to do about it.

It never occurred to me that He would ask ME what should be done; I replied, "I want to illustrate that people and particularly Christians have a responsibility <u>for their own words</u>. The devil cannot <u>make</u> a person say anything; we say something because we *choose* to. I want to show the kids that God wants us to build each other up and not tear one another down with our words."

God brought a scripture to my mind. Luke 6:45 The good man brings good things out of the good stored up in his heart and the evil man brings evil things out of the evil stored up in his heart. For out of the abundance of the heart, his mouth speaks. (NIV)

As I sat sipping on my tea, I thought about that scripture. The words start in the heart and come out the mouth. Grandma knew this, but suddenly it came into context. I control my mouth, and what comes out of my mouth comes from inside my heart. I not only control what comes out of my mouth, I have pretty much to say about what goes into my heart. So, I have *a personal responsibility* about both what goes into my heart and what comes out of my mouth. Interesting.

As I scattered through my desk looking for my "idea" lesson plan book, a skit started coming together in my mind. The kids love to do skits and everybody learns easier when they are laughing. Laughing is like the sugar mint that makes the medicine not only go down easy, but stay in your belly once it's down.

Grandma wrote a skit to deal with the "bad mouth" issue. The kids loved it, they laughed SO hard! If EVERYbody likes it, I may even publish it. There's a lot of mean talk going around these days, it's time good sense take the standard. But---with humor---so it stays in your spiritual belly. If you aren't laughing, you aren't remembering. (Skit is in the back of this book, titled, "Got Mouth?" and Grandma did publish it.

The Great Broccoli Soup Adventure

I'm SO excited! Grandma dearly loves to have friends and family over for dinner. I've been known to spend days, even weeks, planning for a big supper. My heart delights in the looking up of recipes, shopping for ingredients, making, baking and of course, praying over every step of the production. In the Bible the disciples prayed over handkerchiefs and handed them out, well, food is a much better vehicle for prayer, don't you think? Cooking isn't just fun, it's a ministry.

Anyway, tonight a dear friend is coming over for supper. The table is all set and pretty and the menu is written out so grandma doesn't lose track of what she's doing. The first dish to be served tonight is broccoli soup.

I have the broccoli all cooked and pureed, the seasonings have been added and tasting shows this will be the best pot of broccoli soup ever. Of course, Grandpa says Grandma says that about every pot of broccoli soup, but, seriously, this pot IS extra delicious. The only thing that needs to be done now is to add the cornstarch to thicken the soup.

I reach into the pantry for the can of cornstarch and the front doorbell rings; our guest has arrived. Grandpa welcomes him and I hear them talking in the living room. As I take the whole cream out of the refrigerator I reach for the measuring spoons. Carefully I start measuring out six tablespoons of cornstarch and stirring it into the cream, making a thick slurry.

After all the little lumps have been stirred out, Grandma turns to the stovetop where the broccoli soup is simmering and begins to add the thick white goop. Just then our guest walks into the kitchen and I turn to greet him. Then, I see a look of horror come on his young face. Turning back to the stovetop, I see a green foaming cloud growing up out of the soup pot like a monster!

Frantic, I start grabbing pots and bowls and dipping the green billowing monster into other containers as fast as I can. I hear our guest whisper, "Oh, Grandma, what have you done?" I have nooooo idea what I did, I only know the giant green cloud seems to have a life of its own, writhing, flowing out over the top of the pan onto the stovetop, flowing down and billowing across the floor. Then, as quickly as the monster had sprung to life, it died back and all that was left was rivers of muddy green goo—everywhere.

Thankfully there were enough other foods to serve that the soup was not missed, but Grandma was distracted all through dinner trying to imagine what, in the name of peace, had happened to bring my soup climbing up the sides of the pan and out on the floor. After the meal was finished, I went to the pantry to see if the date on the cornstarch was bad, although, even if it was, how would that make a pan of soup into a seething monster? It just—made—no—sense.

Then, Grandma knew what she'd done. Sitting side by side on the pantry shelf, was cornstarch and ---baking powder. The cans were the same color, the same size and I'd looked away as the doorbell rang when I reached for the container. When measuring, the contents were both white and a fine powder so I never even thought about having the wrong can. The minute the baking powder slurry was introduced to the hot liquid and the chemical reaction of "rise" started. Most recipes where baking powder is used, call for only a half to one teaspoon of baking powder and I had made a slurry of SIX TABLESPOONS. It's a wonder the pan had not blasted off the stove and through the roof. Mercy.

Later, as Grandma scrubbed the floor and cleaned the rest of the green putty off the counter top, I thought about how sometimes things that are harmless when used properly turn disastrous when used in the wrong way. There's an important God message in that, I know there is. But, tonight, Grandma is exhausted, I'll think about it tomorrow when I have my quiet time with the Lord. Tonight, I just want to sit down in my rocker and have a cup of coffee.

Grandma Can't Multitask

Today, I was so excited about getting on my new treadmill! Grandpa and I both are getting to be the age where exercise is no longer an option. Old joints get creaky and daily exercise makes sure we don't just stop moving altogether. Physical activity keeps senior minds alert, joints limber and as much as Grandma hates to admit it---after the initial getting used to it all; makes my day happier.

A gym membership is not easy to maintain. Grandma is all about spontaneity; my mind doesn't do the "set time show up every day" kind of activity. I fly by the seat of my pants, doing what needs to be done as it needs doing. Keeping a set schedule has never been one of Grandma's strong points.

With having my own treadmill in the den, I can exercise whenever I find time to do. Even in the middle of the night, if that is what I want to do. I popped gum in my mouth and I was good to go, excited to get healthy at my own convenience.

After about ten minutes of a steady light run, all the wet had been sucked out of my gum. Pulling a new piece out of my pocket, I thought I could simply spit the old out of my mouth into the tissue waiting in my hand while, at the same time popping the new into my mouth--all without breaking my stride. But, the old piece of gum fell out of my mouth, missed the tissue and fell onto the moving belt of the treadmill—and stuck.

The belt on the treadmill carried the piece of gum past me about every five seconds. Every time it came by, I tried, unsuccessfully, to kick it off the belt with my foot. Realizing that the gum could ruin the expensive piece of equipment, I judged the speed and leaned down, hoping to swipe the errant piece of gum up as it glided by.

As I leaned over to grab, free hand holding onto the stationary front, my feet got all tangled up. I lost my balance and threw myself onto the floor; taking out the end table, the lamp, and a basket of laundry. The mess in the den confirmed what Grandma had known for quite some time; that I can't multitask.

After I got everything picked up and back in its rightful place, I was d-o-n-e with exercise for today and was ready for a hot beverage. Many folks like a cold beverage after a workout; but I like the comfort of a hot beverage, no matter what I've been doing. As I stood waiting for the coffee machine to heat up, I was thinking about how simple my life can be when I don't try to complicate it. Simplicity can also be carried over into my Christ life. Like walking while trying to pick something up, when I try to live by the world's standards and still serve Christ, in time, I fall and make a mess.

Not only do I make a mess for myself, sadly, when I try to walk with Christ AND have one foot in the world, I also damage my representation of the Christ life to those who are watching me. Every day, every moment, I have to choose who I will serve, the world or my Lord.

Carrying my cappuccino, I walk through the house in search of Grandpa and his coffee cup. It's been a long morning with several life lessons learned. It's time for a sit down and then---we both need a nap.

Crazy for Evangelism

I'm going to be ok. Really, it's just a few cuts, scrapes and bruises. Of course, now you want to know how I got those injuries. Well, Grandma was asked to do a promotional skit for an evangelism class at our church. I dressed up as a wild woman, big hat, crazy dress, red tennis shoes, and bright red lipstick---and to complete my character's point of view, I was carrying a big cardboard sign with bold letters, "REPENT!"

The plan was that during the opening announcements Sunday morning, on 'cue,' given by the Pastor, I'd come running in the back door like a crazy woman, yelling, "Repent!" Once I'd get to the pulpit, Pastor was going to tell me about the new class that was starting and how I could benefit from it and become more productive in my witnessing instead of acting crazy. Unfortunately, we never thought to tell the usher at the door about our skit.

In today's world where the evening news carries reports of shootings in churches and violence on the streets, I guess we should all give more thought to what we are planning. For future reference, it is important to inform all personnel of plans that are out of the ordinary. When I threw the back door of the sanctuary open and ran in yelling, the usher tackled me!

As soon as the usher grabbed me, he recognized my face and promptly let go of me. By then the momentum of the tackle was in full play and when he let go of me, I sailed through the air and took out the last row of folding chairs in the back of the church. I ended up with a busted lip, a chipped front tooth, a sprained wrist and serious carpet burns on my chin and knees. I was------ a sight! Indeed, the whole event was quite dramatic.

Grandma likes lifestyle evangelism way better. Jesus is a person, He is real, I can introduce Him like I would introduce a friend and talk about Him just like I would any other close relationship. If my neighbor was looking for a good manicurist and I had one, I'd certainly mention her to my friend. When my neighbor is trying to live life in a world of pressures and demands--- why shouldn't it be simple to introduce my savior? No big deal, no stress, just---simply share Jesus.

That is the approach of the new evangelism class that is starting; life style evangelism that is "real." A class showing how simply sharing your personal relationship with Christ can fit into your everyday life. And the next time the evangelism class starts, Grandma will ask them to post it in the bulletin instead of asking me to run in the backdoor like a crazy woman holding a sign. Mercy!

The Adventure Begins

Grandma doesn't know whether to be mad or delighted. They say extreme delight is only one step sideways from insanity. They also say that anger releases the same pheromones as joy; both are referenced as a form of passion. And while I think of it, who are "they" anyway? These often referenced experts, simply called, "they," who have answers to everything but never sign their name to anything as proof of authenticity? Never mind, Grandma will save that for another day's contemplation.

Grandpa is an ornery old man, and I can't believe he baited me so easily. Actually, I'm happy he knew how to bait me or we'd never be headed out on this adventure. Oh, mercy, it is, indeed, a two edged sword. We are –moving-- to Florida. Grandma will give you a moment to reflect on that before continuing. What's even more astounding is Grandma is actually, a tiny bit, excited about it.

I know those of you who know me are stunned because you KNOW how Grandma has always been set against moving anywhere. When I married Grandpa, I said he could move our family out of state only once. Then we live where we are, or he could visit me and live wherever he'd wanted to move to. That has continued to be the rule since day one. Consequently, we have happily lived at the foothills of the North Carolina Mountains for almost 40 years.

Now, our children are grown and our grandchildren are nearly grown. Grandpa had been considering moving back to Florida, where he was raised, for quite some time. However, I've not been willing to even consider the idea. Then, one day, a couple of months ago, my beloved, Walter's hip broke and he fell.

Even though he wasn't seriously injured, it made us realize we are closer than ever to the age where such things as moving will be out of the question. We need to find the place we want to retire to and go there. We'd not been looking seriously yet, until Grandpa found an Island. I bet you didn't even know that Florida had any Islands; Grandma certainly did not.

Well, I could ramble on forever about how one thing led to another but the truth of the matter is, from the first time Grandma woke up watching the sunrise over the ocean and heard those waves softly kissing the beach, it was a done deal. Sneaky Grandpa, he knew I'd be smitten and it would only be a matter of time till Grandma would think moving to the Island wasn't such a bad idea after all.

SO, that is why we are in the throes of packing up our entire life into cardboard boxes and moving. Packing is easy; everything goes in one place, in the box. Unpacking, now that will be a different story. In a strange place where nothing has a place and everything looks out of place even after it has been put IN place---mercy sakes!

Our grandchildren have been putting ridiculous labels on all the boxes so Grandma will laugh when she unpacks. Of course, they have no idea how difficult it will be to figure out what room of the house to unpack boxes that are labeled, "thingamajigs." But, it will make grandma laugh.

Friends have told Grandma that I should call a professional packer to help with all this. One of my friends did exactly that and when she unpacked she found a carefully wrapped plate with a half eaten sandwich. No, thank you. Grandma will pack her own boxes.

I hate change. Even good change is difficult to adjust to. Grandma is so thankful that no matter what is changing in the world or my life, I can depend on one thing. God never changes. Never. So, that means I can focus on my Lord and keep my heart steady. No matter what lies ahead, God has this. And then, there's bubble wrap; I'm sure God invented this product for stress relief. It is purely accidental that it is used as packing material. As long as Grandma has God and bubble wrap, I can do this.

Antique Hutterly for Sale

Grandma has a china cabinet that is in the way. It is big and awkward and looks almost gothic in design. Quite frankly, it is the ugliest piece of furniture I've ever seen---ever. It has been in my dining room for many years simply because it came with the table, which I love. The table is big enough to seat 12 comfortably. Do you know how difficult it is to find a table that large? Exactly.

So, the fact that the table of my dreams came with an ugly gnarly china cabinet is of small consequence. But, the cabinet must go because our new house in Florida, thankfully, doesn't have space for Bohemian cabinetry.

I placed an ad in the local newspaper. Somebody, somewhere, no doubt, is sitting in their kitchen thinking, "I want a giant, ugly, china cabinet, I simply MUST have one." Grandma hopes that person sees the advertisement and comes to pick this monstrosity up—quickly.

I'm sure the only reason this cabinet exists is because of the companion table that it comes with. Like Grandma, nobody wants to discard a piece of perfectly good furniture, no matter how ugly it is. After all, it is---wood and intricately carved. Even though the carvings look like demon possessed muskrats, (what ARE those animals carved in the corners supposed to be?) the wood, itself, is quite lovely.

The phone rings and as I rush to answer, I marvel that somebody could actually call about the cabinet so soon. The man on the other end of the line said, "Yes, I'm calling about your hutterly that is for sale in the Evening Newspaper. Can you tell me what kind of hutterly it is?" Confused, I say, "I'm sorry, what did you say?" The man patiently responds, "The hutterly you listed for sale in tonight's paper, can you tell me about it? What kind of hutterly is it?"

Not sure what on earth the man is talking about, because what he said makes no sense at all, I said, "OH, the hutterly! Well, you caught me as I was heading out the door, could you call back in about an hour?" The man agreed and begged me to not sell my "hutterly" until I'd spoken to him first. Grandma hung up the phone and went to fetch the newspaper off the front walk. Hutterly? What on earth?

There, in bold print, right in front of my eyeballs, is clearly printed, "Antique hutterly for sale. Must see to appreciate. Call (my phone number) for appointment to view." How, in the name of peace, did the newspaper get, "hutterly" out of "china cabinet?" Doesn't anybody proof read anymore? Chona cabinet would make sense, china cavinet would make sense---but---how did they get---hutterly? Grandma is –bumfuzzled at that one.

Then, even more funny than the misspelled word is the fact somebody called to ask me to describe the hutterly—which is not even a real word. My thoughts are interrupted by the phone ringing. It is another inquisitive buyer asking for information about my—hutterly. It is hilarious that nobody is calling to ask what a hutterly is, they are all calling to ask what KIND of hutterly it is. Oh, Grandma is going to have fun today!

Each potential buyer that called I answered as truthfully as I could. "What kind of hutterly?" Why, a very ornate one, with hand carved animals of some kind in the corner. Grandma didn't mention she thought the animals looked like muskrats. "What color is the hutterly?" The traditional color, the value would be greatly lessened if the color had been changed. "What size is the hutterly?" It is standard sized; it's not the miniature one.

Grandma has rarely had so much fun with a piece of furniture. The calls continued throughout the day. People had many questions but nobody asked what on earth this "hutterly" was. I guess because they thought that would make them look foolish—I mean, what kind of uneducated fool would not know what a hutterly is? Human nature is sometimes very ---fallible.

At the end of the day, Grandma has had a marvelous time. The newspaper had no idea how the word swap had happened but happily said they'd run my advertisement for two extra days over the one I paid for to make up for my inconvenience. I did not tell them about the endless source of entertainment the phone calls had provided.

As I sit sipping my evening tea, I begin to understand how so much false doctrine can be running about uncorrected. If people are not willing to ask definitive questions about furniture, why would they question false doctrine? Interesting. Troubling, but, interesting, none the less.

A HOME FOR OLD BIBLES

As I pack one box after another in preparation of moving to Florida, Grandma has a question. What should I DO with all my old Bibles? For that matter, what do we ALL do with our old Bibles? Anybody who has served God for a lot of years has a box or at least a stack of---worn out, falling apart, Bibles.

Do we burn them with ceremony like an old flag? Do we fasten the broken bindings with a large rubber band and relegate this beloved book to gather dust on a bookshelf or in a box? Just what should we DO with our old Bibles? Strange, I've not seen anything written about that. No direction on the subject ever comes from the pulpit. Yet, hopefully, this is a common situation. Because if our Bibles aren't getting worn out-----

One of my most treasured possessions is an old, very old, pocket Bible. My beloved, Walter, paid a few cents for it at a sidewalk sale. Inside, the original owner had written notes, penned thoughts and marked passages. According to the dates the previous owner had penned in the cover, the Bible is over 100 years old. It is very moving to gently flip through the pages and read the personal thoughts of its long ago owner.

As I read through her notes she'd written in the margins, I find that as odd as it would seem, the woman struggled with the same problems, temptations and failings that I do. It encourages me to read her side notes of victory and answered prayer. It makes sense that even though times change, the issues of life are constant.

We are young then old. We grow up and face challenges; we suffer bereavement, job difficulties, and issues with other people. The circumstances of life are constant even though our surroundings are not. Our parents grow old and die, our children, if we have them, grow up and then our grandchildren grow up.

Grandma had never thought of life as being so—so---common. The dear saint who wrote in the margins scribbled about gardens that were desperate for rain, laundry that always needed done, suppers that had to be made, and a heart that was in mourning for the family she loved who were not serving God.

My own heart breaks with understanding as I read her notes about prayers made in tears for children, grandchildren and other loved ones who were busy about their way with little thought of Christ. My heart hopes that her loved ones are with her in heaven.

One day, when I've gone to be with my Lord, I want to meet this gentle soul who lived so strong for Christ. My heart can only hope that one day somebody will have <u>my</u> old Bible and be encouraged by the markings I've made in its pages. An even greater hope
is that my old Bible will be cherished by my family and not be left at a roadside market—unclaimed.

A Time to Break Things

Somehow, during the course of packing and moving, I managed to break my foot. Not a serious break, thank goodness, but painful nonetheless. The local emergency medic center x-rayed my swollen appendage, pronounced it broken and gave me a ridiculous boot to wear.

The nurse told me I was blessed that the break was in the place it was. If it had been only an inch higher it would have required surgery, a metal pin and months in a cast that went clear to my knee. It seemed odd that a blessing could be so painful and inconvenient, but, sometimes blessings don't make sense. Grandma is grateful for all blessings---big and small.

Telling Grandma to sit still and stay off my foot is fodder for comedy and drama because it simply is not happening. Grandpa would happily take care of me, but I'm not one to sit around and be broken; all that being said, I noticed that we were totally out of milk. I told Walter he could either eat dry cheerios for a bedtime snack or I could get take-out for supper when I went to get the milk.

He opted for take-out. I didn't argue. I chose Chinese. I picked up the milk along with a few other items I remembered was needed and then grabbed our Chinese food and headed home. On the way home, my broken foot started punishing me for disobeying the doctor's orders by suddenly cramping severely.

So, I'm driving home from the store in traffic muttering, "owl owl owl owl" and grinding my teeth. Grandma does NOT have time for such shenanigans and refuses to give in to suffering. I hate being pitiful, will absolutely not participate in that kind of behavior. Just. NOPE.

When I got home I figured if I balanced everything just right, I might be able to manage to carry three bags of groceries, (not difficult since the baggers put only one item in each bag so the customer feels they got their moneys' worth) a quart of milk and the box of China food. Nothing was heavy and I only had a few feet to walk to the house. This should not be a big deal.

I figured success was all in achieving the proper 'balance.' I strung the three bags up my left arm and then leaned over the driver's seat planning to reach down, pick up the box of Chinese, rise up, snag the quart of milk with three fingers, kick the door with my one good foot and I'd be on my way. I've always been an over achiever, but this was a bit over the line, even for me. Hind sight is always the clearest vision----.

Standing outside the car, open door at my back, I precariously reached over the driver's seat with my (big) rear end waving in the air, my left arm occupied with the light weight, but incredibly awkward, grocery bags, trying to unsuccessfully reach the China food, grab the milk, balance and stand up.

It would have been so much easier if I'd simply walked around the car to the passenger side and retrieved the groceries from there. But, my foot hurt and I thought reaching would be much less painful than hobble footing. After stretching as far as I could, the box of Chinese was only a fraction of an inch out of my grasp.

I waved my fingers hoping to coax the box to levitate into my hand; I found the box just would not cooperate. Exasperated, I lunged forward on my tippy toes hoping the extra little bouncy thrust would help me reach the box on the floor under the dashboard without dropping the bags hanging on my left arm.

I'd just gotten my hand almost around the box when my right shoulder screamed, "noooooo, nooooo." As Bette Davis, an actress from times gone by liked to quip, "Getting old ain't for sissies." Bravely trying to cope with arthritic shoulder pain, foot pain and the effort of stretching clear across the front seat, I rested my chin on the edge of the driver's seat to try and balance myself.

Thinking if I only had one tiny more little bit of stretch left in me, I bit the edge of the seat with my teeth in the hopes of pulling my body just that one last tiny micro measure I needed to grab the China food box. I forgot that I wear dentures. My teeth flew out of my mouth and fell into my jacket pocket that was dangling just below my chin as I stretched myself like the old Stretch Armstrong rubber doll. But, that extra thrust was enough to grab hold of the box of Chinese!

There I was, leaning over the driver's seat, left arm laden with bags, right hand clutching a box of Chinese, every muscle strained and every fiber stretched, on my tippy toes, broken foot cramping, toothless but refusing to let loose of the box of food. Then, the Styrofoam lid on the box of Chinese broke open and the aroma of Moo Shu Pork flooded into the car as the food dumped out onto the floor mat.

For one brief moment in time I thought I was going to fall apart and throw myself down in the driveway and just---- CRY. About the time I was ready to start sobbing, I got a mental image of what I looked like to the casual passerby and instead of sobbing, I started laughing.

I laughed and I laughed and every time I tried to stop, I thought of the sight I was making and started laughing again. Finally, I gave it all up, dropped everything, pulled my self over the seat and back onto my feet. I limped around to the other side of the car, scraped the food back into the container, dropped it into the trash can, threw the floor mat onto the driveway for later hosing then gathered the parcels and the milk and went into the house.

Grandpa looked up as I walked through the door. "There you are! I was starting to worry, so what are we having for supper?" I took a deep breath and said, "CHEERIOS!" Now, Grandma tries to take every disaster and make it into a lesson. Often, such trials can be teachable moments; but, not always. Try as I might, I could think of no Godly illustration, no scriptural reference---*not—one---stinking ---thing*--that I could use in this moment to build my faith.

Walter looked at me kind of blank then smiled and said, "Oh, I see what it is, you don't have your teeth in. For a minute there I thought you said we were having Cheerios for supper. Why did you take your teeth out?" Then, I had the scripture. The fruit of the Spirit is—*self*—control.

The Tiki Bar Sign and Grandma's Coffee Cup

Grandma is amazed at how much JUNK Grandpa and I have accumulated around the house over the last few decades. Somehow, while life was being lived, I just didn't recognize that so much of the stuff we were bringing home really had no practical use. Since Walter and I are moving to Florida, we have determined that we are going to do some serious clean out. Anything that hasn't been used in the last year is going in the box for a local charity to pick up.

This week, I've been very tough on myself as I've gathered up all the stuff that has no purpose. There are a lot of knick knacks that serve no reason for existence other than to collect dust. For instance, the tiki bar sign over the sofa in the den. Grandpa and I had bought it because it was so bright and shiny. Actually, more influenced the purchase than just the sign being shiny.

We were in the Bahamas; our first big vacation alone after the kids had grown up and moved out. We were having so much fun watching people dance and laugh and mind you, Grandpa and I had done some dancing and laughing as well. We saw the Tiki Bar sign for sale and thought it would be a great memento of our trip.

It had blinky lights that flashed, a silly picture of a fish that had had too much to drink and a few pink flamingo feathers wafting here and there. I know, I know—and yes it actually is as ridiculous as it sounds; but, at the moment, we thought it was perfect. The fact that the sign was so ridiculous was what made us want it to start with. It was so unlike our usual practical attitudes that it was just—outrageously--perfect. So, we bought it.

Once we got it home, we had no idea where to put it; we don't drink so we have no "bar" area. We'd paid quite a bit for the silly thing---the insanity of the moment—. For one fleeting moment, Grandma wished we did drink, that way we could blame the purchase on our drunken insanity. But---nope, it was just the insanity of the moment, no drunkenness to do with it. And *that* is why there has been a garish Tiki Bar sign that has hung over the sofa in our den for the last ten years.

One year our son in-law got us a silly fish that was motion activated so that when anybody passed by, the fish started wiggling its tail and singing a ridiculous song about being drunk. He said it had to go on the wall beside the Tiki Bar sign. Grandma thought it was funny but creepy. Anyway BOTH the Tiki Bar sign AND the creepy singing fish went in the box to be donated to charity. I told my son in-law nobody would buy that stuff, we should just throw it away. He looked at me and said, "You bought it." (Smarty pants.)

It has taken me all week to pack up the relics of old vacations, winter clothes that won't work in the sunny south and miscellaneous odds and ends that are too numerous to mention. Grandma put it all in boxes and set them on the front porch and called a local charity to pick it up. The next afternoon, I sat on the front steps with my pink Bible that I was reading my morning devotions in, my cup of coffee (in my favorite cup that fit my hand so—so—very --comfortably), and my NEW running shoes that I would put on for the first time this morning..

My intention was to finish the chapter I was reading while I enjoyed the last few sips of coffee, then, put on my new running shoes and take off jogging. Good plan, until the phone interrupted. The phone call took longer than I thought it would. Finally, I headed back to the front porch to dump out my (by now cold--) coffee, put on my shoes and finish my devotions later.

To my dismay, the charity truck had come while I was in the house and taken not only the STUFF, but my running shoes, my Bible AND my favorite coffee cup! The feeling of betrayal was overwhelming. I'd freely given of my excess and in return they had taken all I had!

What kind of insanity would have a charity employee take everything not nailed down instead of just the very obviously packed stuff in the boxes? Seriously? My coffee cup even had a few swigs of coffee in it---! And my pink Bible? Couldn't they see the book was laying open faced---like it was set aside by somebody reading it?

As I stood staring up the street where the big truck carrying my cup, my shoes and my Bible was fading from view, I remembered last Sunday's Bible study message. When we truly commit our lives to Christ, it means that we allow God to use us anyway He wants to for any purpose He desires at any time He chooses. When we draw a line around our talents and possessions giving only what we think is necessary, we put limits on what God can do through us AND *for* us.

All of that is well and good, but, my shoes, my coffee cup and my pink Bible? I don't think God had anything to do with this—it was simply overzealous volunteers. But, Grandma can't help but wonder if sometime in the next few weeks, three people I don't know and will never meet---will cry tears of joy over BRAND NEW, never been worn, running shoes, a favorite cup that holds just right in their hand and their very own---pink-Bible. At least I choose to believe that will be what happens—it makes the pain of loss less itchy.

Part 2
The Move

Truth Is---

It's the first Monday since we moved to Florida. We unloaded the truck on Friday, unpacked all day Saturday and most of Sunday and now, this begins our first week in our new home. The truth is, one of the hard parts about moving is all the new places that have to be located and made personal. Like a Dry Cleaner, Doctors, Beauty Parlor and Barber, Grocery Store, and of course, a Church.

God created Grandma for relationship, primarily relationship with Him. But, truth is; I also need the encouragement that comes from relationships in the body of Christ. In today's world, it could be sooooo easy to substitute the surface gratification of social media for making relationships in my own community and at a local church.

Grandma is BUSY; whoever thought that being old meant you had less to do, nowhere to go and no friends to be with was sadly mistaken. It's really crazy that as science and technology comes up with more and more gadgets to lighten my work load, I'm busier than ever.

The truth is; most of these confaluted gadgets are a waste of my time. I can get something done in less than half the time it takes for these new gadgets to get plugged in and warmed up. That is not even taking into consideration how steep my learning curve is. Mercy.

Amazingly, if I feel pressed for time, I can even watch a televangelist instead of going to church. Why, I even have social network friends that are pastors and they post their Sunday services on line. It's like being at church; only I'm in bed with coffee and in my jammies.

In a Christian study, made across denominational lines, it was discovered that the number one--- number ONE—reason why people don't go to church is, "just too busy." When interviewed about their personal walk with God, most said they really loved the Lord. But, with family, job and home, the added responsibility of being at church, on time, every time, was just—unreasonable.

Now, Grandma could share her faith on line and certainly share my witness with my friends. But if I'm not feeding my own heart by hearing the Word of God and participating in active prayer within the church community, WHAT am I sharing? Truth is; something has to be <u>experienced</u> before it is shared. A moving picture on a flat screen isn't experience, it's entertainment; and far too easy to walk away from.

Truth is; going to church provides a witness to God, to me and to the world. It also makes for accountability and heaven knows this old lady needs to be held accountable. Does going to church make me a Christian? No. But going to church gives me the strength and fellowship my human nature needs to live the Christ life and be a strong witness.

Truth is; I need the strength of 'presence' with the body of Christ. What going to church _does_ do is give me a place to worship, share God's Word together, encourage each other—and rest. It's true, Grandma wouldn't want to wear jammies to church, but I don't have to be in my bed clothes to rest either.

Television and on-line church are blessings when I'm sick, or for some real reason, simply cannot make it to church. Sometimes, every now and then, my busy life just demands that I take time away from normally scheduled things. Those times are when having the availability of video church on the internet is a welcomed and appreciated alternative to physically attending church.

But, truth is; Grandma needs to be AT church whenever possible so I can fellowship with others, enjoy the warmth of friendship and the physical contact of hugs and handshakes. I need to be a – _living_ part- of the body of Christ. So, there, the decision has been made.

We just moved to a new community, nobody knows us here and certainly nobody cares if we find a church and attend regularly. If we want to, we could simply avail ourselves of the many "on-line" and "live-feed" worship services. BUT, now that Grandma has thought about it that would not be a good choice after all. I wonder if Grandpa has given any thought to finding a Florida church or has he been thinking about the same alternative as I have been tempted with?

As I sit up on the edge of the bed to go find Walter and ask him about this, the bedroom door opens and the first words out of Walter's mouth are, "I looked at the city directory on line and I found us a church to check out. We need to be pulling out of the driveway at 9:45 Sunday morning to make sure we have enough time to get inside and sit down before the choir starts."

Alllllllrighty then. A strong willed woman needs a strong man, Grandma is glad God gave her one. It is only Monday and already we have a church to visit.

Hello, My Name Is Rebecca

In case you've noticed, it has been a few days since Grandma wrote in her journal. It was very difficult and painful to pack up the intimacies of our life, say good bye to friendships nurtured over a lifetime, and give our grandchildren one last hug. As difficult as the rigors of moving proved to be; our first Sunday in our new city was as emotionally draining as the move itself.

Grandpa and I recognized the importance of establishing life priorities quickly. Because a new environment makes it easy to leave even well-founded habits behind, finding a church home was placed on the top of our list. We knew that satan takes advantage of every circumstance; life is about choices and doing nothing *is always* the easiest choice of all. In full knowledge of that, Monday, Grandpa had found us a church to look into.

As we sat in a church we'd never attended before, Grandma experienced the chill of anonymity. There was no family to embrace, and no friends to welcome me. Standing tall, I took a deep breath and reassured myself with the thought, "Soon, I will put names with these faces and these people will be my friends."

In obedience to the order of worship, I stood, sang, sat, prayed and listened to the well prepared sermon. My tears fell unnoticed, or, perhaps, simply accepted by those around me as a part of my personal worship experience. Grandpa squeezed my hand and sat close with his arm around my back.

We had reminded ourselves that no church would, immediately, feel like "home;" the coveted feeling of "belonging" comes with familiarity. Most people in a church are welcoming because they have been trained through classes or by the personal acknowledgement of the need to be noticed. Many churches have assigned door attendants to reach out to newcomers. I recognized that if my first contact was with one of the few who weren't friendly and I let myself be hurt; who wins in that game? Satan.

As a visitor, putting all the responsibility of "meet and greet" on the *other* person is unfair. Being in "their" church doesn't mean that ALL the duties of protocol and etiquette should rest on them. Perhaps the person sitting behind or beside me may be a first time visitor just like me, it's not like visitors wear a special t-shirt or something. Determined to not fall victim to the wiles of the deceiver, I reminded myself that making friends is a two way street, and, an introduction is the first step of relationship.

When the last prayer was said, I turned to the person closest to me, smiled invitingly, and extended my hand in greeting. After all, who wouldn't respond to the warmth of a smile? In very short time, the shared foundation in Christ was built upon and strangers, as had been anticipated, became precious friends. The fact that making new friends at church is difficult speaks directly to how important friends are to both God and Satan; for opposite reasons. Satan knows that if I have no friends at church, I will be vulnerable to his tools of discouragement, bitterness and loneliness.

God knows that there is personal growth in friendship and strength in fellowship. It's up to me which plan I choose to participate in. Friendships are an important validation of emotional stability; Satan wants me to be weak and vulnerable. Grandma knows better than to fall into that trap. I remind myself that friends also come in all sizes, shapes, ages and colors so I don't need to seek out only those who are like me; EVERY person is a friendship waiting to happen.

Therefore, I will not wait for others to make the first move toward relationship. I choose to make friends because I choose to avail myself of all the strongholds of Godly friendship. Making sure my visitor badge is firmly clinging to my dress front, I turn to the person next to me and say, "Hello, my name is Rebecca Grace, but my friends call me Bitsy."

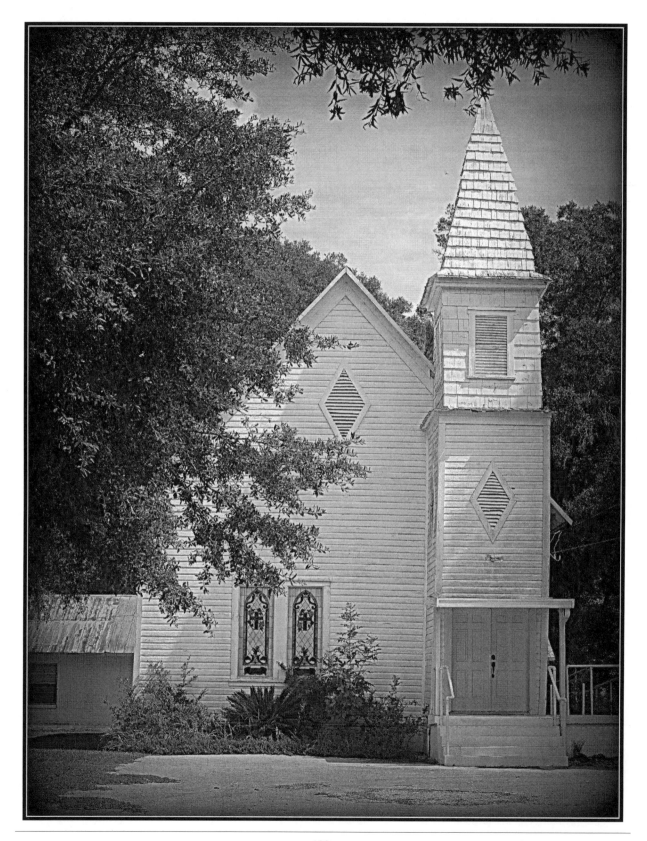

Grandma's Spin Cycle Class

When we moved, Grandma knew that establishing an exercise program in our new environment was second only to finding a good church to fellowship with. It is far too easy to stop doing something in a new place, even when you have been doing it for years, so, I signed up for the gym. Today, I started out my fitness program at the YMCA in Florida with a spin cycle class.

Once I got started in the class, I realized this was probably not the best class to start out with, but, there I was, so boom. The room has about 20 stationary bikes in it. At first glance I thought maybe they gave us each a seat we attached or I'd missed the instruction to bring a bicycle seat---or what. Then the instructor told me the hard, narrow black strip of black was actually the --seat; not the joint where the seat was to be attached.

I'm old, my rear stopped being narrow many years ago--and it never was ---that--narrow. The room was dimly lit and icy cold---I told her it was freezing and she laughed and said in about 15 minutes I'd be sweating like an animal and wanting somebody to throw ice on me. My mind started the grade school chant, "If you feel danger walk away from the stranger."

It was a bit unsettling to realize I was the oldest person in the class by 20-40 years. I began to have even more doubts about my---fitness selection. These women were young, lithe, firm and *very* fit. This morning they had told me to wear loose comfortable clothing to work out in. So, I wore pedal pushers and a T-shirt.

I guess the young girls didn't get that memo, because they all had on black spandex shorts. Without exception, these young girls had backsides hard and tight enough that I could have cracked a walnut on either one of their butt cheeks using only a fly swatter. I doubt I could even find spandex in my size---and if I did, I'd look like 25 pounds of jello struggling to get out of a 10 pound sack and there for sure would be no walnut cracking, not even with a mallet.

The instructor (a young woman so fit her skin looked like it had been sprayed on her bones then allowed to dry) showed me how to set up my cycle and how to mount properly. I'd had a bicycle when I was a kid, but this was nothing like my childhood memory.

I tried to get on the bike but missed and hung myself sideways. She patiently helped me get properly situated so I had one foot on each side of the bike. The seat was much smaller than even one side of "me" and balancing myself so I didn't fall off--or impale myself-- was a gymnastic feat all by itself. The pedals had straps so my feet couldn't get out, fear mounted in my mind.

This bike's seat was higher than the handlebars---so when you ride, you lean over--even stretch out---across the handlebars. I told her it was VERY not comfortable and she said it was fine; I'd be standing up as much as sitting down. She turned and trotted away, her pony tail swinging---and didn't hear me holler--"WHAT? Standing? Wait--come back!"

She mounted her bike at the front of the class without even taking a deep breath--no struggle, she just threw her leg over and boom, she was on and adjusting her mike to call out the cadence as we rode. She told us to set the pedal resistance to mild and start a slow pedal warm up. She showed us how to take our elbows back, rotate our shoulders and move our head from side to side to--loosen up--all while doing a slow pedal. The young girls had obviously done this class before because they were a step ahead of her as she instructed.

I was struggling to keep my big rear ON the seat---and to do shoulder scrunches, head tilts and elbow loosening WHILE I pedaled was just---no. I sat there, trying to steady myself and not fall off the tiny little seat while I started pedaling. Even on the lowest setting, my legs ached to pedal--I could feel a cold film of sweat breaking out on my forehead. This was not the sweat that comes with physical activity--no--this was the cold sweat of ---skeert.

Everybody loosened up now, the instructor called out, "We're going to flat ride for a few minutes, increase your resistance as I call out to do so by adjusting the lever in front of you. The music today is hot, REAL hot---(the young girls cheered) so we are going to climb steady, your RPMs (wheel revolutions per minute) should be between 60-110, if you get tired, do not stop pedaling, just lower your RPM to 50 till you get your wind back then ease it back up."

She smiled really big and shouted, "LET'S RIDE!" The music started screaming some song about "I'm on FIHYAR!" and the girls leaned forward stretching out over their handlebars their legs pumping like engine sprockets on a fly wheel. I leaned forward, started pedaling, chewing on my bottom lip and praying in tongues.

After a few minutes the instructor started hollering, UP, two, three four, DOWN, two three four. On the UP the girls stood up to ride for four strokes then on the DOWN sat back for four strokes--- When I stood up, I felt like concrete blocks were tied to the pedals they were so hard to push, when I sat down the pedals went so fast I knew why they had straps to hold your feet on.

Again and again, up, down, up down. Then the instructor hollered "HILL!" The fastest hard rock music I'd ever heard was playing; we all stood up, leaned forward and pedaled like demons were chasing us. I could not hear the words to the music; all I could hear was my own voice saying, "Jesus, Jesus, Jesus--" over and over.

My life was passing before my eyeballs---I knew I was going to die. I mentally made final prayers for safe keeping of my loved ones. My butt was numb, my legs burned like fire, and my arms ached. About the time I knew I was going to pass out, the instructor hollered, "even road!" And everybody sat down but kept pedaling.

I figured the hour long class must be nearly over---I glanced up at the wall clock. It had stopped right after we got started because it said we'd only been riding for 15 minutes. The air conditioner must have shut off when the clock stopped because I was sweating like crazy and it felt like it was the middle of July on the beach with no sea breeze blowing.

I grabbed my water bottle from the holder and tried to put it to my parched lips---but water went all over me, not in my mouth. I didn't care; in fact, I actually enjoyed the cool water as it splashed onto my fevered body.

The instructor yelled, "if you're new to the class, don't hurt yourself, ride with resistance, pedal as hard as you can, resting as needed but do not stop pedaling, drop your RPMs back to 50 (we'd been doing 90-110) and hold till you get your breath back."

So, for the rest of the class, I just stayed in that "drop back" position. The rest of the class climbed the hills without me----while I just rode steady. I finished the class---and had to have help getting off my bike---but--I finished the class. I did. I. Finished.--the---Class. I wanted to fall on my face and worship God for allowing me to live--but knew if I did--I'd have to spend the night there, face down on the floor.

As I left the classroom, the instructor told me how proud she was to have me in her class that she couldn't wait to see what a great rider I was going to be in a few weeks. I sat in the car for a while; parts of my body were numb that should never---ever---EVER---be--numb. I figured it would be wise to sit for a few moments till I could feel at least one butt cheek before I started driving. Oh, mercy sakes, I just realized---how is this going to feel in the morning? NGNNGNG

Living In the Highlighter

I love my new kitchen in Florida. It has windows that allow sunlight to pour into the room. There is a built in bookcase on the back wall. On my kitchen bookshelf is a row of diet books. Grandma has read the books, agreed with them, highlighted them and dog eared their pages. You KNOW how Grandma loves to read self-help it books. But, when it comes right down to it, I put the book back on the shelf and keep right on going.

This is going to change now that we have moved to a new place. Grandma lives in a new state, a new city, and a new neighborhood. This is the perfect time to begin a new life pattern. There is no pattern to be changed because I've not set a daily routine yet. So, this is the perfect time to get serious about a healthy lifestyle.

To actively lose weight requires discipline, planning and action. The hardest part is simply, doing it. Discipline is never easy. Even when I try to move helpful hints out of the highlighted pages, there is always the mental conflict and the weakness of human nature to deal with. And Grandma's human nature is seriously weak when it comes to such things.

Like for instance, those small chocolate squares that used to be so popular. Ayds appetite suppressant chocolate diet candies that were all the rage in the 1980's is a good example. Grandma got a box of them. The instructions said that when you are hungry and want a sweet treat, simply peel the foil off one of the small squares and pop it in your mouth. The complex combination of vitamins and minerals would satisfy that sweet tooth with only a tiny few calories.

Grandma discovered the little fudge bites were particularly satisfying when twenty of them were melted down in the microwave in a little custard dish then poured over vanilla ice-cream. After Grandma had consumed three boxes of the Ayds appetite suppressants and gained four pounds, I realized this "tool" was not working for me.

Then, there were the ever popular liquid meal substitutes that came in a vast array of tempting flavors. Flavors like "chocolate malt" and "banana orange." Only 400 calories per small can. The taste was actually decent, but the serving size was way off. It took at least three cans to make lunch feel satisfying, at least for a while. That meant that lunch was 1,200 calories—a big mac only has 1,200 calories and tastes a LOT yummier and keeps me satisfied the rest of the afternoon. Boom. No struggle in that choice.

Grandma has even joined the gym a few times. With each gym membership renewal I lost about forty five dollars a month. While enjoying the discipline of going to the gym, I also tore my rotator cuff, sprained my ankle and broke my toe. None of these accidents were the gym's fault. Grandma is old, clumsy and at times, over ambitious.

I have noticed that living fully for Christ has many of the same pitfalls that dieting does. It's not only about reading and knowing "how to." And it's not just going through the motions while making substitutions to make the process more pleasant. It's about doing everything possible, with the Spirit's help, to actually make life application.

Similar to finding a diet that works for me, I must find a time during my busy day to sit quietly with my Bible, read and pray. The same discipline that I apply for accomplishing everyday things in my life can be applied to accomplish a time of devotion AND a time to go to the gym.

I must plan it then I must actually DO it. Grandma wonders why it is just as hard to plan and go exercise as it is to plan and read the Bible. I guess because they both require---discipline. Discipline is not punishment; it is a routine that is done to bring change. Going to the gym regular requires both planning AND the discipline of---doing.

Nobody is going to make me follow a diet and exercise program. I must do it. Nobody is going to make me find time to read my Bible and have a conversation with my Lord. I must---do—it. Alllllrighty then. Grandma has written, "I must do it," so many times it has almost become a chant---. Going to stop writing now and put action into words.

Not just with the time of devotion and prayer but also with the eat less and exercise more. Yes. Going to do both of those things---starting--now. I'm (finally) going to take those words that I've highlighted in all of those healthy living books and make life application. Here I go. Pray for me; I'm putting my pen down and standing up. I'm taking the words that I've so faithfully highlighted so often and—living them. Mercy.

Shopping for Necessaries

Today, Grandma went shopping for "necessaries.' In other words, I set out to get shoes and hopefully, a new outfit. First, I did the shoe shopping. Now, mind you, grandma does not do shopping of ANY kind very often because, I'm just not a "shopping" kind of person. My idea of a great day shopping is going into the store, going straight to the item that I'm needing and heading for the checkout line. Unless, of course, it is a kitchen gadget store; then you may need to send somebody in after me after the first three hours.

When Grandma grew up in West Virginia, and later lived in North Carolina, it was chilly in the winter, even cold at times. This drop in temperature meant that Grandma had to wear "real" shoes for at least a few months each year. I miss the old days when I could go into a shoe store that was actually service oriented.

Unlike the shoe stores of today that tout cheap shoes but whereas the shoe itself may be cheaply made, the price tag is not cheap. The old fashioned shoe stores had quality shoes and nobody said anything about cheap. Shoes lasted years, not months and when the bottoms began to wear out; we took the shoes to a cobbler to have the soles replaced. Shoes had leather soles, leather sides and cushioned insoles. The shoe store clerks wore dressy clothes, like they were going to church instead of spending the day measuring feet.

And yes, the clerks actually measured your feet. They used a weird looking metal appliance that had slides to get accurate size measurements; it was called a Brannock Device. Google that to see what it looked like---and you'll understand why everybody had shoes that really *fit* in those days. Shoe fitting was a science, not a guessing game.

Today's clerks know nothing about shoes, nothing about fit and nothing about style. They simply stand at the counter, ring up your purchase and take your money. If you ask for advice or direction, you are met with a disinterested shrug and a mumbled, "I dunno." Grandma longs for a good old fashioned shoe store and can't help but wonder if any of the youth today have ever even had a pair of good shoes that fit perfectly and don't wear out; probably nope.

Since moving to Florida, I have noticed that flip flops are the main shoe of choice. It seems that even brides in Florida wear flip flops. Grandma knows this because she has seen lavishly bejeweled flip flops in bridal stores. I wonder if the reason flip flops are so popular is because nobody knows anything about style, fit and purpose anymore.

Without any leadership in shoe selection the customers just moved to the easiest choice---one style fits every event. Take a beach flop, glue some sparkly stones on it and boom, you have a wedding flip flop. One shoe conforms to every event.

However, Grandma has found that those cute little bangled flops displayed so enticingly in the window are a size 6. When I go in and ask the clerk for the same shoe in a size 10 wide, I'm usually told that particular shoe is only available in up to a size 8. On the rare occasions that I find the shoe I was wanting in my size, it doesn't look like it did in the display window.

That delicate little sparkly flop in the window, when found in my size, looks like a river barge. Those fragile sexy little toe straps sparkling with rhinestones look like a dog collar with hubcap studs when they come in a size 10 1/2. Those tiny little sized shoes sparkle and shine and attract admiring looks. But, the river barge sizes bring gawking stares, snickers and jokes about glare.

While we are on the subject of clothing, why is it all the larger sizes of dresses come in ridiculous orange and purple patterned prints? There are times that Grandma likes to wear loud crazy prints but that is not my choice for most days. I like fashionable clothing, with collars, necklines, sleeves and a discernable waistline. The skirt of a good dress should flow; not be tight because when I'm not on a diet, Grandma is a large woman and nobody wants to see all "that."

Nobody makes stylish clothing for large ladies. All the clothing looks like it was made by Omar the Tentmaker and comes in only two prints; huge brightly colored flowers or wide stripes like an awning. Consequently, Grandma has given up on dressy clothes and stays with slacks and a blouse. And more and more often, my clothing choice for the day is a pair of capris and a T-shirt. Since we've moved to Florida, this seems to be acceptable attire for beach living so Grandma fits in with the locals. I like that.

But, enough rambling on and on. Truth be known, it would have been better if Grandma had just gone to bed this evening without thought to writing in her journal. Nothing wild or crazy went on today, just the ordinary, which, the way my life usually unfolds, is a small miracle. Grandma is thankful for quiet days.

I shall have a cup of Earl Gray Tea on the porch and relish the thought that today I did nothing foolish, nothing wild and unusual happened, and all is quiet in the neighborhood. Thank you, Lord. Wait, there was the mousie that got loose from the pet store and ran into the dress shop making all the young women scream and jump on the clothing racks. But, Grandma is not afraid of rodents; I just took off my new flip flop and smacked at it when it ran by.

Oh, and for you clothing mavens, Grandma settled on a brightly colored blouse. And yes, I know that the flowered top will make Grandma look like a country field in full bloom. It was either that or look like the awning on the front of the big bank downtown.

Growing Up Is Not Mandatory

My two year old grandson, George, is visiting us in Florida. His mama and I had taken containers of cold water with us to the beach. The sand was hot and George was jumping and chanting, "Hot, hot, hot!" Now, you'd have to have been here to understand how crazy cute that was.

We laughed as we watched little George open and dump out both of our containers of cold water; one in each hand, in his attempt to cool down the hot sand. The sight of the toddler dumping cold water onto the sand around his hot little feet was just—adorable!

He was so cute that we didn't mind the inconvenience of not having cold water readily available. If his older brother had done the same thing, he'd have been scolded. The action was cute because of George's innocence—cute because of his childish immaturity and *total unawareness of consequences*.

Grandma loves it when the Holy Spirit quietly whispers revelation in the midst of everyday life. Children <u>want</u> to grow up; they're eager to enjoy the benefits of maturity. However, they soon find that with the benefits of maturity comes responsibility and work.

Spiritual growth also has responsibility that goes along with the benefits. Often times it is at this point, when maturity leads to responsibility, that Christians leave the church. Maturity, whether social or spiritual, doesn't just happen; it is a <u>choice</u>.

Grandma has never been a fan of "growing up." That childhood exuberance, the passion for adventure and discovery should always be part of our lives. No, Grandma never wants to grow up. But I do want to be—mature; there is a difference. Growing up is not mandatory, but maturity is.

Whose Box is This?

We have lived in our new home in Florida for a couple of months now. Grandma is slowly getting used to all the different ways, places and details. Moving is never easy and the older I get, the more difficult it becomes. However, there are a few things that would be easier if they just made sense.

Like the mail box out front of the house. Every time Grandma goes to get the mail, the previous resident's mail is in my box. Seriously, Grandma changed our address with the post office; it is not that big of a deal, people. It's just---not. Yet, the mail that comes in my box out front continues to have former resident's name on it.

If Grandma knew where they'd moved to, I'd go change their address myself. I keep writing, "MOVED! No longer at this address!" on the envelopes and putting them back into the box with the flag up. Hopefully, when the mail is re-directed to the proper address, the folks will go to the post office and have their information updated so Grandma no longer has the responsibility of mail forwarding.

Today, I went to get the mail, but it had not gone yet. As I turned to go back to the house, the gentleman across the street went to MY mail box, opened it, put in some outgoing mail, put the flag up and smiled at me. Grandma stood there, wondering why on earth the man across the street would put his outgoing mail in my box---. Then, it dawned on me. He—would---**not**---do---that.

Since moving to Florida, Grandma sometimes feels like she has moved to the state of confusion; this is one of those times. Stepping back from the mail box, I looked down at the numbers painted on the mail box post---the numbers were NOT my house numbers. Turning to look across the street, where my neighbor was going up his front steps, I notice the numbers ARE his house numbers.

Embarrassed, I call out, "oh, I'm SO sorry, I thought this was my box, it is at the end of my driveway—." The neighbor turns, laughing and says, "I know." So, now Grandma knows my mail box is NOT at the end of my driveway---our neighbor's box is. So, who can figure THAT one out? (rolling my eyeballs)

The Importance of Scheduling

Organization is my middle name. Okay, not really, my middle name is Grace; but I'm serious about planning my time. All of Grandma's appointments are neatly scribed in my sunshine yellow day planner. To me, planning and organization are a lifestyle, not a haphazard attempt at maintaining order.

I'd thought when we moved to Florida, my schedule would be less demanding; silly me. How could I not have realized that the everyday things I did in NC still needs done in FL; I just had to find all new places to "do" in.

Today, I realized that I had a conflict between the doctor and my hairdresser. Knowing that both were important, I wrestled with what appointment I should postpone. Do I put off the doctor and keep my hair appointment or do I let my hair go and keep the time set aside for filling my annual physical? Obviously, the doctor wins; but, since I really need a haircut, I go ahead and re-schedule my appointment for later in the day. This mop has simply GOT to be trimmed; I look like a ragamuffin on steroids.

Looking at my tightly scheduled day, I (again) prayed that God would show me how to make time for Bible study and prayer in the daily stress of life. When schedules are this tight, there has to be some way to re-arrange and plan more efficiently. Perhaps it isn't time that I struggle with; perhaps it is simply planning.

As part of my renewed commitment to seek God, I had written "God with Bible" in the margin of my day planner. So far, I've not found a slot to fit this planned time for communication with the Lord IN my day, but when I slow down for lunch, maybe I could do my devotions then.

Or, even more time thrifty, I could carry my Bible on the front seat of my car, already marked and open. When I pause at street lights for a red stop, I can read the scriptures for today. I'm a fast reader; I should be able to get at least three of four verses read before the light changes.

Prayer could also be slipped into my busy schedule without much effort. As long as I didn't close my eyes, I could pray as I drove. Hmmm, in fact, I could pray while I walk, ride the elevator, grocery shop; making time for prayer isn't going to be as difficult as I'd thought. Nice.

This new awareness to plan to use my extra, otherwise wasted, moments for time with God is going to work. By days end, feeling that I'd finally gotten a handle on how to work God into my busy day, I turned the lights out and went to bed, exhausted. Success was, obviously, possible, but perhaps required more planning than I'd anticipated.

Once again, I'm sitting at the breakfast table, day planner in hand, trying to organize my time. I liked the success I'd had with "pray as I go," but the stop light Bible reading just wasn't working out for me. I need more time in the Word than this "stop n'grab it." Suddenly, God spoke to my heart; honestly, His voice was so clear that I jumped and almost spilled my juice! "Make an appointment for time to spend with me."

Stunned, I put my pen down, shut my day planner and whispered, "Whaaaaat?" God's voice continued to speak into my heart, "Would you get your hair cut while you were at the doctor? Yet, you pray and read your Bible while you are busy doing something else. Open your appointment schedule and write my name in one of the spaces." Startled at how obvious the solution to my problem with time is, I sit quietly for a moment.

After giving me a few moments of quiet contemplation, God continued, "Determine to never cancel your appointment with me. If something unexpected needs your immediate attention, like a grandchild needs to be taken to the doctor or Walter needs you to take him to the airport, reschedule, but don't cancel. Just like you'd re-schedule a doctor appointment, actually reschedule your appointment with me."

The answer was so easy; I guess I've just been too busy to see it. When I seek to make God part of my life, I must plan to actively include him in my day. The things that are important to me, I plan for them. It only makes sense that I would actively plan an appointment with my Lord. I'm a very organized person; I plan for the things that are important to me.

Grandma's Never Fail Filing System

All afternoon Grandma has been working on computer housekeeping. My documents section has become so cluttered that I have to take the time to divide and conquer or just give up. I had hoped to do this before we moved, but packing actual objects took precedence over shuffling virtual reality files. My mind does not work well with computers. I've found with repeated exposure and a lot of head banging (mine--) that I can almost squeak through and accomplish the basics---ok, maybe not.

I believe that I wrote a journal entry earlier about taking a computer course at the Community College a few years ago—and how Grandma was banned from the computer lab unless I had adult supervision. One of the things that really messes me up, and it is a uniquely 'Grandma' thing, is saving files in my computer. Always, I end up with multiples of the problem I had to start with-- which I find to be frustrating.

Whenever I lose anything, Walter will very patiently show me the wonders of Google Desk Top Search one more time--and then very patiently explain to me about how my computer is simply a giant compact file cabinet. While he explains the file cabinet analogy to me, my mind vividly pictures my brain as a huge trash compacter pressing in and in and in---. My mental interpretation of my beloved's instructions only makes matters more complicated.

Every time he and I go through this exercise in frustration, I'll move my relocated lost file to where I KNOW I'll be able to find it next time. Only, since I lost it *last* time, I decide that before I move it *this* time, I'll copy it to another file and put it in an obvious place so if I lose it *next* time, I'll at least have the security of knowing I actually do have it SOMEWHERE--I just have to find it. This makes perfect sense to Grandma, but makes Grandpa crazy.

In my non techno old befuddled mind, I refer to this "multiple save" as the 'fearful fruitbat filing system.' According to Grandpa, saving all those times is just---crazy as a fruitbat. Ergo, the 'fearful fruitbat filing system.' Thanks to this fruitbat system, I have 6+ copies of some things, and still can't find—even-- one.

What I've learned to do when I take time to attend to 'housekeeping' is; open a Desk Top Search. I patiently locate each and every one of those files, each with variations in the title, and put them each in the new file. When I've located all the copies, I delete all but one copy so the file now has only one item.

Since the new file only has one item, I'm afraid I'll lose it so I make another one and keep it in the only logical place---in the file with the first one--with a similar but not identical name. Walter says this is simply doing the same thing all over again--. Grandma says this is—loss prevention insurance.

This flaw in my thinking causes both Walter and my adult grandson, Gerald, much grief whenever they try to help me find anything that I've lost. Oddly, my system seems totally logical to me--but when Gerald very patiently says, "Grandma, why do you have this document saved 8 times each time by a different title?" Saying, "so I won't EVER lose it," doesn't really seem to be an adequate response.

Last year, my personal brand of fruitbat filing left me with copies of WMA music files in multiples of 3, 4, sometimes even 5 or 6. Gerald, trying to teach me how to convert WMA files to MP3 files deleted numerous copies of copies--trying to just glean my files down to a workable level. And then, there are the teny eight thousands of word document files that I have named, filed, renamed, filed and saved numerous time to ensure their safe keeping.

SO, I said all that to say this: I've done better this year. Some--ok, a **little** better. I'm trying to organize all my files and go as far as I can before I throw myself on Gerald's mercy and beg him to help me out--again. I know better than to ask Grandpa to help me, he'll just shake his head and say, "Ask Gerald next time he comes over, he's young and smart."

Everything that I want makes perfectly good sense--until I'm with my grandson, Gerald, and he says, "What do you want me to do?" Then, my mind goes totally blank and whereas mere nano seconds before, I had a logical plan and an absolute goal, now I have nothing but the sound of the wind whistling through the hole in my head.

In order to simplify this exercise in frustration and cut down on the time Gerald will have to take out of his busy schedule to help me accomplish what I want done, I've made a detailed list. I keep it beside me here at the computer and every time I realize a problem I'm having, I write it down.

Miracle of miracles, since we've moved to Florida, I've even managed to solve some of the problems on my own. (faint) You can't imagine the joy, the exhilaration, the rush I get when I cross something off of my list, labeling it D-O-N-E. Since Gerald lives two states away now instead of two streets away, I'm really making an effort to keep my "need help with" list down to only a few pages.

Of course, right after I do that, I make a note on my computer of what was wrong and how I fixed it and save it several times under different titles so next time, I'll be able to solve it more quickly. At least, as soon as I remember one of the names I filed the list under ---.

Hell Is for Everybody

After Grandma retired a few years ago, I decided to take a part time job as a cashier at a local retail store. It would be a great chance to meet and greet people; an opportunity to make new friends and it would get me out of the house for a few hours a week. Not to mention, provide a little spending money to spoil my grandchildren and take my friends out to lunch more often.

As a part of my training to work in a retail store, I had to watch a compilation of video clips. The challenge was to try and identify the "shoplifters." I watched as a selection of customers entered the store. The cameras followed the individuals through the store as they shopped. I was assured that two of the persons who had entered were, actually, honestly, thieves. At the end of the video, I had to choose the persons whom I thought were stealing.

It was easy to tell who the thieves were. I could pick them out a mile away, as they say. The scraggly guy with raggedy jeans, torn shirt with natty hair and beard, obviously was up to no good. He went up and down every aisle, picked up lots of things, examining them, but put only a few items in his cart.

The teenager with black lipstick and black fingernail polish, dressed entirely in black---*obviously* her, I could clearly see she was evil as soon as she walked in the door. She spent a lot of time at the makeup counter, opening bottles, checking color charts. My third suspect was a dorky looking teen who kept looking over his shoulder; obviously feeling guilty.

At the end of the video, I pointed out the customers I thought had stolen something. To my total surprise, only one of the three persons I selected as suspicious was actually a thief. The second thief I had not even suspected. Stunningly, the shop lifter I did not presume was a middle aged woman, dressed well, acting—normal.

The obvious lesson was that shoplifters have no particular "look;" they come in all socio economic levels, all types of clothing and all kinds of hair styles. In other words, keep my eyeballs open and watchful, appearances can be—deceptive.

As I closed my locker, preparing to go home after the video lesson, the Holy Spirit spoke to my heart. He pointed out to me that the same truth applies to those who don't know Christ as their savior. There is no particular "look" that an unsaved person has.

Obviously, the dude standing on the street corner with long hair, tattoos, body piercings and a dirty T-shirt needs Jesus and the business man standing beside him, dressed in a suit and tie doesn't; right? Wrong! Everybody needs Jesus, not just the ones who look "needy" when measured by my own lifestyle. Satan is an equal opportunity destroyer; he has no economic or social preference of who he wants to keep from having intimacy with Christ.

Grandma thinks maybe it is easier to speak to "needy" people than it is to speak to my own peer group. Nowhere in the Bible does it speak of it being difficult for a poor person to recognize their need for a savior. There is such a warm fuzzy feeling about telling that poor family in public housing with five screaming children running through the house—about the love of Jesus and how He is the answer to all of our problems. But to speak to a person, living in a nice home, driving a nice car with all of the accruements life well lived can offer, is—well---off putting. Why is this?

Hell does not embrace only the destitute and addicted. It also welcomes housewives, business owners, lawyers, store clerks, mayors, governors and barbers. The Bible says that it is almost *impossible* for a rich person to get into the kingdom of heaven. Was that just an observation, or was that meant as a challenge?

Yet, how often do we see an evangelical stand outside up town stores and custom car shops to hand out tracts? When was the last time any of us spent hours in fervent prayer for our doctor, our lawyer, our politicians, or a wall street executive?

Have you noticed the facebook "stories" that folks love to post about how a poor, dirty person walks in the church and is shunned? The story speaks of how that high and arrogant church treated the poor person terribly. This story is always followed by a couple of hundred "likes" and a multitude of comments about how churches are so arrogant, so cold, so uncaring—why—"you couldn't pay me" to go to church with all those hypocrites!"

Yet, Grandma has been in church all my life and while I'm sure there might be just a few of those "hoity toity" type churches out there---I've never been to, nor personally seen or heard of one, other than in the "what churches are really like" put down rants. This makes Grandma wonder---if the majority of churches are NOT like that—why is the same pitiful story posted on facebook so often; and make note—it is –the –same story.

Every church I've been to has gone out of their way to welcome all people, but especially those who look like they might feel—awkward. Where exactly do these "put down" comments *come from*? Perhaps from satan himself---who works over time to discourage people who are NOT in church from ever –going to church.

Every person we meet is an opportunity; no matter what they look like or where they live. So, Grandma has a question that remains unanswered, why IS it often easier to do street witness than to tell coworkers, neighbors, family and friends about Christ?

Perhaps because I have no fear of rejection from the person who is obviously not as well off as me; and I will probably never see them again after right now, anyway. I have no "skin" in the game, so to speak. They accept Christ---what a testimony I have to tell—they reject Christ and it is no skin off my back---hey, I gave them the opportunity. Bless their hearts.

When I present Jesus to my own family, neighbor or co-worker and they reject Christ, I feel the rejection <u>personally</u>. I also have to live with that knowledge of that personal rejection every day as I continue to live and work beside them.

Of course it <u>IS very important</u> that I continue to make every effort to win the poor and homeless to Christ but it is *equally important* that I share Christ with those I live and work around; my peer group. There is only one Hell and ALL—as in EVERYbody-- who does **not** have Christ as their savior will spend eternity there. It makes my breath catch to realize that many of them will be dressed in a business suit or a party dress and sadly---some will even be wearing---church clothes.....

Grandma has no idea what has brought this memory to mind. I've not worked at the store in over a decade. When Walter retired from mechanical engineering, he'd opened a small store front employment office. In fact, the last few years, I've been helping Walter as he found work for locals who had lost their job. I haven't worked in retail in—years. Why on earth would such an old memory pop up like that? Interesting.

Interesting how things rise to remembrance when you least expect it; maybe this is a direction from the Lord. It's a good reminder and something worth thinking about, because, *everybody* needs Jesus.

Grandma Wants to Learn to Yodel

Grandma is just too busy. There, I said it. For years, I've suspected this to be true, but I denied it and just kept on going full bore. Somehow, I'd always thought that after I passed a certain birthday, the busyness of everyday life would curb off. I'd have time for the things I'd always wanted to do. Things like learning to yodel. Don't laugh, but Grandma has always wanted to learn to yodel.

As a little girl I watched the classic story, "Heidi." Actually, I read the books first, and then watched the movie. For those not familiar, Heidi was a sweet little girl who lived in the Swiss Alps. She and her Grandfather and a few young friends who lived round and about had all kinds of adventures together. During one segment of the story, there was yodeling. Right then, Grandma knew that sometime in her life yet to be lived, she would learn to yodel. That time is now.

As with any new project or program that is started, first, I need to get on-line and find any information available on the "how to." To Grandma's surprise, there are gracious plenty tutorials on how to yodel. Who knew, right?

The biggest issue to overcome with yodeling is learning to accept the sound of your own voice. According to information given on the internet site, one must also accept the knowledge that until the art of yodel is accomplished, there will be unseemly, at times even unhuman, sounds that will be made. After having slept with Grandpa's snoring for 40 years, unhuman sounds do not intimidate Grandma.

Obviously, this new skill will have to be acquired while I'm alone in the house. Perhaps, even alone in the neighborhood---sound carries. I know this because I've heard football game day noises emanating from neighbors homes. I did a walk through the house and made sure all the windows were shut. We are still fairly new to the neighborhood and we don't want people thinking we are—crazy.

After fixing a cup of coffee, I went through a few of the lessons, not participating, just reading and listening. Finally, having completed the reading of all the lessons and having listened to the examples of professional yodeling; Grandma was ready to give it a go and get her yodel on.

I stood up, threw my head back and followed the directions given in the first lesson; fearless, paying no mind to what my ears hear. My neighbor's kitty cat that I'm keeping for a few days, jumped like she had been smacked on the butt with a fly swatter and ran from the room seeking shelter from whatever wild beast had invaded the sanctity of her shelter.

Those forewarned unhuman sounds turned out to be more funny than scary. After a few attempts at yodel interrupted by bouts of uncontrollable laughter, I decided I should switch from coffee to warm tea, with a touch of lemon to sooth my throat. As I put the hot pot on, I opened the kitty treat jar in the hopes I could lure the puss back out into view. Nope.

Just as the teapot started whistling, the doorbell rang. It was my next door neighbor. She had been weeding her flower garden when Grandma had practiced her yodeling. Her concern for my well-being brought her to my front door. She'd seen the commercial about old ladies who fall and can't get up. I appreciated her concern, thanked her warmly but did not bring up the yodeling. I'm pretty sure I'm back on her prayer list again. She stays on mine, bless her heart.

Drinking my cup of tea, I wondered if yodeling once was enough to move the goal out of my bucket list and onto the table of my accomplishments. Yes, I think it is. How many times does a thief steal before he is labeled as a thief? I think once. Grandma can now move onto another goal in her bucket list; sword fighting; or not.

Now, where is that kitty cat? Oh, mercy, hiding behind a pot of flowers on the sunshine shelf. Where is my camera when I need it? Maybe I can find it before kitty decides to abandon that cute pose.

Wedding Adventures

Grandma loves weddings; one of my friends just enjoyed the wedding of her great granddaughter. If you have never been in the melee of wedding preparation, you have not fully experienced stress. Having "married off" daughters and helped in the production for weddings of daughters' in-law and granddaughters' in-law as well as the weddings of friends, church members and extended family; Grandma could write a book about humorous wedding stories. And then there are the "not so funny at the moment" stories as well. Mercy.

Many wedding mishaps involve the wedding cake. One of my wedding adventure memories is of a friend's daughter's wedding when the giant cake fell through the table. The wedding was one of the events of the season. There were hundreds of guests invited, full sit down catered fine dining meal and a HUGE cake that weighed well over 100 pounds.

The bride's mother left instructions that the cake was to be set on the middle table in the reception hall. Unfortunately, when the bakery delivered their masterpiece, there were six tables set up. There is no definite "middle table" in an even number of tables. If there had been five tables, then two on each side and the fifth in the middle--.

Somebody, nobody ever figured out exactly who, had set up a small table with a lovely cloth like all the other tables—to arrange the napkins, plates and silverware on. The cake delivery was made early in the day, before the tables were serving their determined purpose. The bakery delivery person walked into a banquet room with six empty tables, one of the middle tables being –small.

The cake was placed on the small table—I imagine the reasoning being the cake would have a table all to itself. There is no way of telling how long of time the poor table bore its heavy burden before collapsing. Two hours before the wedding, the bride's mother and her friends arrived to make one last eyeball check only to find the cake in a heap on the floor.

A panicked call was placed to local bakery and large grocery stores that had a bakery for simple white iced ---cupcakes. With that short of notice, no one bakery could supply 600 cupcakes, so every bakery in town sold all their white iced cupcakes that afternoon.

The bride was breathtaking, the ceremony precious and the attractively displayed white cupcakes were spoken of as, "adorable," "trend setting," and "unique." The bride's mother spoke of them as---damage control. The errant bakery shop refunded half the full price for the cake---. Stuff happens.

Then, there was the bride's cake that was supposed to be a delicate shade of pink, almost a white but just a hint of color--. The bride's mother had taken a scrap of the brides' maids dress fabric, a bright fluorescent pink, to the baker as a reference to make sure the lighter shade of pink was not a clash with the brides' maids' dresses and bouquets. It had been noted that the pink was to be---*barely a hint of color*---so as to go with the color scheme.

Somehow the instructions got bum fuzzled and the cake was made to MATCH the swath of fabric. So the bridal cake looked like it was from the wedding of the Pink Panther. Good times, good times. It was quite tasty—just—*very*—pink.

Then, there was the lovely formal wedding where the color scheme was black and white. An evening candle light wedding, very formal, the bride and groom in the traditional white and all the attendants wearing black. The female attendants wore black velvet, close fitting gowns and carried a single white long stemmed rose. Very elegant.

The formal black and white color scheme was carried through the reception. The wedding cake was very elegant, a magnificent center piece of smooth black fondant adorned with white pearl swags and tiny white rosebuds. The cake truly was a lovely and elaborate formal display. The only issue was that the black icing stained every body's teeth black. Grandma knew the photographer—and she had her hands full fixing the teeth of wedding party and guests from gray to white.

But, not all wedding mishaps involve cake. Imagine the upset of the bride's family when they walked into the reception hall to find a huge wreath of flowers that had the words, "Rest in Peace," bannered across the front. However, that had to be better than the other side of the miss-delivery. Somewhere a deceased person was resting beside a huge wreath emblazoned with a banner that read, "Congratulations!"

Oh, mercy, so many crazy wedding happenings! Grandma has seen silk flowers set on fire by the ushers lighting the candles, brides' maids with tennis shoes and socks, brides that threw up on their bouquet, punch that was a muddy creek color and a horse that pooped while pulling the white tasseled carriage the happy couple rode from the church.

So, if your daughter or granddaughter has a wedding mishap, know that you are not alone and the stories you have to tell years later will be hilarious. Every wedding has a story; Grandma had a black eye at my youngest daughter's wedding. It happened while exiting the ladies' room right before the ceremony. Never lean over to adjust your hem in front of a door knob <u>and</u> nobody should ever open a door without knocking---.

Grandma's most favorite wedding story of all has to be from years ago; the little ring bearer who had been taught by his momma, or his Sunday School teacher, maybe even his grandma, that when you are scared, sing out a song to Jesus. The wedding decorations were lovely; the wedding party started down the aisle. The little ring bearer, wearing his tuxedo, carrying his little satin ring pillow, came down the aisle--.

Half way down the aisle, the adorable little man child with the spiked hair and the wide blue eyeballs started singing at the top of his lungs, "I'm under the rock! Jehovah hides me, go tell people they can't harm me, I'm under the rock!" I don't even remember the rest of the wedding, just that precious child's brave song.

All brides are beautiful and all weddings are magnificent. Grandma loves weddings; and if I can find some of the beautiful wedding portraits from some friend's granddaughter's weddings, I'll include them in my journal.

Grandma's granddaughters have not married yet. My sweet Emily Jane is dating a nice young man she met at church. He is full of the spirit; a precious man of God and has a praise song for everything. Wait--- a praise song for everything. Nah, impossible! Hmmm I wonder if he was ever a ring bearer in a wedding?

You Don't Need a Lucky Shirt

Since we moved to Florida, Grandma has had a hole in her heart and in her life. One of the things that is hardest to bear since we moved is the absence of our young grandchildren. The older grandchildren are certainly missed too, but an adult grandchild is more like a young friend than a child and consequently, can come see us as an adult would.

Our oldest grandson, Gerald, is full grown and drives to Florida now and then to visit and of course, enjoy the fishing and the beach. Molly is a junior in college and she comes to visit over Christmas and Spring Break so she can enjoy the beach and go shopping with me.

But, the younger ones, little Henry, sweet little George and precious little Mary, are all still young enough to take for ice cream and to the park. Oh, ok, maybe not the park too much anymore, even the little ones are on that border line of being too old for going to the park now. But who doesn't love a trip to Dairy Queen?

Also, since we've moved, Grandma has not gotten involved with the Children's Ministries like I had been before. The young ones are so full of energy, it is time that I stepped back and let younger adults help with the little ones. The absence of youthful laughter and antics has left a dent in my heart almost as deep as the one my grandchildren have left.

However, I had a neighbor ask me to volunteer with her as an after school helper. The children are ages 8-11 and their parents work late so the school has an after school program. No crawling on the floor, no jumping or running, just help the kids with their homework, if needed. Grandma likes this; I get to spend time with the kids but don't have the physical demands of play like I did in Children's Church.

The first week I volunteered as an after school helper, I met a young man and his younger brother. The oldest, Jackson, loved to play sports, especially football. When we finished the homework, we sat and talked about life and of course, football.

He was not a big young man; he was of rather slender build, more wiry then muscular. He did not let his moderate stature slow him down on the game field; he was in it to win it. When he got hold of that ball, he did not let go and he did not stop till he crossed to goal line. Period.

One afternoon, while I was helping my young friend, Jackson, with his homework, he told me about a problem he'd had that morning. It was sports day and he ALWAYS wore his "lucky" shirt on sports day. He said usually, he stuffs this lucky shirt in his book bag and puts it on AFTER he gets to school.

But, today was an important recess football competition day. He felt that he needed to wear the "lucky" shirt from the beginning. Unfortunately, or fortunately, depending on your view point, his mom caught him walking out the door wearing it and insisted he change. I asked him why his mom did not like the special lucky shirt. He took a deep breath and started the lengthy story of his special football winner shirt.

This "lucky shirt" was beyond dirty. It was absolutely "stand in the corner for a science project" filthy. It smelled so bad, it <u>reeked</u>. It had stains on it, was permanently wrinkled and smelled like a big sweaty arm pit. His mama was HORRIFIED that he even OWNED such a nasty thing; much less wanted to wear it to <u>school</u>.

She confiscated it and was going to throw it *in the trash*! But, Jackson was so upset, that his mom told him he could keep it to PLAY in; not for school wear. However, the shirt would, at least, be washed and pre-treated with stain remover each and every time it was worn.

Back to the event from Jackson's perspective; Jackson rubbed his hands through his short, spiked hair, slowly shaking his head. He anguished a bit, then, he told me, "You won't understand Ms. Rebecca Grace, I know you won't." I told him he'd be <u>surprised</u> at what a fat old grandma could understand, give it a try. He sat in obviously pained turmoil for a second or two, then, taking a deep breath, he told me the full down and dirty truth about his lucky shirt.

He was FAMOUS for this shirt and his team <u>always</u> won when he wore it. It started when the shirt was just an ordinary shirt that he liked to wear. The team won a few events---then, he discovered that this lucky shirt became more and more "lucky" every time he wore it. On the rare event the shirt would not be worn, the team had lost.

He admitted he was a pretty decent player to start with, but, when he came on the playing field wearing this lucky shirt, the boys on his team cheered, the opposing team booed and made threatening noises---it was—from young Jackson's point of view, "freaking awesome."

Jackson said once on the playing field, he ran after the lead on the opposing team; they *always* ran from the lucky shirt. Once the victim was tackled, Jackson would lie on top of him and put the victims face in the armpits of the lucky shirt. EVERYONE on his team would cheer! EVERYONE on the losing team would pretend to gag and scream! NOBODY could withstand the horrible "fumes" of the lucky shirt!

I asked Jackson how on earth this lucky shirt smelled <u>so bad</u>. Jackson sat there, looking sheepish. Gus, his younger brother, sitting across the table from us seriously admonished, "Tell her, Jackson, you got to tell her, man." Jackson took a deep breath; for two days before the sports event, he would NOT shower. Not even wiping off with a damp cloth. Total free standing comando, as he called it.

He said the hardest part was staying away from his mom because if she hugged him, she'd tell him he needed to get in the shower NOW! Between sporting events, he kept the UNWASHED lucky shirt wadded up in a plastic garbage bag in the bottom of his closet to "ripen."

Jackson turned his face away from me, obviously suffering from extreme adolescent anguish. The secret of the lucky shirt—revealed to a stranger. Grandma sat in silent contemplation; this young man had a reputation as a sports hero because he had a *shirt* that SMELLED BAD?? We sat quietly for a moment; Jackson said, "Do you understand the problem, Ms. Rebecca Grace?"

I solemnly acknowledged that I kind of---sort of—did-- understand. As we sat in silence for a moment, I prayed for wisdom on how to handle this---stranger than fiction---confession. This dear young man thought his game prowess was because he wore a nasty dirty shirt. He had no hint that he could actually play a good game--.

With what I hoped was divine inspiration, I told Jackson that was a cool really neat "stunt"--in a weird "guy kind of way." BUT, when you win a sporting event, it most likely would be <u>because your team played the game *really* well</u>; not because you smell bad and torture the opposing team with your BO. Even though I'm sure an unshowered adolescent in a skanky shirt would be quite--- off putting, there had to be some skills involved.

Jackson thought about that for a minute and finally agreed. He said the lucky shirt thing just "happened"---and he just "went with it." I hugged him and told him that playing fair and playing well would get him a lot farther in life than the temporary fame of owning a shirt that smelled so bad it had a reputation all by itself.

After quietly thinking for a moment, Jackson told me he <u>had</u> won lots of times **before** the lucky shirt, it was just that the lucky shirt became a mascot and made him *famous*. I reiterated that fame that came from honesty, hard work and fair play would take him a lot further than a lucky shirt would. Lifting his adolescent face to mine, we locked eyeballs for a moment, neither of us saying anything. In his eyes I could see the reflection of what, I recognized would, one day, become a strong man of God.

I told Jackson that playing his very best; playing with integrity, would earn him fame that would be far more lasting than a football season. He nodded his head in agreement. His face breaking into a big smile he told me the big church on up the street had a football team and he was thinking about seeing if his mom would let him go to church there so he could play with them. Jackson confided that she'd been saying she wanted to start going to church. I laughed and told him that would be GREAT because that was where I went to church, please introduce me to his mom so she would have a friend to sit with.

As Grandma sat on the porch sipping a cup of strong espresso later that evening, I was thinking about how young Jackson didn't think he could be a winner on his own. Just like when Gandma thinks there has to be a reason that causes God to love me. Sometimes I forget that God loves me just the way I am, not because I'm good but because **HE** is good.

PART 3: LIFE CHANGES FAST

The Widow's Might

It will seem odd to finally sit down at my desk and begin to write again this evening. Has it been almost a year since I put words to paper in my journal? Eight months, it has, indeed, been almost a year. It's crazy how things can change so suddenly. One moment life is busy, planned and dare I say it, controlled? Then out of the blue everything is thrown into a spinning cyclone, chopped up and regurgitated onto the floor. Nothing is the same, the days are all jagged with no pattern or plan. Grandma's mind feels like it has left town with no forwarding address.

On many mornings the constant motion of my emotions leaves me feeling nauseous and weak. This morning, after another sleepless night of tossing and turning, I threw the covers onto the floor and sat up on the edge of our bed. My bed. How has "our" become "my" so quickly? Will I ever be able to think in the singular again? My heart aches as day number 245 since the death of my beloved husband, Walter, begins.

One of Grandma's most favorite rooms in our, no, MY house, is the suite bathroom; huge windows flank both walls of the eastern corner. Morning sunshine floods into the room washing away the last stains of the night with almost blinding natural light. Right now, I need this shower of light every morning to cleanse my heart from the gray sadness that clings to me after another night of sleeping alone. Growing up, I'd had sisters to sleep with, then, marriage and my beloved husband to sleep with. This is the first time in Grandma's life I've-- ever—slept---alone for more than just a couple of nights now and then when Walter would go out of town on business.

Resolutely, I once again determine that I will return to "normal" as much as possible as quickly as possible. The awareness that each day I'm creating a new—normal—and in time, will adjust is no comfort this morning. In time, I know that life will have a pattern again. The pain will subside, actually, even now, sometimes, ok; rarely---I find myself smiling and enjoying things. Oddly, I hadn't thought I'd ever be able to smile—or laugh—or enjoy ANYthing ever again. But, by God's comfort and mercy, I AM. Slowly---.

The heart attack had taken Walt so suddenly; there'd been no hint of ill health. Sometimes, I still strain, listening to the silence, thinking the nightmare will be over and I'll hear his voice call to me one more time as he walks in the front door. Now and then I even speak his name then remember, when only silence answers me, that he is gone.

In the bathroom, contemplating the mirror, I wonder who that haggard old lady is and why she's wearing my pajamas. Shaking my head in wonder at how fleeting life is, I turn the shower on. Waiting for the water to come to temp, I go to the closet to select something that a kind and compassionate, yet discerning, administrator at a successful employment agency would wear.

Morning ablutions completed, I dress in a softly patterned dress with a flowing skirt that gives me the illusion—and believe me—it is ONLY an---illusion--- of grace. Finally downstairs, in the sun bright silence of the kitchen, I sip bold black espresso. Sharing our first cup of espresso was always one of the best parts of our mornings together. STOP IT. Opening my executive day planner, I ritually pen, "This is the day which the Lord has made, I WILL rejoice and I WILL be GLAD in it" in the wide top margin.

Pausing before looking at the details of the day, I pick up Walt's eyeglasses still lying on the corner of the table and hold them in my hand. I need to donate these, I heard there is a place in town that accepts no longer used eyeglasses to refurbish and be given to homeless people. Walter would like that. As the first anniversary of his death looms near, I still struggle to live my life without him. It wasn't supposed to be like this; I was supposed to die first. Walt would have been much more adept at accepting the rigors of life, alone, than I.

The thought of him so near, I found my nose searching in vain for one more scent of his after shave. My mouth aches with the memory of his lips placed firmly on mine each morning as he left for work. As he went out the door, he'd always wink at me and say, "I'll see you later, babe." I firmly place the spectacles back on the table. Maybe later, I will donate the glasses, today; I need them to be on the table as if he was going to reach for them to read the mail.

Work, I must get to work... Once at the office, I have no choice but to set aside the affectations of loneliness and dismiss all the comforting props of a grieving widow. I must get to the office quickly or one more day will be wasted in unproductive crying. Life goes on and so must Grandma.

One of the things I've done since Walter's death is to keep the office opened late, just in case some poor soul lost their job today and looking for some bit of hope before heading home—stops by the employment agency. Who am I kidding; I keep the office open late so I don't have to go home and face another evening alone. After a while, I may sell the business, my heart is just not in it without Grandpa. But, for now, every day is a struggle, I can't even think of such things at this time. My mind is too---fragmented.

However, one of the things that helps Grandma to keep her lips from coming unraveled is to do even the most common of things—differently. MY way; like coming in the front door of an evening instead of the side door where the car is parked. Things like setting new hours for the business to open and close give me a sense of control.

Each thing I do differently, my way, makes this strange life more real. Changing some things has given me the illusion that I'm in charge of my life. Grief would demand that I stay in bed all day, every day and not go into the office at all; that would NOT be a good change.

Working outside the home had never been one of my responsibilities. After Walt had retired from being an engineer, he'd been successful in setting up and running a small employment agency. After the children had grown and gone, I worked with him at the office, scheduling appointments and acting as a search hound for hopeful clients.

Walter had felt each client was his brother or sister and he had an obligation to do everything possible to help them find work. It was good to be close to Walt all day, to hear him laughing and teasing with the clients. The tears gather behind my eyeballs. STOP IT.

Walt had been known to hire a few folks himself, those that were "hopeless" just to give them hope. A few weeks running errands, answering the phone and filling out forms at the business for a small pay check while they waited for a real job was often preferred over the endless empty days of continued unemployment and the meager benefit check the government would provide.

The last ten years, Walt, in his firm but gentle way, had shown me every aspect of the business; all the intricacies of running the company. I'd had no idea that I was being groomed to run our small business alone. Both God and Walter had been faithful, without my even realizing; I'd been fully equipped for the task now at hand. It's crazy how sometimes God's provision can be best seen looking in the rear view mirror instead of through the windshield.

Lost in a reverie of random thoughts as I stand at the kitchen sink, rinsing my coffee cup, a wave of fresh grief surprises me. The sudden assault of emotional pain causes me to lean on the counter top to keep from sinking to the floor. My hands reach out to grab onto something, anything ---and then wrap themselves around my face and I sob. This moment will pass, though I'm a bit overtaken that this moment of absolute loss has hit me again.

Mistakenly, I'd thought these moments of raw, consuming agony were done. It had been a couple of months since a wave of pain like this had hit me. At first, these waves of emotional pain had come regularly; leaving me limp, sobbing and drained. The weeks following the funeral, I'd often spent hours curled up on the kitchen floor sobbing into the uncaring silence. The cold, hard reality of the ceramic tile had been a place of certainty in the fevered frenzy of my mourning.

Many times, in the painful weeks and months since, I had begged God to allow me to die as well. Contrary to poetic license, time doesn't cure anything, but it has taken me further away from the raw agony of bereavement. Only God's grace and mercy have sustained me through the suffering and loneliness.

Forcibly turning from the pain, I pull myself to my feet, walk over to and open the door then step out into the disinfecting morning sunshine. God will give me strength for another day; I force my mind to focus on the unemployed that wait on me to find work to sustain their homes, their families.

Grandma knows that I'm old, but I've never---felt---old before. The grieving process continues to "mature." I've read books about grief, but it feels different when you live the experience. For the first time, I feel so alone. No matter how I feel, life must go on. I have no choice. I must be patient with myself, give myself time. Smiling, I realize those are the exact words Walt would say to me if he was here to cheer me on.

Then, I realized that Walter would be proud of me; I'm going to be okay. As I unlock my car, I acknowledge that tonight, I will return to writing my journal. I will do my best to get home in time to go to the park, sit on a bench and enjoy the sunset before I go home to write. Life goes on, so does Grandma, even when I just want to---quit.

Look at Me

The storm outside was spectacular; thunder, lightning, pounding rain and strong wind. My entire life right now is stormy. And Grandma is not talking only about the weather. These past few months have been a perfect example of how being saved does *not* mean life is guaranteed to be without turmoil or upset. There have been a lot of days where I've had to make a conscious choice to look beyond the storm to God's peace.

One particularly difficult day, God reminded me of an actual thunder storm that my (then) very young daughter and I went through together. She was four and we were playing with Barbies on the living room floor, trying to ignore the tempest outside. I knew that if I could keep her distracted, the commotion outside wouldn't be so frightening. So far, my plan was working.

It sounded like a bomb went off as a lightning bolt and the ensuing thunder crashed, taking the power out! With a startled yell, my frightened daughter jumped into my lap looking for comfort. With a "mommy's right here" tone of voice, I tried, unsuccessfully, to distract her from the noise outside. She was just too scared; my efforts were futile.

As she sat trembling on my lap, the thunder resounding again and again around us, I took her face tenderly in my hands and said, "Look at ME." She turned her eyes to mine and I began to sing Sunday school songs to her. Her voice wavered at first, but as we sang, "Yes, Jesus Loves Me," her voice grew stronger and she stopped shaking. The storm was still raging around us, but we sat, focused on each other and our song.

Now, a life time later, my daughter is grown and married and I sit alone, terrified as the storm that has consumed my life crashes around me. Shaking, I lean against the wall as emotional pain sweeps over me again, sucking the air out of me with gale force winds. The last several months have been brutal as I've tried to make a new life pattern, without my beloved Walter.

At first, I'd held tight to my faith, quoted scripture, but the waves of emotional pain left me weak. Music didn't help, Bible study didn't help—trying to calm my insides down was like trying to nail jello to a piece of foam board. Every person has the expected array of lifetime casualties; sickness, financial distress, death, we all know the "list."

But knowing of these common life events is far different than experiencing them. It's crazy how I thought such things, though harsh, would leave me standing. I know God is my rock, my steady fortress that holds me, but, Grandma is NOT standing. Through the years, I've experienced the loss of loved ones many times; it never felt like this.

Where IS God's protection when bad things, things beyond the normally expected issues, happen? The addition of these "surprise," things, piled on top the expected life issues have left me struggling and barely handling--. Bits of memorized scripture pop into my mind, offering peace like a cool glass of water in a hot dry place. I gulp them down and thirst for more but can't seem to be satisfied.

Through the last few months, even ordinary expected upsets send me into a tailspin; a leak in the roof, my car breaking down. Things that used to be accepted as just---stuff—are now major sources of anxiety. My closest friend has started calling me Jobet; her self made female version of "Job" in the Old Testament who underwent harsh life challenges one right after another. Her analogy amuses me but a leaky roof can hardly be classed as a harsh life challenge. But, I *feel* as though it—is.

The scriptures that had, until now, brought comfort and encouragement mocked me as I read them. The peace I'd found in prayer during other trials brings no emotional strength; inside, there is only silence. As I press myself against the wall, my skin is cold, my heart racing and waves of nausea pound me.

Emotionally, I felt as if all the pain that I'd pled the blood of Jesus' over, all the trials that I'd rebuked satan and stood strong—all –of—everything, was bound together and hurled against me in one huge blow. As I melted into a heap on the floor, feeling the cool linoleum against my face, I began to wonder that; perhaps, there was no God after all.

What if it really was all a joke? What if faith and love and peace really is all just an illusion, and there is no God? But, that can't be, I've felt my Lord's presence, I've heard him speak into my heart, I've followed the leadership of His Holy Spirit. These moments of intimacy and direction were NOT contrived or made up. They were actual experiences, actual events. God is as real as the emptiness and pain my heart is experiencing now.

All my strength was gone and I was left with only an emptiness that was profound. I felt as if I was outside, looking in. The only sound I could hear was the whistling of the wind as it stormed through my soul leaving a vacuum. Silent tears flood from my eyeballs. Nobody. It seems not--- even---God—knows the depth of my pain.

As I lay in a puddle of my tears in silent defeat, I suddenly feel the presence of God as I've never felt before. The air vibrates with the power of His being. I'm expecting a loud booming voice that will shake the floor beneath me but instead, a quiet but incredibly strong voice whispers into my heart, "Look at ME." As I raise my tear stained face to heaven, the silence is deafening. My mind rushes back to that long ago moment, when my daughter was in my lap, terrified. I remembered my own gentle commanding words, "Look at ME."

With the last ounce of strength I have left, I close my eyes and focus on all the scriptures describing the power and authority of my God. Tears flowing down my face, Grandma begins to sing, "Jesus loves me, this I know, for the Bible tells me so. Little ones to Him belong, they are --- weak—but---HE is—**strong**."

Oh, mercy sakes, I miss my beloved, Walter, so much. I have no idea how I will live without him, but I know that—I—will because-- there is no other choice. Inside, I feel so gnarled and old; like the ancient twisted weather worn trees around my darling Walter's grave.

How can I, even though surrounded by family and dear friends, feel so alone, like a solidary tree set a part from the forest? The storm inside has calmed but I can still feel the wind whistle through the hole in my heart; however I know---*I am*.

Midnight Cupcake Madness

Grandma can't sleep. Instead of taking pills to make me sleep, I've decided to bake. Even though it has been—many-- months since Walter went to heaven, I'm still not used to sleeping alone. So why not do something productive since sleep is so elusive? Everybody knows how much Grandma likes to bake, so, of course, baking would *have to be* involved. Therefore, I'm up at 2 a.m. baking.

How absolutely marvelous this idea is! I will not bake something ordinary; what point would there be in baking at midnight if I was to bake a casserole? Instead, Grandma will bake cupcakes. These will be special cupcakes that are not ordinarily baked. After all, these cupcakes are being baked in the middle of the night while other people are sleeping soundly in their beds.

These cupcakes will be scented, not flavored, ordinary cupcakes are flavored; special cupcakes are scented with some exotic flavor. I have special flavors bought to be used only on my midnight cupcaking nights. Flavors like raspberry cream and pineapple flair topped with a light whipped cream icing or perhaps a decadent chocolate ganache.

Nothing about these midnight cupcakes will be ordinary. Nothing. From the top of their swirled, puffy, fluffy light heads to their decadent tender interiors, these cupcakes will be works of culinary art. Some will even have luscious cream fillings---if I feel so inclined.

When the eater tastes, they will shut their eyes and be taken to another world, where cupcakes are lavishly served for no reason at all. "Cupcakes? Today? Why are we having cupcakes today?" Because we can; here take enjoy, eat a cupcake.

The other day, on a cooking show, Grandma saw an amazing thing---caramel threads that were molded into a golden cage that sat over a plate of cupcakes. There is nothing else going on, it's 2 a.m. what better time to experiment? I'm going to make a caramel cage to sit over the plate of exotic cupcakes. What drama there will be when I bring this artful dessert creation to the table at Bible study tomorrow night.

First I got a plain glass bowl out. Next, I made the caramel, easy enough; even for a beginning baker. Just use a good candy thermometer and fight the urge to stir a lot. Stirring can make the texture of the caramel wrong. Once the caramel reaches the right temperature, take it off the heat and let it sit for a few minutes. It has to cool in order to hold its shape.

Once the caramel is cooled but still warm enough to flow off the spoon, Grandma carefully began to drizzle the thread of caramel around the inside of the bowl. Around and round, up and down, back and forth until the inside of the bowl is a "cage" of caramel. Then, I set the bowl aside to finish cooling.

I noticed that some of the lines were a bit on the thick side and didn't look delicate. Have to work on that. As I make a cup of tea, I sigh; my journal has become my crying towel. Dear readers please forgive Grandma, I will get back to journaling without tears and pain---I will. In the interim, also please forgive me my endless rambling about everyday life. Life goes on and so will— Grandma.

Once the candy cools, I can gently move the caramel framework out of the bowl and set it on a plate. A smaller caramel cage can be used as a covering over one of Grandma's cupcakes scented with exotic flavors. Drama. Yup, lots of drama. This bigger caramel cage that I just made will make a lovely decorative enclosure over a whole plate of cupcakes.

It turned out so well, Grandma decides to do it again. Only this time, I'm going to be more free handed in swinging the caramel thread around the bowl so I can make a finer line and a more delicate pattern. I want this caramel cage to be very lacy and fragile.

Thinking ahead, I realize the thin threads of caramel will have to set up pretty quick or it will simply break and slide off instead of staying a continuous flowing line. So, I set up a small table fan at my work station on the kitchen counter.

As the caramel is heating to temperature again on the stove top, I practice holding a spoon and throwing imaginary caramel around the bowl while I reach over and turn on the table fan. Genius! I believe this is going to be the perfect solution to my thick caramel lines. On a thought, I got an extra spoon so I could drizzle two lines at the same time for a more intricate design.

My work station all organized, the caramel at perfect threading temperature, I lift both of the spoons over the prepared bowl to drizzle and turned on the table fan. Somehow in setting it all up and doing a test run with no caramel, Grandma managed to turn the table fan on high AND the dial got moved to oscillate.

As the delicate caramel strings came off the two spoons, the fan wind caught the threads and caramel starting flying all over the kitchen. In surprise, I dropped both spoons trying to catch the floating strips of caramel. Realizing the spoons were falling, I grabbed for them. The wind off the fan caught the new ribbons of caramel and the strings started flying around onto the cabinets as if they were in search of the other caramel strings.

As I reached across the countertop to turn the fan off, my reading glasses that had been on the tip of my nose fell into the pan of caramel. I'd thought the finished caramel dome would be dramatic—that was nothing compared to the drama of flying caramel strings, an oscillating fan and caramel covered reading glasses. Mercy. Grandma is ready to go to bed now. Staring at the ceiling will be a welcome distraction after all of this!

Of all the beautiful cupcakes Grandma has baked, I think these are my most favorites. The little flops are so stinking CUTE! Perfect for a beach party and oh mercy are they yummy!

These are a few of Grandma's friends, both young and old; they all love to bake as much as I do. I'm actually thinking about starting a cupcaking club. Seriously.

Grandma's Gift of Great Worth

The sun is setting over the meadow and the sky is ablaze with crimson and yellow. Sitting in stunned silence, Grandma doesn't even notice. A tear slips down my tired face and splashes onto the new pink Bible I'm holding in my lap.

I can't believe that I've been robbed. This was not the typical break in, like what happened to my friend, Martha. No, this thief did not smash a window and leave a trail of evidence. This thief hacked into my bank, invaded my account and emptied my savings.

The bank had called this afternoon to say there was nothing they could do. Over the weekend, a collective of hackers that call themselves, "Nobody," had stolen thousands of account numbers from Strident, a US based security bank.

It wasn't just any savings account that had been robbed; this account had been opened, many years ago, long before Grandpa had died, for our granddaughter. Grandma had saved that money for a college education; my Molly wants to be a nurse and go on the mission field when she graduates. I scrunch my face in my hands and turn my thoughts toward Jesus. Nothing takes HIM by surprise. Even though my confidence is shattered and my bank account drained, God knows all of this. I will trust Him.

Allegedly, this hacker group had been able to get into the big security think tank because somebody in the security department had failed to properly encrypt client credit information. I'm praying for that security person; obviously, they will be losing their job. Everybody has moments when they could do more but don't. Rarely does that moment of slight do so much damage to so many. Bless that clerk's heart.

This, this, "NOBODY," has not only cost an innocent person their job but broken this old woman's heart and, I'm sure, many other hearts as well. Grandma is just thankful that Grandpa is in heaven before all this happened. He'd have been absolutely—crushed, just as I am.

I will trust and wait; and try my best not to be angry at this group of hoodlums. Anger can lead to bitterness and bitterness can make a rift in my relationship with my Lord. I will not allow somebody else's sin to harm my walk with God. I'm not ignorant of Satan's devices; Grandma is way too experienced for that kind of tomfoolery. Sin is the gift that keeps on giving and this old lady is not opening THAT gift!

Sitting upright, I straighten my skirt. Molly will arrive in a few minutes and I don't want her to see me in such a state. Tonight was supposed to be such a great event; the night where, after years of planning, I revealed my secret savings account. Molly would have been ecstatic when I told her she'd have the money she needed to pay for her first year of nursing school. Now, what am I going to say?

Years ago, when she was just a girl, she had told Grandpa and I how she felt that God was calling her to be a medical missionary. Her eyes had shined with the glory of God as she had confided in me. Mercy; my old Grandma heart had been so filled with thanksgiving and praise, I thought it would just POP!

Molly had said she had no idea how she would ever have the money to accomplish such a goal but she knew that God would provide a way. Hugging her close, I'd prayed with her and said, "If that is what God's plan is for your life, there will be a way." That afternoon, I'd talked to Grandpa then I'd opened the secret savings account.

This morning, all I'd told her was that I had a very special surprise for her, a gift of great worth. I'd gotten her a beautiful pink leather Bible to take to college and later, the mission field. In the front of the book, I'd carefully penned my personal favorite scriptures; verses that had comforted encouraged and directed me through my own life. I was going to present it to her when I told her about the savings account.

The doorbell rang; I wiped my tears on my sleeve and turned the knob. Molly rushed into the room, grabbing my old bones and spinning me around in a happy dance, she exclaimed, "Grandma! You were right! You said if God wanted me to be a medical missionary, He would make a way! And He DID! Look! I got a full paid scholarship for my first year in nursing school; books, room, board, EVERYTHING! And Grandma, there's more; the scholarship even covers transportation and a bit of spending money for the whole year!"

Tears of joy on my wrinkled face, I presented my granddaughter the pink Bible, a gift of great worth. One more time, God had taken what had been planned to destroy and made it of no consequence. One more time, my Lord had known what was ahead and made beauty out of ashes. One—more--- time.

Grandma's New Friend Has Four Feet

Grandma has gotten a doggie. I know, I know, you remember how often I've said that I'd never have another pet. Pets are just too much trouble, too often underfoot and cost WAY too much money. However, my friends who live alone have told me to get a pet; I'd be surprised at how much company and laughter the addition of a pet would bring to my life. They were absolutely right---Grandma would be surprised. Very surprised.

I wasn't too committed to acquiring this –pet—even though my friends reminded me often that I said I would do it. Then, today, this doggie showed up. Grandma opened the door this morning and there dog sat. It sat there just like it had been waiting for the door to open. Obviously, pup had been on a rough journey, fur all dirty, toenails over long and oh, so *painfully* thin.

The first item on the rescue agenda was a good meal and some fresh water to drink. After a quick trip to the corner grocery to get dog food, I placed the dish of food on the floor in front of doggie. She sniffed at it and started to eat but stopped, sitting back up and looking at me as if asking permission. I told her, "Eat, it's ok, it's yours."

She came over to me, licked my feet then went back to the dish and began to eat in gulps, confirming my thought that she had not eaten in days. Obviously, somebody had taught doggie manners. Her pet parents must be frantic to have lost her. I posted a photo on the local community facebook page in hopes that her "doggie mommy/daddy" would see it and come pick her up.

Grandma feared that doggie had escaped from the pet parent's car while they were vacationing in FL. Maybe they had just been driving through Florida, they had stopped at a roadside rest and doggie got away. Obviously, doggie had been on the loose for at least a week. A trip to the vet revealed she had been spayed but no ID chip was embedded so no hope of figuring out where doggie lived.

To make a long story short—and I know you were hoping I would—dog's family never showed up so I kept her. Best doggie companion EVer. I had her out in the yard to go potty the other morning and the neighbor across the street was out trimming his hedge. He's always fixing something to his yard, so I was watching what he was doing.

Doggie was sniffing in my flower bed, trying to find that ---perfect---pee spot to relieve herself in. While I was watching the neighbor, I tugged on dog's leash and said, "Are you going to pee?" The neighbor looked up at me and said, "Excuse me?"

Realizing that doggie was hidden by the bushes, and he just saw me standing there looking at him, I thought fast and said, "I said, beautiful day, isn't it?" He looked a bit puzzled then agreed it certainly was. Grandma is surprised I could think that fast before I'd had even one cup of coffee--- .

This morning, I saw a photo about being careful when taking your pup for a walk on hot streets. Poor doggie in the photo, bad blisters, broke my heart! So, I went to the pet store and got a set of doggie boots to protect her little feets.

I wish I'd videoed the whole episode because it was---hilarious. I finally got the boots on her--she walked shaking her paws, concerned look on her doggie face. I took her out on the hot street---the sound of the boots frightened her and she kept trying to get away from herself---poor doggie---but hilarious, looking behind herself and walking faster and faster.

Finally, she got used to the sound but kept shaking her feet as she walked---oh mercy, I laughed and laughed. Then, she sat down to scratch her ear and as she raised her back foot to scratch, she saw the boot and she SCREAMED and tried to run---then she couldn't get away from it and she was just---beside herself.

Finally, I just gave up and took her back to the house---. As soon as the boots were off, she ran and hid under the bed, shaking. The next time I put the boots on her, she went limp. It was like she had no bones---just melting down onto the floor. I kept trying to sit her up but she continued to have no bones, laying like a limp pile of noodles.

When I tried to give her a pep talk and encourage her to sit up so we could stand up and go for a walk, she would look down at the boots, lick my face then collapse into a pile of boneless fur. So much for boots to protect her doggie feets; we will be walking after dark when the street has cooled off during the summer months.

Oh my! Grandma just remembered, my dear friend up the street walks her little doggie every night! Now, we can walk our pups together; what fun! This afternoon, I will call her and arrange to meet her at the rock wall flower bed.

The Mourning Class

At my Pastor's advisement, Grandma went to a Bible study on grieving last night. The last few months have been terribly rough. Some days, I feel like I'm going to be ok, some days I feel like I will never be able to live again. This is too hard, but as Pastor said, there is no way out, I must walk through this valley. The other side will come; I just have to keep walking on.

The grief class was helpful. All of us there had suffered loss. Some had lost spouses, some siblings, some parents, friends and some, their child or grandchild. Heart breaking, the pain Grandma is going through is not even close to the heartbreak of these dear souls. After sharing our stories, comforting each other and quite a bit of crying, the Bible study leader led us through a study of scriptures on God's presence in loss and helpful thoughts for "good mourning."

Life has a time for laughing, a time for crying, a time for celebration and a time for mourning. All of these events are known by God and scriptures are written to help through those times. No mourning ever "feels good," but it can be walked through in a way that brings a healthy recovery, in time. We are not ignorant of the devils devices; old slew foot would have Grandma sink lower and lower, cut off from friends and family and slip into a deep depression. Satan loves it when God's children hurt and can't recover.

As part of the healing process, the leader told us one of the healing tools is to write a note about our departed loved one, or a poem about God's comfort, or a song if music is your talent. Grandma thought that was silly, *seriously silly*. However, as I followed the leader's directions, this action actually did help. Grandma's heart felt a bit lighter as I read the words I'd written. This is my poem about God's comfort, written with many tears.

Grandma's Poem of Mourning

I love you, my Lord.
My heart cries out in Thanks for all the good things you have given me.
Bring those blessings before my mind now so that I can see them clearly through my tears.

You are Almighty, omnipotent, trustworthy, and endlessly kind.
My heart remembers the times you have given me direction.
Your Spirit within me whispers reminders of past provision, comfort and healing.

Even though; my heart is breaking with the pain of life and the harshness of reality.
You are the rock that I stand on.
You are the strength that holds me together.
You are my God, my Lord, my comforter and my dearest friend.

You will give me strength to go on.
Give me clarity of mind so I know my direction.
Bless me with friends who will hold me when I cry.

I will rise from the ashes of pain and I will once more dance,
laugh and write your praises.
I love you, my Lord.

_____

As I sit quietly, sipping an espresso, after the class on mourning, my mind goes to God's Word. The Holy Spirit whispers to me a particular few verses. Until now, the words hadn't been anything more than ---verse.

Now, my heart embraces the words and I focus on the depth of meaning hiding in them. Only those whose heart has been broken can fully understand the sweet words, "He leads me beside still waters. He restores my soul."

Life Goes On So Will Grandma

Today, I'm going through Walter's things. They say that it is best to wait a few months after a loved one departs to sort through their "stuff." It has been 10 months now since my beloved Walter went to heaven. I like saying that, it is so much gentler than saying, "Walter died." Sometimes I think the healing is processed by the words you choose to use. At the top of the box sitting on the bed before me is Walther's Eulogy that was read at his funeral. Correction, his "celebration of life;" the words that I choose--matter.

One of my responsibilities those painful hours after Walter's death was to gather information about my husband's life for the funeral message. As I typed the words for Pastor to read, I realized that "we" write our own eulogy. The person who is left to assemble the life remembrances is really only doing the work of an editor, choosing what is to be read and what is set aside.

Like Walter, many of those who die hadn't known "today" was the day of their death. Those who were old and sick, of course, knew their time was at hand. Walter wasn't sick, but he was getting up in years. He never let that slow him down; he could work longer hours than any young man. He had to, he owned his own business.

We'd joked together about who was going to "go" first, teasing each other about joining one of those on-line dating sites within a week of the other's funeral. We called it, "old humor." As we age, thoughts of eternity and heaven are more on your mind than when you are 20, vigorous and life seems endless. But, sadly, Pastor had preached at funerals for both old AND young, the sick AND the healthy. Death is no respecter of persons, has no age limits, no time that is pre-arranged within our knowledge.

This gave me pause for thought; I too have no guarantee of more time. True, in my mind, I'm far too young to think about dying, but obviously, the length of my life is known only by God. If today were to be my last day, what would my life leave as a testament to be shared as *my* eulogy?

Would there be mention made of how I influenced others to follow Jesus? Will there be friends from my church and my neighborhood crying tears of loss? Will my children mourn my passing or be relieved I've finally gone on? Will my grandchildren and, if I live long enough, my great grandchildren, make tearful pledges to love Jesus as much as "Mamawl" did?

The decisions that I make today will write my eulogy and determine the legacy and example I leave for my children and my grandchildren to follow. Time passes quickly, and life can be too soon over. When Walter got up that fateful morning, he had no idea that was the last time he'd put his socks on, the last time he'd kiss me good bye. (My breath catches in my throat. STOP it.)

Each day that I live NOW is part of my own legacy; all the more reason why I must pull myself together and live on. Perhaps my time remaining will be short; tears of hope well up behind my eyeballs. STOP IT. It's morbid to think of my own death as a relief from the emptiness my heart feels. Life goes on and so will Grandma; I tenderly fold the paper with the eulogy typed on it and put it in my Bible.

Grandma has MUCH to live for; many things to accomplish, many books to write, many friends to have fun with. Life is a mission field; there are still those in my own family who don't know Jesus. Walter had always given generously to both those around us and to missions; we both believed that investing in lives was far better than fancy living.

So many things remind me of our life together. Simple things that ordinarily would go unnoticed bring a flood of tears. A particular song on the radio—oddly it isn't the words of the song that brings the ache in my heart. It's the memory of being together when we heard it and knowing the song will never be "our song" again.

The two chairs sitting side by side on the beach, arranged there by a beach front home owner. To the owner, just chairs waiting for tomorrow. To me, memories of my darling, Walter, and I sitting in similar chairs watching the waves touch the shore as the sun came up.

As I sort through memories, tenderly folding clothes, packing things in boxes, tears gather in my eyes. This time, I don't stop it, there is a time to cry, a time to mourn and one more time, I will cry till I'm done. Doggie crawled up on the bed beside me and licked the tears from my face.

Grandma's Friends

A recent article on 'self-discovery' claimed that if I want to know what my Christian walk is like, keep a diary. An honest journal of what my busy days consist of. I'm to be honest, nobody will see this journal but me and the idea of the project is to examine myself, according to the scriptural direction.

At days end, simply jot down the activities that have consumed my day. No need to write anything big and fancy; just a few brief words about what I did today. No explanation, no reason for each activity, just flat out, what I DID.

The majority of journal entries will be everyday life events; family upkeep, on the job time, sports, reading, television. Which is as expected; Grandma thinks this will be a good idea since I'm trying to get my life back in order after Walter's death. Since his leaving, I've had to carefully outline my days so that I don't fall into bed and just stay there---grieving. Walter would NOT want me to be a puddle of pudding with no life---.

Routine: Every day morning stuff---shower—dress—take meds—eat—do quiet time devotions and pray. Bake, write, edit, take baked goods to friends and shut ins, do errands while I'm out, straighten up the house, do laundry, read, watch the cooking channel go to bed. Mercy sakes, Grandma had no idea that my day is so---**very**---ordinary. I just need to get organized and *start* doing things again.

I have many friends, I need to start accepting some of the invitations I've been offered. I would rather have life the way it was, but that is not going to happen, so it is time to get involved in creating new adventures. This is not easy, but life goes on, so must Grandma.

One of the things I've been intending to do is organize the photos that I've collected through the years. I have a big box of photos of friends. Friends have a big impact on our lives; they influence our attitudes, activities and pleasure pursuits.

Grandma tries to surround myself with friends who are close to my Lord so that we can share the things of God, pray together and hold each other up. Relationships are an important part of a victorious Christian life, the "third thread" to hold the button on that Grandma wrote about earlier in her journal. I also have friends that I'm mentoring, friends who are just learning to live the Christ life. Discipleship is important.

I have some GREAT friends and you might be surprised to find that Grandmas still work, laugh, play, love and enjoy life. Many of my friends still have careers! Some have retired and become involved in hobbies or do volunteer work. The point is, *none* of them "sit and do nothing," waiting for that last good night.. Old age is not a destination, it's a journey. Walk with friends; it makes the trip safer and more enjoyable. First thing in the morning, I'm going to start arranging pictures of a few of Grandma's beautiful friends and putting them in my journal.

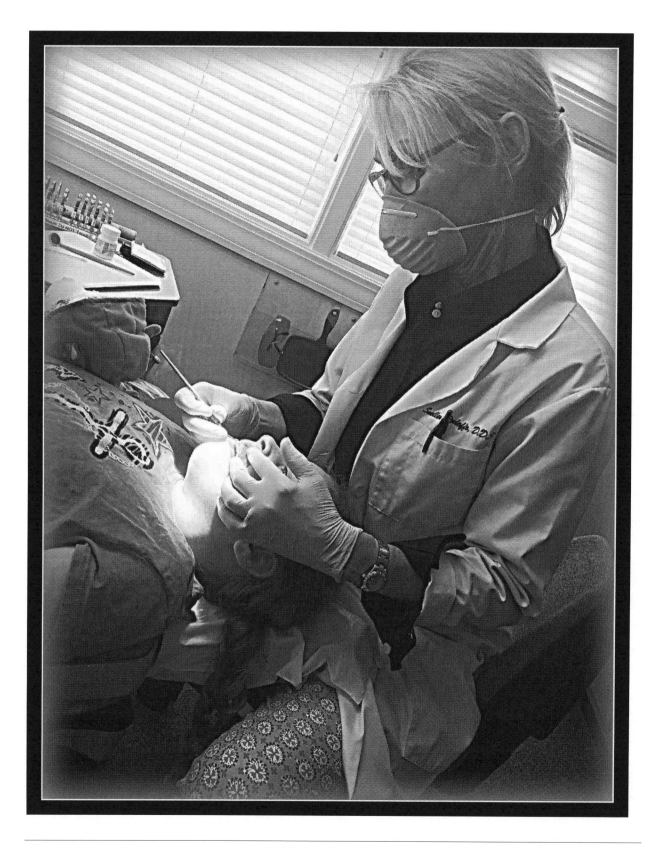

The Floppy Red Frog

Grandma should have known today was going to be one of "those" days when I first got up this morning. Early, still sleepy eyeballed, I was reaching in the fridge for a yogurt for breakfast---that early, I leaned against the fridge to balance as I leaned over for the bottom fridge drawer.

As I reached my left hand that was on the fridge for balance slipped and I hit the water dispenser on the door--cold water allll up my arm. That made me jump and when I jumped, I hit the ice lever and added crushed ice to the cold water on the floor. Believe me, Grandma was fully awake from then on.

About lunch time, I went to the grocery store to pick up some groceries and a sandwich for lunch. The rainbow bridge doggie resale is beside the store--so I thought I'd pop in and grab a new floppy toy for doggie. She LOVES floppy toys~ and the doggie resale has used stuffed animals for $1-$3. Sure beats the floppy toys at the pet store or retail store that are ten bucks.

I'd parked the car out in the parking lot a ways because the grocery store was slap packed out--. The weather forecasters were predicting a BAD storm coming up and folks were rushing out buying batteries, bread and milk. There's just something so enticing about eating milk sandwiches by flash light while a storm rages.

Grandma never could see the sense in eating bread and milk in a sandwich---besides, it's not like everything already in the fridge is going to vanish when the wind starts blowing. Anyway, instead of hiking to the other side of the parking lot--I stuffed the floppy red froggie in my giant grandma purse and took it in the grocery with me.

The lines were--crazy. I'm standing in line with at least half the people on the Island--and my mind turned to the doggie and her thrilled reaction to her new toy when I got home. I pulled the red frog out of my granny bag purse and wondered if the short arms will flop or will just the long back legs flop? Hmm---. Doggie loves really floppy ones.

I started violently shaking frog all over every which way--watching how the arms and legs flopped and thinking how much doggie would LOVE that. Then---I felt eyeballs on me. I looked up and all the people around me had stopped talking and were watching me violently shake that silly floppy red frog.

Slooooooowly, I put the floppy frog back in my purse--and just stared straight ahead. The elder women behind me whispered to her friend---"I want one of those to shake, ask her where she got it." But then it was my turn at the check out, so she didn't ask me---and I didn't volunteer. It's MY red floppy frog---.

Commitment to Fitness

Is it mid-January, already? Mercy sakes! Time has passed so quickly since Grandpa died. At first, time was at a standstill, but now, time seems to pass more quickly. The days all stream together as I create a new lifestyle and routine. They say the first year is always the most difficult because EVERYthing is---different. Grandma thinks the difficulty will last longer than a year, but, I'm doing better. Each day another day lived-- new.

At first, there was so much activity, so many friends and family to console me, comfort me and even give me guidance. There were often times that I just wanted to scream---LEAVE me ALONE! Of course, in time, they did. And then, there is life standing before me, empty. Nothing I did before works now. All future plans have been canceled because---they were made together and "us and we" are no longer pronouns in my daily vocabulary.

From the time I get out of bed till the time I fall back in bed and cry myself to sleep; nothing—is---the—same. There are days when my heart hurts so bad I can't breathe; then other days are without any feeling what so ever. Just---emptiness. Numb. I try to pray but it's like my mind has turned itself off. I can hear the wind whistle through my soul and then, the silence is deafening.

My friends who have walked before me in these painful, tight fitting widow shoes; call me, come over and sometimes, just sit beside me while I say nothing. There is nothing to be said. Of course life must go on, but, how does that happen?

My friend, Sandy, tells me that I must find things that I did on my own when Walter was still living and start doing those things again. The familiarity of those things will help bring "normal" back into focus. Of course she is right. Sandy is ALWAYS right---sometimes that is annoying. But this time, her "rightness" helps me to get my life focused on a new normal.

Today, I will focus on re-affirming the good things in my physical life. It's time to renew my annual commitment to lose 50 pounds. However, in theory, I actually met and surpassed my goal last year because I lost 55 pounds. The problem is; I lost the same 5 pounds, again and again. My commitment wears thin as the real goal continues to be out of my reach. This year HAS to be different because this is the year of doing all things different.

Last year, I reassessed my methods; I can't do the same thing over and over while expecting different results. Fifty pounds seemed a reasonable weight loss goal to spread over a year, so, instead of adjusting my goal, I decided to change my approach. Once more invigorated by the prospect of a thinner me, I vigorously began a new approach; I bought a gym membership again.

Quickly, I discovered that more commitment was required than simply signing on the dotted line. My old gray head held high in determination, I disciplined myself to a rigorous regimen of exercise. Nothing, absolutely nothing was allowed to deter me from my goal of fitness.

Reviewing my accomplishments after a few months of daily trips to the gym; I discovered that I had gone to the gym four days each week faithfully. And, I'd lost a steady thirty five dollars a month. Not the goal I'd hoped for, but certainly proof I did have some level of discipline. At least I'd kept the commitment of sticking to a plan.

Discouraged, I decided to try a different approach. Commitment didn't work, planning didn't work; perhaps it is my goal that needs to be over hauled. Instead of struggling for perfection through strict discipline and unyielding commitment to a plan, perhaps I need to simplify; eat less, exercise more. Maybe the answer isn't a big change but a small attitude adjustment and a little life style follow through.

Sometimes, my goal to serve God can get as bogged down as my weight loss plan. It's so easy to commit myself to what I THINK God wants for my life. God has a plan; however, not necessarily the same plan that I have. *My* plan was to live happily ever after with Walter by my side. The question is, am I committed to *what I'm doing* or surrendered to God's perfect will? I don't understand why this has happened. It makes—no—sense. Enough---life goes on and so must Grandma; back to my new fitness goals.

It is important to remember that God is sovereign in every area of life, but---and this is the kicker---He LETS me do whatever I want. That includes the level of my faithfulness and commitment to EVERY life goal, not just spiritual goals. With new clarity about life commitment, I pull a clean pale blue piece of stationary out of my desk drawer.

Picking up a writing pen, at the top, I write, "Fitness Goals." Somehow, Grandma thinks this contract will be far more difficult than the one I make with God every New Year's Eve. Never the less, Grandma signs her name on the bottom line. And now, in spite of my best intentions, I will go make a cup of espresso, sit in my beloved Walter's favorite reading chair beside his boat collection and cry till I'm done crying—one—more---time.

For the Love of Carolyn

Carolyn stands on tippy toes as we watch the milk being steamed into froth. I step out of her way; she is much shorter than me, though both of us are full grown women. We watch the rich chocolate join the foamy milk as they are carefully married by experienced hands.

Enrapt in anticipation, we watch as the barista uses a wire whisk to whip thick cream. With a flourish, he piles white whipped to an ethereal lightness on top of the liquid chocolate. A comforting hot beverage made extravagantly rich enough to pamper queens, placed humbly in our outstretched hands. We giggle like school girls as both of us simultaneously stick our tongue into the cream.

My friend, though only slightly younger than me, has hair that glows golden red in the sunshine. Wisps of silver catch the sunlight, making her hair look like it has been professionally highlighted instead of ---graying. Her personality is still voluptuous, her laughter melodious as it bubbles from her bright red lips. She exudes an inner strength and determination that adds another layer of richness to her extravagant personality.

Throughout our friendship, she has always been the one with the bright personality that lights up a room when she walks in. At one time, as girls, Carolyn had wanted to be a missionary, a medical missionary. But, as the sirens of life beckoned to her with all of their colorful, exciting promises, she turned from that calling and went her own way. More than a few times, she has even reminded me of her "calling" and how she felt a much better choice had been made. A life of glamour, excitement and wild living had been more rewarding and---she felt—certainly more fun.

We sit at the wrought iron table on the patio of the coffee shop and drink the hot chocolate, each laughing at well told stories of the other's foibles. How can we allow so much time to pass between our meetings when we love each other so easily? It seems the older we get, the more years collect between our conversations.

We grow silent, basking in the simple joy of fellowship. I reach across the table and take Carolyn's hand. Uncomfortable with the insistent touch, she knows what is coming and averts her eyes away. I persistently, gently, embrace her hand until she raises her face and looks at me. I whisper, "It's time, dear friend, stop running and come home."

She once more averts her eyes but I squeeze her fingers and she's forced by the heart strings of friendship to raise her eyes to mine again. It's like she is looking into my soul, opening every door of my heart, pulling out into the light every wayward deed I've ever done.

I blush at the awareness of her knowledge of the things I've participated in. Things forgiven by my Lord long ago, yet still loud and colorful in our shared past, come to my mind. Refusing to look deliberately away, I let my gaze slowly slip down to my cocoa. Carolyn's eyes are like hot coals, burning into my soul with mocking self-righteousness.

Carolyn and I may never meet again; life can be unpredictable. Oh, we will continue to write, certainly. It was, in fact, a note from her that brought us together today. But, we will each go our separate way, each to live our lives according to our own will as usual. Yet, today, maybe because of Walter's fairly recent death, I'm painfully aware of how fragile life is, how temporary physical well-being is and how quickly time can pass. My friend, always small in stature, seems to look even more fragile today.

Resolutely, I meet her unwavering, accusing eyes with my own and whisper, "We can't undo the past. We can't go back and erase our sins, but, God can erase them from HIS memory. You know my sins are covered by the blood of Christ and you also know yours *can be* as well." Again, her gaze falters and her hand falls to her lap and begins to stroke her other hand, as if comforting it.

Whenever I've written to her, I spoke of how faithful God is and the joy of living fully for Christ. I've told her about my happy marriage, my children and then my grandchildren. I've always remembered to send her birthday card and holiday greetings. And I'd even remembered to call her about Walter's death.

Her response has always been to send me a note declaring how her life is full, her purse fat and her days her own. She has never married, preferring rather to keep things, how is it she says? "Uncomplicated." Enjoying a series of lovers, always breaking away from them before any real affection can be cultivated; she has been quite the playful tart.

Rather than challenge her life choices, I have persistently offered a reminder of childhood friendship, a heart touching witness of Christ and what He had been to her, to us, through the years of girlhood. The years of our youth, before we tasted the bitter sweet nectar rebellion brought us in our teen years, lay silent without mention of remembrance.

Hopefully, the churched joy of childhood compared beside the harsh results of rebellion would leave a yearning in her heart. Sin seems to be fun for a season, but soon it turns bitter, often leaving scars that last a lifetime.

Long ago I discovered that rebellion is a gift. It is a gift that both my friend and I have been entrusted with; a God given gift. I made the choice to use that gift FOR God rather than against Him. It has taken strong self-discipline and the direction of the Holy Spirit, but, I have chosen to rebel against the world, not against the things of God. I have stumbled now and then, but quickly stood back up and walked on with my Lord. My Lord is faithful even when I'm not. He is my strength when I have none.

Of all my friends, dear Carolyn is one of the few that has never backed down in their reckless pursuit of self-fulfillment. I've reminded her again and again about Christianity not being a religion, but a relationship. She always makes a reciprocal wave of her hand acknowledging my commitment yet postponing my words of persuasion about her personal need for a savior.

Promising to stay in touch, she'd once again run from me, laughing and toss, "I don't have time for your Jesus talk, maybe later." She has never looked back over her shoulder to see the tears on my face as she ran full throttle away from me and God--again. When I'd called to inform her of Walter's death, she said she had been wanting to come visit, and we'd planned today's meeting.

But, today is different than our other visits, this time I notice that I have a sense of urgency to be with her that I'd not experienced before. Puzzled that God's Spirit within me is even more insistent after all these years, I wonder why this sense of immediacy. Now, a bit frightened by the troubling in my heart, I nervously rise and face her. I look at my watch and ready myself to leave.

Once again, my aching heart searches for some new way to ask her if she'd like to pray with me before we part—knowing what her answer will be. Then, I see her head lower and a shadow of fear plays over her face. Her eyes glisten with tears as she turns her head away from me as if she doesn't want me to see this moment of weakness. What is this? I'm stunned at her unexpected change of attitude. I sink slowly back into my chair.

This is not like Carolyn. As I reach my hands across the table for her hands, I whisper, "What?" She slowly moves her hands away from mine, at first clenching her fists, but then, in what looks like a surrender of will, she lays them flat on the tabletop and looks directly into my eyes. Words come pouring out, angry words at first then words of anguish as she tells me about the cancer that has been found growing out of control inside of her body. Her words hit me like a bag of ice leaving my face feeling cold and bruised.

Sobbing into her hands she asked me, "Isn't it wrong to wait till the last possible moment to commit your heart to Christ? Waiting till you're sick and staring death straight on before finally running to Jesus is so-so—hypocritical, isn't it? I've played a dangerous game and seeking salvation now would be, presumptuous, wouldn't it? Does God even still want me after I've turned away so many times?"

My heart aches as I tell her that death is eminent at any moment in our lives; the dark specter that stalks us all every day from the womb till---we are finally done. God calls us to repentance each of those days. God loves all of us with a love so deep it reaches across every obstacle.

Sin also includes what the world would label as silly, human frailties. Greed, self-righteousness and arrogance; there is NONE that can say they have never sinned. Only God's mercy and sacrificial offering on Calvary covers every sin, from the most horrible to the most common.

There is no person who doesn't need the cleansing blood of Christ for redemption. Reaching across the table, I wiggle my fingertips up under her hand that is laying in limp defeat. I take a deep breath and whisper, "Pray with me now, dear friend, Jesus is waiting."

xxxxxxxxxxxxxxxxxxxxxxxxxxxxxxxxxxxx

Months have passed since that glorious fall day when I held Carolyn's hand as she asked Jesus to come into her heart and she received forgiveness for her sins. I have not heard from her since that day; not unusual, usually months, even years pass between our meetings. Each day I have prayed that my sweet friend would be healed from the cancer. Any day I expect the phone to ring and I will hear her rich, melodious voice tell me of her miraculous cure. Silence. Maybe tomorrow---?

It's still early as I stand on the beach ready for my morning swim; I'm distracted watching the seagulls dive into the surf. My reverie is interrupted by the ringing of my cell phone, in my beach bag. Immediately, I know in my heart that the call is from Carolyn, I can feel it, and my heart begins to dance. Taking my sunhat off so I can hold the phone against my ear, I speak into the handset, "Hello?" An unfamiliar voice responds. "This is Monica Shelling, you don't know me, I'm a Hospice Nurse in New Haven, Connecticut."

Strength leaves me and with rubber legs, I sink to the sand, watching the surf, the gulls, the fluffy white clouds as they drift carelessly across the pale morning sky. The voice on my cell tells me that Carolyn has died. Nurse Shelling had promised my friend that when she passed, she would call me and give me the "good news" of her safe arrival in heaven.

I can imagine my beloved Walter's surprise as Carolyn sachets through the gates of heaven. He'd always said she was too hard, too stubborn to "come back to Jesus." Squeezing my eyes tight shut, I smile softly; *finally*, Grandma is right about something; nothing is too hard for God.

My fingertips caress my lips in self-applied comfort as tears begin to slide from my eyes. My head is nodding in acknowledgement even though I know full well the voice on the other end of the call can't see it. "Ma'am? Hello? Ma'am? Are you there?" the nurse inquires. I clear my throat, "Yes, yes, I'm here, thank you. Did—did she die peacefully?"

Nurse Shelling tells me that Carolyn slipped the bondage of pain and crossed into the heavenly realm with praise for her Lord on her lips. "Oh, and ma'am?" the voice continued, "I feel led to let you know that before she died, Miss Carolyn told me about Jesus—and the other nurses--- her doctor and anybody who would stop to listen. And—I accepted Christ as my Savior and so did three other nurses!"

Now the floodgates of self-control are useless and tears gush from my eyes, streaming in rivers down my face and I---laugh. The hospice nurse continues, "Of course, you knew that your friend was a very wealthy woman, she had amassed quite a fortune. Since she had no living relatives, she left over one MILLION dollars to the Baptist Medical Missionary fund, with instructions that the monies be used as scholarships for young men and women who want to go to medical school before heading to the mission field."

I'm mesmerized by the morning sun's reflection on the waves and the sea gulls dipping in the surf. I feel like cool, living water has been poured over the burning ashes of personal loss in my soul. The animated voice on the other end of the line continued, "AND, she left a hundred thousand dollars to you with instructions that the monies be used for your granddaughter, Molly, to finish going to nursing school in preparation for the mission field. The monies remaining after education are to be applied to your granddaughter's mission's work.

She said you had told her that Molly was working toward the goal of becoming a medical missionary. Miss Carolyn said that should be enough to get her the rest of the way through college and the first few years on the mission field as well. I gave the lawyer your name, phone number and address; he will be contacting you soon to make arrangements for your granddaughter's endowment."

Thanks were given for the call, appreciation for the information expressed, and the phone call was ending. Just as my phone was slipping from my face, I heard nurse eagerly interject one last comment. "Oh, wait, WAIT, I almost forgot, Ms. Carolyn also left you personally, the odd sum of $4.29. She said to tell you it was for hot chocolate." Why, of course she did; in the midst of my heartache, I'm unexpectedly overwhelmed by joy. My heart embraces the memory of my beloved friend's odd sense of humor and--I laugh.

I slumped back in the sand, eyes closed, listening to the rhythmic sound of the waves as they kissed the sea shore. Tears of joy freely streaming down my face, I try to absorb all that has happened the last thirty minutes. I've lost a friend, but have the comfort of knowing we will meet again.

I've learned that before my friend died she had become a Spirit inspired missionary and led four nurses and who knows how many visitors and personal attendants to Jesus. In an off road kind of way, Carolyn had embraced her original calling as a medical missionary. Only instead of being the nurse, she led nurses to Jesus. Do I think this was God's plan for my friend all along, to be called, go into rebellion then return and actually do the work that God intended for her to do, to start with? *Absolutely not.*

God's perfect plan was for Carolyn to go to the mission field as a medical missionary. However, God is omnipotent and omnipresent. He gives us direction but lets us choose the path we take. When we choose to walk away, His plans for our life do not change. We are free to make our own choices.

When we return to God, the original plan has not changed, but we have. God is faithful to take our brokenness and mold it to fit His sovereign will; that we love Him with all of our heart and do works that will bring Him honor. God is faithful even when we stumble.

I sit up, brushing the sand from myself and sachet down the shore, laughing; only Jesus could make such a glorious finale out of a life redeemed at the last minute. Only my Lord. Only ---Jesus. The gulls watch with curious eyes as I put my sunhat back on and walk up the beach singing.

The White Water Rafting Adventure

Slowly, Grandma is reconstructing my life to reflect the current state of affairs. After so many years living with Walter, to be suddenly single is a difficult adjustment to make. A neighborhood friend, who had herself been widowed awhile back, shared with me that one of the most helpful "recovery tools" is to plan—and do---things that Grandpa and I never did together. This would help establish a starting point so I could move on.

Of course, keeping memories alive with daily ritual and customary calendar is important, but I must also find a new "normal" for-- me. While Grandma was thinking on that, a dear friend at church invited me to go---(sit down—seriously, sit down, because if you know Grandma, this is going to knock you on your tuckus)—white water rafting. As soon as you stop laughing, I will tell you about my new adventure, but I understand you need a few moments to recover from the initial revelation.

The white water adventure was to take three days, one day driving to the NC Mountains, the second day to go rafting and the third day to return to Florida. Grandma's idea of great water adventure has always been to pull the plug and fight the current in the big tub at the health spa. "Adventure" is the word at the bottom of the left hand corner of page ten in Funk and Wagnall's Dictionary, nothing more. Grandpa always teased me that the "A" word was not even in my vocabulary.

When Wilma first invited me, my first thought was to say, "Thanks, but, no thanks." However, she kept telling me about how much FUN it would be—out in nature. Many years ago, Grandma had been camping with Grandpa and it was the most horrible 12 days of my life. My idea of roughing it is a five star hotel with no hot tub. Walter assured me the small RV that he'd rented for us to "live" in would make camping out just like being at home.

My first thought was, "Why would I plan a vacation that was just like staying at home? Isn't the whole idea of a vaca to get AWAY from every day stuff?" Grandpa had insisted we would have SO much fun---and I bought into the fantasy. By the end of the first day I figured out that RV camping was exactly like staying at home only you do everything in cramped quarters on tiny little inadequate appliances. To make a long story short, and I know you want me to do that, let me just give you the low lights of our week in the woods.

The RV had a bed that folded down from the ceiling and rested just over the dashboard; great caution had to be made while sleeping. Grandma sleeps like a rotarooter chopping vines in a drain pipe; caution is not on my sleep time agenda. Somehow I fell off the side of the pull down bed and plastered myself on the front windshield. Stretched out on the glass like a cartoon character, I could not wriggle down onto the dash nor could I squirm back up to the fold down bed. Finally, after much yelling, I woke up Walter and he helped me out of my predicament.

Then, there was the day we were traveling through the great red wood forest and I was roasting a chicken in the oven as we drove along the winding road. A deer ran out in front of the RV and Grandpa hit his brakes, avoiding the deer. Unfortunately the sudden swerving maneuver threw the roasting chicken against the oven door and pot, chicken and veggies flew out of the oven, sailed across the small kitchenette and, thankfully, the cooking pot fell to the floor and only the half cooked bird continued the flight across the RV to slide down the big plate glass window on the dining room pull out.

And the day we had stopped for lunch on the rocky beach, cooking wieners on the grill. A group of seagulls swept out of the sky and each took a wiener off the grill and flew off over the beach. I have no idea why the charcoal flames didn't burn their little bird feet. The nearest grocery was a 20 minute drive, so we ate empty buns with catsup and mustard. Grandma could continue with disaster stories, but, let's get back to the white water rafting trip and just suffice to say we never went on another camping trip together.

To start with, on the day of our great rafting adventure, we had to be at the starting site at o'dark thirty in the morning. Then, there was no coffee, only energy drinks that were sweet like syrup and had fruity undertones. My overall impression of the canned energy was that somebody had chopped up citrus into old stale coffee and sealed it in a colorful tall can.

The girls were taking small sips and raving about how there was so much caffeine in there, they'd never sleep again. Grandma held her nose, chugged it, tried not to gag and waited for the caffeine hit to strike. It didn't. I made a mental note that none of these girls had a clue what a good espresso was. It was just starting to get daylight, I was chilled, hungry and desperately needed a strong black very hot coffee---it was going to take extreme effort to keep the Fruits of the Spirit, love, joy, peace---, active in my life today.

The first order of business at the rafting site was that we were all given a paper to sign that warned us that rafting can be dangerous, though not common, there have been deaths. We had to sign our name at the bottom saying we understood there could be loss of life and we would not hold the rafting place responsible if that should happen. At the bottom of the page was the proclamation that NO refunds would be made under any circumstances---.

Grandma wonders why they didn't give us the contract to read and sign BEFORE we paid our money. Never mind, I know why---and I was starting to feel cranky over the whole thing. I don't know Wilma well, I made a mental note that I did NOT WANT to know Wilma well---she obviously was one of those athletic nuts that like to live on the edge of adventure. Grandma didn't seek after adventure when I was young, I sure don't go looking for it when I'm old. My only hope right now is that I won't drown while white water rafting.

As we were led to the rafts, those who had previously been on the white water adventure talked with great animation about being thrown from the raft, getting shoes caught and lost in rock formations and returning with badly sprained ankles, wrists and a wide variety of scrapes, cuts, and bruises. One young man even boasted how he had broken his nose and sustained a mild concussion on one wild river ride.

The rafting adventure was without disaster, but it was also without Grandma. As I'd stood marveling at scars and grand tales being told by those who had been on the river before, I decided that I just did not have that much foolish daring in my bones. I didn't have it when I was a youngster and sure didn't grow any as I aged. Grandma was a good sport and didn't ruin the adventure for the rest of the folks with who knows what kind of disastrous happening that surely would have gone on if I'd gotten in that raft.

Staying on the shore, even if it meant losing the money paid, was the best decision I think I ever made. Mercy sakes; I hate being cold—one of the reasons I moved to Florida was to get away from being cold—and the possibility of being suddenly tossed into the icy mountain water and struggling to survive? Grandma is all for experiencing new things, even things Grandpa and I never did before; life is an adventure. But, this was just *way* off my good sense meter.

When the worn out rafters arrived at the other end of the adventure, Grandma was waiting with hot beverages and sandwiches I'd bought for everybody at the "trail's end" snack shack. The hot drinks and food were eagerly received with cold trembling hands by the survivors. The great adventurers were so cold Grandma couldn't tell if they were talking in tongues of if they were just so cold their teeth were chattering too bad to speak coherently.

Grandma has no proof, but I think maybe along with the well-known "Jesus said" verse, "I was hungry and you fed me, I was naked and you clothed me—" is an addendum about being wet, cold, sore and exhausted on a rafting trip. I know my dear Walter is looking down from heaven laughing his angelic tukus off. He probably is elbowing all his heaven friends and saying, "see, I told you my Bitsy wouldn't go through with it---."

Grandma has learned an important lesson through this trauma; just because a friend has been through the same thing I have (widowed) does not necessarily mean "her" idea of things to do to move toward a new "normal" works for ---me. I've never liked adventurous things and I feel safe in saying I never-- will.

Being married to Walter had nothing to do with the stunted development of my adventuresome spirit. What was I thinking? I'd hoped to include a photo of Grandma enjoying her white water adventure, but, that didn't happen. However, I do have some friends who ARE adventure seekers.

Grandma has friends who have not let age hinder their youthful enthusiasm and high spirited spunk. I'll post a photo of one of my friends having an adventure—I know exactly which one.

There certainly must be some kind of spiritual lesson in this story somewhere, but Grandma is ready for a hot meal even though all I did was stand by the river and pray. Maybe later the "God part" of this will come to me, but not—now. Mercy sakes, let me go look for the photo of my adventurous friend, before I forget.

Life Can Be Dangerous

While at the doctor's office Grandma was fascinated by a book about the top one hundred most dangerous things people encounter in everyday life. The book was very worn so it was obviously well read. It revealed some amazing facts about everyday life.

Are you aware that 5,700 persons in the USA are injured by musical instruments each year? Grandma wonders how that would be written up on a medical record; patient was viciously attacked by an out of control tuba? Patient suffered serious injuries resulting from being caught in their violin strings? The patient swallowed their trombone? (that last one is something Grandma has always wondered about---where DOES that trombone slide go to---?)

Grandma was completely stunned to discover that there are more people injured by Teddy Bears than Grizzly bears! Who knew those fluffy teddy bears could be so dangerous? And how on earth are ten persons a year **killed** by vending machines? Does Grandma even want to know HOW those vending machine deaths happened—probably not.

My mom always said Go-carts were VERY dangerous. Interestingly, according to statistics, 287,933 persons are injured annually by dining room tables and 26,700 injuries are incurred from the use of shopping carts. While only 10,500 persons are injured annually in Go-Cart mishaps. Though my Mom's intent was noble, there was more risk in eating supper or pushing the cart at the Kroger Store than racing down the street in the Go-Cart. Where were these statistics when my brothers and I needed them?

Then, there's this; on average, 100 people choke to death on ballpoint pens every year. Seriously? How does THAT happen? And who would ever imagine that more than 6,000 people go to the emergency room each year with pillow related injuries? Pillow related injuries? Grandma didn't even know you could be seriously injured enough by a pillow to need ER care. I wish Walter was still alive so I could tell him all these crazy statistics, he'd have found it as silly as Grandma does. Who knew, right?

In the Us there are an average of 19 shark attacks each year and one shark-attack fatality _every two years_ while twenty Americans are KILLED _every year_ by---horses, another 20 people a year are killed by cows and a shocking 186 individuals are killed each year by a ---pet dog. 1-17 people die from a mosquito related death each year. A mosquito, seriously?

Thinking on all that, Grandma has been entirely too scared of things that rarely ever happen and way to trusting of ordinary things that can do serious harm. It's a crazy world we live in. Mercy SAKES!

On a whim, just curious, I looked through the index to find statistics on how many persons were accidentally injured while attending church services. Church is one of those places Grandma goes to all the time, is it possible my house of worship could be more dangerous than walking in the jungle?

There were no stats listed for accidental injuries acquired while sitting in church. However, injuries and deaths suffered through contact with musical instruments and table legs could have occurred at church and just not been made note of. Never the less, the next time Grandma invites somebody to church, I can add that church is one of the safest places to be. Who knew, right?

Grandma Has Anger Issues

The other day, Grandma's new fangled wireless keyboard was giving me fits. Being technologically challenged, I tried everything I knew to do; pray, beg, cry, stare at it without blinking. But, I just could NOT get the silly thing to work. Of course, knowing my ineptitude with all things technical, it could be that the problem is simply a screw loose in front of the control panel. Think about that for a minute---Grandma sits—in front—of the keyboard. Yes, now you understand.

Finally, in a fit of exasperation, I picked up the keyboard and SLAMMED it down on my desktop as hard as I could! (I may also have emitted some kind of unspecific sound; like a primal scream, or a deep throaty growl) My uncooperative wireless keyboard immediately began to function normally and hasn't given me one bit of trouble since. I think techno geeks refer to this particular repair method as the "Slambamit Technique."

My keyboard finally working again, Grandma fixed a cup of tea and sat down to recover her composure. Obviously, I have issues with unresolved anger. The outburst of anger was not just because my keyboard failed to function; there was a deeper issue inciting my fury.

I'd noticed that lately, it didn't take much to drive me into the hot zone. Unable to put my finger on exactly what I'm so angry about, I'd taken the problem to God and asked Him to help me find my issue. Life has many issues that we all stuff down and try to ignore. Once the problem causing my anger is determined, I can give it to Jesus and He'll help me work through it.

God spoke into my heart that when I get edgy and annoyed, I should respond to the Holy Spirit instead of reacting to the flesh. He also revealed to my heart that this anger, regardless of what is causing it, is not healthy for me---my relationships---or my testimony. During the course of the day, the Lord brought to mind some relationship problems that I'd not gotten over. Grandma is bad about holding a grudge.

Holding a grudge against somebody is called –unforgiveness-- and according to the Bible, if I don't completely forgive people who have wronged me, then God can't forgive me for the sins I've done against Him. In fact, the Word says that unforgiveness is so damaging to relationships that if we have a grudge, God won't even hear our prayers.

Grandma doesn't have a problem with forgiveness; nope. I have a problem with ---forgetness. Indeed, there are some things that simply can't be resolved unless an asteroid comes flying out of the sky and crushes the person I'm angry with.

Of course, this is not the way God would have me handle my issue with anger---or people who annoy me. However, I'm in good company because two of the disciples wanted Jesus to call down fire from heaven and kill their opponents---fire from heaven---asteroid---same thing. Jesus rebuked them, so I consider myself having been rebuked as well. Humpfff.

It really is hard to stop being angry with somebody who has hurt you. If you can do that, Grandma salutes you---or prays you will repent of lying, whichever shoe fits. Such things take time---but all good things take time. Be patient with Grandma, my learning curve is steep; I know God is faithful to give me strength to forgive AND walk on.

Where are the Memories?

Grandma has a lot of "grandma" friends who are praying for their grandchildren. Indeed, I'm among those silver haired prayer warriors. The world is so different now than when we were growing up. Grandkids no longer play with toys; even young grandchildren have electronic devices. When I have difficulties with my cell phone, any of my grandchildren can tell me how to fix whatever is wrong---and that includes my six year old grandson.

Whatever happened to match box cars, tonka trucks, Lincoln logs, etcha sketch, tinker toys, jax and baby dolls? Nobody wants carefully chosen gifts anymore; nobody wants models to build or baby dolls to dress. The older ones don't even want jewelry or clothes; they aren't interested in sweatshirts or bicycles. They all want money, just---cash. And then, they very rarely even call to say thank you for sending the money they said they wanted. It's like making memories no longer matters; relationships no longer matter.

Some of my most treasured childhood memories are of hand selected gifts from my grandma. I can tell you exactly what every dolly she gave me was wearing when I opened the box and lifted "her" from the tissue cloud she was hiding in. What will our granddaughters remember of gifts we've sent? There's no intimacy, no sweet memory of beloved dollies or sparkling necklaces and earrings. No joy in remembering the bubble bath oils that came as round colored marbles that would melt in the hot water of the tub and fill the room with fragrance and sooooo—many--bubbles.

How much memory can be attached to a $20 bill? Not even a fifty or a hundred dollar bill holds memories. How much loving forethought can keep a special Christmas gift alive through the years when the gift was simply---paper with numbers on it? Years after we Grandmas have gone home to Jesus and the girls have grown to be women, our granddaughters will remember no special gift that Grandma gave them. Indeed, will our granddaughters even remember their grandmother got them a gift-- at all?

I don't understand. The children these days do not relate to the concept of making memories to cherish; it's like they are emotional vacuums. They do not put special had picked, had signed, personal holiday greeting cards in the back of their dresser drawers to be held, smelled and finger traced for decades passing like "we" did.

Grandma still has many of the birthday cards *my grandmother gave me* and my grandmother has been in heaven for—many—many years. I seriously doubt if any of our grandchildren have kept a card that we've sent them. In fact, I often wonder if the cards are even read before they are thrown in the trash right after the cash is taken out and pocketed.

Grandma heard a psychologist on a television talk show say that many of today's youth have no conscience, no passion, no goals. I think it is because they have no memories. Memories are important. Memories are what keeps love and faith alive through the generations.

A dear elder friend begins his testimony with the acknowledgement that he is alive and serving God today because of his grandmother's prayers. Prayers that were made like this Grandma's prayers are made—with tears formed in a heart that aches with longing to see everybody I love—love Jesus.

Since society has essentially erased all traces of intimacy between the generations now; how will today's children—even--- **know** --that their grandmother prayed for them? And even more sadly, who will pray for THEIR grandchildren?

Saga of the Dead Mousie

On the third day of the smell of putrefying flesh, arising from a mousie that had died somewhere in the walls of my home; I began to pray desperately. The first day, my prayers had been quiet prayers for guidance, as I tried to track down what was smelling so bad. The second day my prayers started out as hopeful and escalated to pleading as my frustration *and* the stench intensified. On this, the third day, prayers have become cries of desperation and pleading and have been punctuated with gagging--.

The very things that I pray for deliverance from are sometimes the tool that God would use to illustrate His truth to my heart. So, along with my fervent prayer for deliverance, I'd been searching my heart and thinking, "*IS* there any lesson I can learn through the smelly carcass of a dead mousie?" I can't imagine how or what, but if there *is* a lesson to be learned, Grandma prays it is learned quickly. Ohmygoodnessakes.

The stench is unbearable. Since no epiphany seems to be emerging, perhaps there was no lesson that could be had after all? Could there be no spiritual truth to be gleaned; was it simply an event? Maybe, there was no real life illustration that could be made of this experience, no connection to the mysterious ways of an Almighty God?

Could it be that Walter had been right, sometimes, stuff just simply---happens? But then, how could something so nasty have absolutely no benefit, no teachable moment? Grandpa used to say, "Now, Bitsy, not everything that happens in life has to have a God connection. Sometimes, stuff just, happens." It would be a hoot if after his death, I find this to be—true; he'd so have enjoyed being right—again.

Hours of searching for a small rotting mouse corpse, spraying air freshener as I crawled around in closets and behind appliances has only made the house smell like the rodent died in a fruit basket. The advice of dear friends and loved ones who have had similar misadventures have brought the fellowship of suffering, but no actual relief. As so often with life's upsets, friends have sympathy, even empathy, but no advice that works in my particular situation.

So, at my wit's end this morning, I simply asked God for mercy. No more searching for some way of connection to a spiritual truth; just simply, a cry for mercy. This had to come to an end. There is no way this nasty smell can go on endlessly. There simply HAS to be some type of resolution. As I waited for God's mercy, in whatever form it would appear, I swatted the millions of flies that had suddenly shown up out of nowhere on every window in the den.

How could so many flies arrive and not be noticed till they are all there? Were they waiting in a pre-arranged staging area till maximum capacity was reached and THEN, they all went to the windows? Why had I not seen these tiny intruders until just moments ago? Why had none of my neighbors called and inquired of the black cloud of flies that must have suddenly droned over my house and entered through who knows what crack in the exterior facade?

Totally defeated, I decided enough was enough; they say everything happens for a reason. However, Grandma had noticed that often times the reason is because I did something stupid. But, this time, I could find no reason for this mess, stupid or accidental. It just simply---is. I will go out to find a bug exterminator that could come and kill the flies, and who knows, maybe he'd know where mousies like to crawl to hide and die?

As I prepared to leave the house in defeat, I searched my mind one more time to see if I could think of any remedy I'd ever heard or read about that would help me to at least, get rid of the stench. Spraying the air freshener had only given the smell of decay a fruity over tone. Resolutely, I knew there was nothing I could do that I had already not done to make the nightmare end by myself.

I sought and found the help I needed from an exterminator and finally, the ordeal was over. The flies were gone. On the fourth day the stench quieted and by days end, was gone; but the dead mousie was never found. The exterminator said more likely as not, a smell that big had come from a big dead possum, perhaps even an armadillo that had crawled under the house, near an air vent, to die, not a little mouse.

In retrospect, a lesson was learned after all. Sometimes, stuff just happens for no reason. No mistake to be made right, no lesson to be learned, just, boom, a mess. Of course, it is always wise to examine my actions and attitudes to see if Grandma did something unwise to cause the mess so future messes can be avoided.

In this case, I heeded the exterminator's advice and made sure there were no holes large enough for animals to enter in the underpinning of the house. But, sometimes, there is no lesson, just— stuff happens. God's mercy and strength sees us through the insanity of the moment.

Worshipping Till You ----Laugh?

Grandma's church has called a special day of worship. I need this. So much has happened; so many things that hurt have left me weak and vulnerable to depression. The day of praise and worship is very timely. I love it when God plans things before I'm even aware that I need them.

The sanctuary will be open to pray and leave at the worshippers' leisure. Some stay a few moments, some a few hours and a few stay all day. Grandma is not sure how long I will stay; my attendance will be however long it takes me to lay my heavy heart down.

Worship is a personal thing. It is not something that I can do on demand. It is a response to relationship; not something that happens on cue from a song leader. This is why a special time of prayer with no time constrictions is always a blessing.

There is a special awareness of God that grows from spending time with Him. It seems whenever problems pile on the last thing we think of is to worship, yet that is the one thing that will keep our lips from coming unraveled from stress.

Worship as a result of relationship is expected, but, how can a hurting heart be able to worship in pain and praise through circumstances? When things hurt, that pain consumes every fiber of my being. So, how can I possibly worship when pain is screaming so loud in my life?

The best way I know how to get back on steady ground is to reach out to others and pray for their needs. As I enter the sanctuary, there is soft music playing and almost instantly the tears begin to fall again. Grandma doesn't know which is more difficult; life without Grandpa or the struggle of making a new every day normal alone. Oh, mercy sakes, I didn't plan on spending the evening sobbing at the altar.

God is close to those who have a broken heart and as I weep, I feel my Lord's comfort. Please, forgive Grandma, my heart still hurts. I will return to writing about my humorous life antics---in time. I appreciate your patient understanding as I get back on my feet. I know a lot of my journal entries these last months have had little life humor and much life pain. Thank you for your patience; life goes on, so will Grandma.

After having cried till there are no more tears---again. Grandma sits silently in worship, thinking of all of God's blessings. The tears have washed the pain away one more time and my heart asks God to touch me, to touch me as I've never been touched before so that my days will be productive again. I want to laugh, I want to minister—I want to be blessed. I need a heart healing touch from my Lord so I can continue to live fully in Christ.

While I sat quietly, I did not hear my dear friend, Myrtle, come up behind me. She threw her arms around me and I came up out of that seat shouting "**JESUS!**" That startled my friend and her arms still around my neck, she does a tumble over the back of the pew and her body hits my back and we both fall into the aisle! We lay on the floor, shushing each other in gales of body shaking laughter. Mercy sakes. Grandma knows, beyond any shadow of doubt, that Walter is looking down through the clouds in heaven, knee slapping.

Grandma Learns to Juggle and Wrap

You know that a few of the things in Grandma's bucket list are to call an auction, sword fight and to learn to yodel. I learned to yodel---mind you I did not say I CAN yodel. I said I know how. Knowing how and doing are two different events. But the learning of it has been done so I can officially move it out of my bucket.

A dear friend invited me to the senior citizens "carnival" at her church. She said schools and children's church are all the time having carnivals for the children but her church is hosting a carnival for the senior citizens. She said there would be classes of interest to seniors and exciting things that seniors don't think of doing but would enjoy once the activity was introduced. Sounded like fun, and if you know Grandma, I love to have—fun.

The sign up time for classes was at an end, so Marj read the list of classes to me over the phone and I made my selections. Each senior citizen could choose two classes. The classes I chose were a class on how to wrap and a class on how to be a clown.

Grandma was excited about their offering both of these classes because I'm so bad at wrapping that the last few years; I've just gone to the Dollar Store and bought bags. I've always wanted to be a clown, one of my dear friends is a clown and goes to the Children's hospital and makes the children laugh. That is a ministry I'd love to get involved in. The clowning class was quite a handful, I had no idea it took so much skill to be a clown.

First, we learned how to dress like a clown. This was easier than I thought it would be because the instructor told Grandma my outfit that I wore to class was a great clown suit. Grandma didn't know whether to feel accomplished or---insulted. I do love bright colors and large prints and this morning my red flowered top and my blue striped pedal pushers are what was clean.

The fact that I had on two different colored socks was an accident, but today, it worked for me. Grandma has never been overly concerned with clothing choices—comfort and convenience has always and will always continue to be my primary consideration. Fashion has never been a factor in my wardrobe choices not even when I was young; maybe I was born to be a clown?

From costumery we went on to learning a clown act—several classes were offered; hoola hoop dancing/spinning, cake/pie throwing and introduction to juggling. Grandma chose juggling because I know how to bake, make, throw and *wear*—a pie, no need for lessons. Pffft I could teach THAT class.

The instructor handed me two tennis sized balls and told me to toss them from one hand to the next. Easy peasy, even Grandma can do that. It was going well until the teacher tossed a third ball into the juggle. I let the first two balls drop to the floor and caught the tossed third ball. Not what I was supposed to do—but---it is human nature to drop what you are doing and grab whatever is thrown at you.

After thoroughly explaining to me the proper way to receive the third ball into the juggle, the instructor one more time threw the third ball at me—and one more time Grandma dropped the two and caught the new—one. After several tries, it became obvious that my old brain simply was not going to wave common sense and reinvent its neuro paths. You don't spend almost 70 years dropping things to catch something thrown at you and then suddenly change that reaction to embrace an entirely new---ball game.

The class moved on, and Grandma tried desperately to get it right. After juggling three balls, the class was thrown a fourth ball, then a fifth. Every time a new ball was thrown at me—I dropped the two I was juggling and caught the new ball. Of course, after the introduction of the third ball, I was left with only one ball. Frustrated, I began to bounce the one ball instead of tossing it hoping the instructor would notice that I was doing the best I could.

When the number of balls rose to five, the rest of the class was juggling very well. Grandma was found to be tossing the one single ball back and forth hand to hand and dropping it to catch the next new one thrown in each time. Right before Grandma was ready to start throwing the ball back, the class was over. I did not get a certificate; they advised me to stay with what I know---the pie in the face. This was well and fine with Grandma.

The second class I chose was wrapping. The instructor said to come to class wearing knee pants, a colorful t-shirt and a ball cap. I love casual, and it looked like wrapping was going to be a comfortable, far less stressful class than the juggling class had been. Grandma was startled to find the wrapping class was about singing, not gift wrapping. Why on earth they would call a rhyming beat song a wrap song when there are no packages involved is strange, but, whatever.

Grandma cannot sing, not *even* a little bit, so I'm again regretting I'd not taken the cake and pie throwing class, but, here we are. My mind was a little relieved when they said we were not going to sing, we were going to talk loudly---in rhyme and rhythm. That sounded easy enough, I always loved nursery rhymes.

Then, I learned that there were no written words. The person who was said to be wrapping made them up as they went. ARE YOU KIDDING? You want Grandma to move while I make up words that rhyme? Grandma has to turn the radio off in order to drive the car. First, the class was shown some moves to go with songs.

Grandma has never been able to dance because I can't listen to music and move my feet at the same time. This segment of the class did not go well. Not at all. They said the song had a beat and my movements were supposed to match the beat. The beats sounded more like little boys having a fart contest than music, but, that may be just my old age kicking in.

How, pray tell, does one match a move to a (fart) beat when the beat has already been made and moved on? Consequently, Grandma's "beat moves" were more like swatting at gnats than dancing. The other senior citizens were doing pretty well with their beat moves---some better than others. I'm pretty sure if somebody had videoed us, people would have paid to see the movie.

Finally, the instructor told us that if we had problems making up words as we moved, we could sit down and write a poem. Then, we could use the words instead of making them up as we went along. Grandma thought this was a much better idea---I'm a writer, not a dancer, not a singer. As it turns out, a wrap song is only a very few lines of words that are repeated, and often echoed back by those watching the wrapping dance.

Writing the song did not take long at all. The instructors were surprised that I made my wrapping song about God, but, since Grandma is a devotional writer, what else could they have expected? Anyway, they loved my song so much; they decided to use it as the wrapping song.

Since I wrote the song, I was allowed to sit out the wrapping dance, so it all ended very well. (Grandma has been informed that it is not a WRAP song, it is a RAP song—sorry for my lack of knowledge)

This is a picture of my dear friend I spoke of earlier; she goes to the Children's Hospital to help the little sick ones to laugh. I pray for her ministry, she and her husband both have a precious heart for caring.

Common Sense Maintenance

The other day, Grandma saw a bumper sticker that stated, "Going to church doesn't make you a Christian any more than standing in a garage makes you a car." The statement is, obviously, very true, but certainly this is an odd analogy.

The car wearing the bumper sticker was in good shape, though it had a few miles on it. So, I can only figure the people <u>do</u> keep their car in their home garage and probably take their car <u>to</u> The Garage for maintenance and checkups on a regular basis.

If a car goes to The Garage for regular checkups, there's less likely to be a big repair bill somewhere down the road. Most owners' manuals even give a suggested maintenance schedule for oil changes, tire rotations, belt and filter replacements and even windshield fluid refills. Of course, compliance to the suggested schedule of maintenance is entirely up to "me."

Thankfully, Grandma's garage includes a car wash bay with a vacuum to suck up any unwanted trash that I've collected. It can be startling the amount of unwanted trash a grandma can accumulate. The mechanic, if asked, will even advise me on what kind of fuel and oil to use for maximum life expectancy. Most big garages even offer professional services by skilled people for dent removal, paint touch ups and upholstery repair, in case your car needs special attention due to the rigors of the road.

Surely everybody knows that car buffs hang out together in the garage and talk "cars;" sharing "been there done that" experiences about what they've learned along the highway. Grandma has found that I've avoided a lot of mishaps by simply taking heed of another driver's road experiences.

And who doesn't enjoy showing off a special hood ornament, a quirky license plate or a sentimental window decal? Many even tell of road accidents and how in hind sight, they could have been avoided. When one driver tells of their experiences, all the drivers are attentive. It is human nature to share with each other, both the good experiences and the bad. A lot of direction for safe traveling is shared at these gatherings.

It IS true; being in the garage doesn't make the car a car. Although, I've never heard anybody who kept their car in the garage or took it to The Garage for regular maintenance say they thought it was a mistake or a waste of time to have done so.

However, I have heard some folks say they wish they HAD kept their car in the garage and taken it to The Garage so it would have had less road damage and longer use—but—I don't think anybody ever put that on a bumper sticker.

Oh, mercy sakes, Grandma just realized---I need to get the oil changed in my car! Walter always took care of those things. I laugh as I realize my own ineptitude at up keep and maintenance. I'm glad that all that came to mind or Grandma's car would certainly have been a casualty of life. Hmmm, maybe even I should think about a new car. Sports cars have always caught my eye as have vintage roadsters. The possibilities are ---inviting.

Since I'd sold the family business shortly after Walter's death, I have some extra money to entertain such an intriguing idea. Grandma will have to think about it. Tonight is the monthly meeting of the Back Porch Grandmas; we gather at a friend's home who has a rocking chair ministry.

Yes, I know, now I have to explain. Let's just say there are a lot of broken things that find order again while a group of Grandmas silently rock together watching the sunset. Some pray, some read their Bibles, some just---think. There's a lot of healing that can happen rocking on the back porch in the stillness of a summer's evening.

Hot Car or Antique Roadster?

This is the first time that I make a major decision by myself. No. Let me re-write that statement. Today is the first time in 40 years that I make a decision without Walter. All of these years, we have made major decisions together. We'd talk about it, pray together about it, talk about it some more, pray some more, then---finally, all things considered, we'd come to a decision--together.

Today, Grandma has come to the new car store to look for a very special car. Up until now, cars have always been bought on a "needs" basis. Luxury, appearance and want to has never entered into the decision making process. Cars past have always been shopped for and purchased on the basis of usefulness, cost effectiveness, and common sense.

Today is different. Today, Grandma stands in a sports car store parking lot. There are no cars here that have anything to do with budget, common sense or necessity. These---are---pure---pleasure--cars. None of these cars have any redeeming quality other than "feels good, looks good and---goes fast." I can almost see Walter shaking his head and snickering in amusement. Surprised at myself, I'm starting my shopping at a sports car dealer, not a vintage car dealer. Interesting since Grandma loves both types of cars.

Closing the door to the 1993 Jaguar XJR 15, I pull out of the car lot for the first test drive I've ever made alone in my life. Smooth as cream. Out on the open highway, looking in all directions and seeing no traffic to compete with, I press on the gas. From 0 to 60 in 3.1 SECONDS! Oh mercy sakes!

This is screaming HOT and it can be mine; Grandma has never even dreamed--. Jaguar's ultimate supercar, the XJR-15's smoothly chiseled lines rank with those of the fabled C-Type, D-Type and XJ13 for sheer sculpted beauty. Is it time for all that commitment to wise living, careful planning and judicial budgeting to be set aside in favor of indulgence?

As I step on the gas, the adrenaline rushes through my veins like fire and I'm thrown back against the cool leather of the driver's seat. Oh, YEAH! I can feel the power of the road through the steering wheel and the roar of the engine as it pours its energy out through the rear wheels. This is---pure—adrenalin. Walter was never much of a hot car man; his desire always went toward the heavy trucks. He wanted usefulness; a vehicle that could carry his boat, haul his tag along camper; a MAN'S vehicle.

As I accustom myself to the feel of an accelerated heartbeat, I notice that the road has a rhythm all its own. My mind is sedated by the scenery as it races by and I begin to think about my life. My children are grown; most of my grandchildren are adults now. My beloved Walter has gone to heaven; I have no responsibility to anybody but my ownself. I'm not a wealthy old woman, but I have enough. I'd sold the family business shortly after Walter's death. I can't live extravagantly, but I can indulge myself now and then.

The suspension on this car is amazing! I barely feel the rise and fall of the road beneath me. I could get used to this; I could love it, just saying. My life overview continues. Do I have any current obligations that would suffer from this indulgence of self? My church is starting a new building project. Heaven knows, we need the youth facility! Last week, they had teens lined up around the walls of the gym. I've always supported the youth.

Saturday, I got an e-mail from the Pastor, asking me to make a commitment to the building fund. I will, of course, always support the Children's and Youth ministries. That is a given, a known and has nothing to do with this car. The road turns abruptly and the car handles the transition without complaint. I *love* how this feels. My personal assessment ends. I think I've made my decision.

As I pull back into the car lot, the sales guy grins like a Cheshire cat, giving his buddy a 'thumbs up' as he sprints to greet me before I can even open the car door. For a moment, I sit in the silence, contemplating life's commitments and the life that is my own that lies ahead of me. What does Grandma want; it is my decision and mine alone. As I open the door my hand runs over the immaculate red finish of the hot red sports car. Not even Walter knew my love for sports cars, though he suspected, I'm sure.

The sales guy gushes, "Allllrighty then, my friend, what could possibly prevent you from being the owner of this fabulous sports car?" Smiling as I firmly place the key in his hand, I look away and softly say, "memories." As his face falls, I continue, "do you know of any vintage cars that need an old lady to tenderly love them? Like, say, an antique Roadster?"

The Final Chapter in Grandma's Journal

This morning marks a milestone in my life. As I was going about my daily activities I realized that my day is filled with busyness. Of course, my day started as always, enjoying a hot cup of espresso as I watched the sun rise over the ocean. Then, I had a sit down conversation with my Lord where I told him of things on my heart. That was followed by a time of quiet Bible study listening to what God had to tell me. This has been my morning routine for as long as I can remember.

I have errands that need doing, lunch with a friend, after that, visiting an elder friend then taking the doggie to the dog park for some much needed exercise. This afternoon, I may bake some cookies and go to the Farmer's Market. You may be wondering what is so special about this day. That is my point; nothing and everything.

It has been days, perhaps weeks, since I had to sit down for a good cry. Thoughts of my beloved Walter still do come to mind regularly, and probably always will; we had a life together. But now, instead of tears, the memories bring warmth and even smiles. Last week, Grandma had gone to look at sports cars. My thoughts of Walter were warm; there were no pains of brokenness, no heaviness of heart.

These months since Walter died have been so difficult. There have been some days where I didn't think I could go on living. Yet, I lived. Each day created a new normal and slowly, the blank spots began to fill in. God, and my friends, have been so patient with me. Now, I find the new normal has become common and no longer tears at my senses.

I have a friend who tells me that I need to do something crazy and exciting, like go on a world tour. This was the same friend that talked me into going white water rafting earlier this year. No, I'm not going to follow her, well meant, I'm sure, directions. Grandma has never liked to travel and I'm quite certain Grandpa's death has not instilled a new wonder lust for exploration.

Another friend told me I should check into an on-line dating site. According to the Bible, marriage is until death do us depart. Walter was as dead a month after his funeral as he will be ten years from now. That is a harsh realization, but none the less true. Dead is—dead. It is the grieving process that matures, not the death.

According to Jewish traditions, (I'm not Jewish, but as a Christian, the Jewish faith most nearly matches my own) a widow mourns deeply, to the point of not being able to function in daily life for three days after a spouse's death. Then, the bereaved is commanded to mourn for a week; after that, a less deep but still great grieving and a freedom to express the deep sense of loss in both private and community life. After a month, it is up to the bereaved spouse as to how long his/her grief continues.

Grief is personal; each individual sets their own standard. Some grieve for years, decades---some never cease their grieving. The more or less length of grieving does not reflect on the depth of love for the departed. Some need more time than others. Never, ever judge a person by their time spent in mourning. I think perhaps a person is not even aware when that time to make new relationships happens; it is just a natural progression of events.

For right now, Grandma is going to continue living one day at a time. Each day offers new opportunities for ministry and worship. I have no idea if there will ever be another love in my life. One thing I'm sure of, Walter can never be replaced. But, on the other hand, Grandma's heart knows that new relationships are-- possible. Life goes on and so will Grandma.

No man can ever measure up to my beloved Walter, so I choose to never use him as a measuring line. A man must stand on his own merits. Grandma will continue to love the Lord so much that the only way any man can find me is to be walking closely with Christ himself. Meantime, life has many adventures ahead. If I enjoy those adventures alone, my heart is happy. If I enjoy those adventures with the blessing of companionship, Grandma's heart is happy. Either way, my happiness depends on my relationship with my Lord, not my circumstances.

Tomorrow morning, Grandma is meeting with a gentleman from church that Pastor recommended to talk about vintage roadster cars. This brother in Christ is an expert on vintage cars and even owns one himself. He will have sound advice for me concerning the purchase of a vintage car as well as the upkeep of such a unique investment.

Grandma hopes the day is beautiful with blue skies and fluffy clouds so any test drives can be done with the top down. I'll bake some cookies to take so I have a gift to offer the gentleman for his time. With this last page, Grandma is finishing my journal. Maybe, at some point in time, I will begin to journal again. For now, I'm going to go get a cup of coffee and sit down under the tree out back.

My Walter built a wooden bench around the tree so I could sit there and enjoy the sunset. I call it my "thank you bench." It's the perfect sit down place after a busy day to thank my Lord for today's direction, healing and comfort. Please, get a cup of coffee, or tea, if you'd rather, and join me---and please pray for me, as I continue to grow and worship through this stage of my life.

The Pages Grandma Promised You

Grandma's Famous Extreme Chocolate Chip Cookies

- 2 1/4 cups all-purpose flour

- 1 teaspoon baking soda

- 1 teaspoon salt

- 1 cup (2 sticks) soft butter or butter flavored Crisco,

- 3/4 cup granulated sugar

- 3/4 cup packed brown sugar

- 1 teaspoon vanilla extract

- 2 large eggs

- 2 cups (12-oz. pkg.) semi sweet or milk chocolate chips or use several different kinds of chocolate—white, milk, semi sweet, chips, chunks

- 1 cup chopped nuts

Turn on oven to 350 degrees. Line a baking sheet with parchment paper or use a non-stick pan or lightly grease a regular cookie sheet

Combine all the dry ingredients in a bowl (not the chocolate chips) and set aside. In a mixing bowl, cream together all the wet ingredients including the eggs. Mix (by hand or with a mixer) till fluffy. Add the dry ingredients a half cup at a time, mixing in till all the "flour" is incorporated.

Remove bowl from mixer if using a mixer—and fold in the chocolate chips by hand till well mixed through the batter. Drop by heaping tablespoonful onto the prepared cookie sheet pan, spacing about two inches apart. To make bigger cookies, use an ice-cream scoop.

Bake in pre-heated oven for 15-20 minutes till set and lightly browned. Cookies will continue to cook when removed from the oven because of the heat inside the cookie—so don't wait till the cookies are crispy to remove them from the oven.

Let sit on pan for a minute before removing to a paper towel to finish cooling. Important note: cookies are an excellent prayer carrier. Pray God's blessings for encouragement over the cookies then gift them to people you want to bless.

Skit: GOT MOUTH?

Props: Ahead of time, purchase 'ugly teeth' AND wax 'sugar lips' from your local party store; usually in the costume or party favor section. Make sure you have a set of teeth AND a set of sugar lips for each person in your class—and a few extra for visitors. (if you have a tight budget or can't find sugar lips, use a piece of candy in place of the sugar lips---but you need to have the 'ugly teeth'.)

Before class, open the store packaging and put the lips(or candy) and the teeth, one of each, in snack sized plastic storage bags. Keep baggies out of sight till end of class, following instructions at the end of this lesson.

Microphone for the reporter: take an empty cardboard bath tissue roll and tape a ping pong ball to one end. Paint 'microphone' black or silver or wrap in aluminum foil.

Skit Characters: Mouth and Reporter

The mouth character can be a person wearing bright red lipstick and a big hat to cover up the eyes so that the mouth is the focus. Exaggerate the mouth with the lipstick and wear a baggy 'pull down' hat that covers eyes so the BIG mouth is very bold.

The reporter should have a tablet they refer to for interview questions and a microphone (a good place to keep a copy of your script for reference)

Scene opens with news reporter introducing the special guest, "Mouth."

Reporter: Mouth, it is so good to have this opportunity to interview you for the National Tryntobe Good Paper!

Mouth: Why, thank you, it's an honor to be here.

Reporter: I guess my first question is, what is your job; what exactly is your main purpose in life?

Mouth: (pause) Well, my number one purpose in life is to keep your lips from coming unraveled. Shocking, I know, but think about what it would be like if everybody was walking around with no lips (pull lips inside of mouth so point is made.)

Reporter (momentarily look confused, touches their own mouth): Oh, I see. Ok. That's not exactly what I thought you'd say, but I guess it makes sense.

Mouth: What exactly did you think I'd say?

Reporter: Well, huh, I thought you would say your purpose in life is something spiritual, like praising God or witnessing. After all, you are a Christian mouth, right?

Mouth: Well, I can do that. It all depends on what the person that owns me wants me to do. I do exactly what the person wants me to do, I don't do anything by myself—and nobody but the person who owns me can make me do anything.

Reporter: (looks at the audience) This isn't going like I thought it would. (looks back at Mouth and takes a deep breath) OK---but what about when you say something bad or MEAN or lie--- doesn't the devil MAKE you do those things?

Mouth: No.

Reporter: No? Ummmm (turn toward class and look shocked!)

Mouth: NO! The only thing I can say is what the person who owns me CHOOSES to have me say. I can say praises to God. I can say kind things and build people up. OR I can say ugly things and lie and be mean.

Reporter: Amazing. So, then, you're saying it is entirely up to ME what MY mouth says?

Mouth: Entirely up to you. Every word you speak—you choose what it is. Your mouth has nothing to do with it---physically impossible for your mouth to say something on its own. (reach out and gently punch reporter in the arm) HA—who knew, right?

Reporter: But---how do I choose, how do I make sure I say only things that would praise God and lift people up? I mean, sometimes, words just come out and I shock myself, I mean really, I don't mean to say those words, just, bleah (open mouth like something is falling out), they fall out and ---once I say them, I can't pick them up and put them back, can't erase them. They're just--- just ---there---and even when I want to, I can't take them back.

Mouth: Yeah, I get blamed for that all the time, but, seriously, (throw arms open wide and shrug) not my fault. The Word of God says in Luke 6:45 that out of the abundance of the heart, the mouth speaks.

So, if you have Jesus in your heart and you fill your heart with hope by reading God's Word--- when you speak, it will be easier to choose good things to say. But, we still make a choice. Haven't you ever heard that old saying, "Think before you speak."?

Reporter: But, Christians still say bad things, I've heard them (hangs head and shuffles feet and mumbles) and and well, I've said some mean stuff too---I guess. Ok, yeah, I have, I know I have. But, I couldn't help it, the words just fell out and and—(looks pleading and defensive)

Mouth: Ummm, no. You could help it. The words were in your heart so you told your mouth to say them. And it's not just mean and hurtful words that can hide in our heart. Sometimes, our heart wants to say bad words to--- you know, fit in or be cool.

Reporter: Like when my not so Christian friends are standing around, my Mouth might just say bad words to be---well—like them. And, and, the words just fall out without (voice fades off—waves hands and shrugs) You know what I mean, the words just kind of fly out. (shrugs and looks defensive)

Mouth: Absolutely (reporter looks suddenly hopeful)—NOT! I can not do anything on my own—and nobody tells me what to do but my owner. Your mouth says exactly what is in your heart. If you feel small and inadequate, it's because you have not hidden God's Word in your heart so you don't understand who you really are.

You are a child of God, created in His image, pure and holy. When you know who you are and whose you are, your heart no longer needs to tear people down to make yourself look big. Your heart is confident and doesn't need to use dirty words that you think will make yourself look important.

Reporter: Oh. So, if I choose to put God's Word in my heart everyday, it will be easier to choose the good things to say? Hmmm sounds like it might help if I choose friends who have God's Word in their heart too—so I won't be tempted so much.

Mouth: Now you've got it! Being a Christian is all about choices. Every moment, you have to CHOOSE to do AND say the things that honor Jesus ---and that includes choosing who you hang out with, what you watch on TV, the movies you see, the words of songs you listen to.

When you hear bad words or mean words, that is your sign to walk away. Life is full of choices and choosing to not let our ears be garbage cans is a good start. Out of our heart comes---words.

Reporter: WAIT, what about when I'm mad? It's *really* easy for my Mouth to say bad words then! (grimace)

Mouth: But, when you have God's word inside your heart and the Holy Spirit to whisper, nOOooo, don't say that-- the choice can still be hard, but you can make the right choice—. Give it a minute to think then choose to say good things instead of bad things and---- sometimes the wisest choice of all is to say---- nothing.

Reporter: (look thoughtful) hmmmmm.

Mouth: EXACTLY! A "thinking" noise will relieve the pressure of the moment—and is a much better choice than a curse word or a cruel response.

Reporter: (hang head and shake in resignation then shrug) It's so easy to say mean things—even easier than saying bad words! How do I stop saying mean things that hurt people---you know that's really popular these days—it makes me sound cool. Or---maybe not—but everybody else is doing it so---that's not so bad since it's –you know, (voices trails off) going on-- all the time---(sigh)

Mouth: Again, the best way to overcome a mean mouth is to stop and <u>think</u> before you say things. Don't say things that tear down or put down. God wants us to build each other up with our words, not tear each other down. *Ephesians 4:29* says, "Do not let any unwholesome talk come out of your mouths, but only what is helpful for building others up according to their needs, that it may benefit those who listen." Again---God's word in your heart---.

Reporter: So, if I choose to spend time reading God's Word, all those 'God things' will be in my heart and it will be easier to choose to say good things, kind things. I'll still have to choose to say the God things—but at least I'll have the Word of God hiding in my heart to draw from.

(smacks self in forehead) WOW! Thank you, Mouth, I've learned a lot during this interview! I know I'll have good things to say in my article for the paper! Oh, and what was that scripture again? The one about my heart storing up good things because I put them in there.

Mouth: Luke 6:45 The good man brings good things out of the good stored up in his heart and the evil man brings evil things out of the evil stored up in his heart. For out of the abundance of the heart, his mouth speaks.

Reporter: So, we can see what's in our heart by what comes out of our mouth? Kool extremely kool. Thanks again—I need to run. Lots of things to do today, but I have to make sure I take time to put God's Word in my heart. SEE YA!

Treat: Have helpers give out baggies with the candy and the bad teeth. Explain how just like we choose to put the silly bad teeth in our mouth, or the sweet sugar lips, we choose which words we say. (Have the class put the set of bad teeth in their mouth)

Tell students that sometimes we think we look really cool to our friends when we have a bad mouth—and sometimes we think we are hot stuff when we smart off or "dis" somebody.

Instruct students to look at each other (with bad teeth in their mouths) This is what 'cool bad words' look like to God—and to people who hear them. Not so cool, heh?

An ugly mouth does not show Jesus to the world, and it does not please Jesus. (have the class remove ugly teeth and put sugar lips or candy in their mouth) You choose sweet words, just like you choose sweet candy. Choosing sweet words makes your mouth say kind things. Think about it. Words can hurt or they can help. Out of the abundance of our heart we speak.

Prayer: Lord Jesus, forgive me for the times that I've said ugly or mean words. Help me to choose to put only good things in my heart so I will know good words to say. I will plan a time each day for reading your Word and talking to you so that it will be easier to choose to say good things. Thank you, I love you. Amen.

Post note: The skit was a fabulous success not only in Children's Church, but also in the Youth Group where there was a similar problem with "dissing" each other. The kids laughed and laughed particularly at the "big mouth person." You are welcome to use this skit as you like, with Grandma's blessings. It is also available as a Kindle book.

OTHER BOOKS BY ANNIE KEYS

If you enjoyed this book, please go to Amazon and give it 5 stars then recommend it to your friends. Thanks!

Other books by this author that you may enjoy from Amazon are:

Life Is Like Buffalo Breath, a fun devotional illustrated with animal stories and photos. Particularly appealing to anybody who has a pet or loves animals.

Sick Is An Attitude; Living Well With Diabetes not a devotional; a self help book for Diabetics

Food for Body and Soul, a unique devotion book using food and kitchen stories to show Biblical principles. This beautiful 8x10 book includes favorite family recipes and cooking helps. A very attractive addition to any cook's book shelf.

Food for the Soul, the same devotions as in the cookbook but without the recipes.

Whatcha Got? GOD Has Answers, 42 devotionals that addresses many of the issues we all work through every day. This very popular devotional is written with humorous stories to illustrate timeless Biblical truths.

Got Mouth? The skit that Grandma mentioned and copied in this journal, available only as a Kindle publish on Amazon.

Watch for these books to be released at a later date.

Special Day Devotions, devotions written especially for all the holidays

Come Dance With Me, devotions on finding intimacy with God

Thank you for reading

<u>The Grandma Chronicles</u>

Made in the USA
Columbia, SC
06 November 2018